THE SHEPHERD AND THE KING

BOOK I

BRYAN R. SAYE

The Shepherd and the King

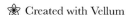 Created with Vellum

Dedicated to my wife,
Jessica,
who always pushed me
further than I thought I could go.

A NOTE TO THE READER

While great care has been taken to mirror the Biblical accounts of David and Saul, this is first and foremost a work of fiction. Much of the material contained within these pages was drawn straight from my own imagination and not from Scripture (though Scripture is certainly what fueled my imagination). Where inconsistencies arise between what is found here and what is found in the book of 1 Samuel, it is my fault alone and I beg the reader's grace.

With that in mind, every attempt was made to capture the themes of David and Saul's lives and remain consistent with Scripture. Artistic license was certainly taken, such as the ordering of events, certain timeframes, and the size of the many armies found in these pages.

Scripture references were taken from the New International Version, though in some cases there have been minor changes to help fit the narrative and flow, such as one occurrence of using Yahweh instead of Lord.

In the end, it is my sincere hope that the reader will find themselves lost in the lives of these two men. For more information about David and Saul, see 1 Samuel 15-31.

PART I

The Lord *has sought out a man after his own heart and appointed him ruler of his people.*

DAVID

FORTY-TWO, forty-three, forty-four...

David frowned when he didn't see the forty-fifth sheep and began counting over, hoping he'd made a mistake the first three times. Another minute proved the only mistake he'd made was losing a sheep. His eyes drifted to his father's house on the low hill at the edge of the sheep pastures. The late-afternoon sun was close to the horizon behind it, bathing the small home and green grass in soft, orange light. He felt a looming sense of dread. He had little desire to be around his family in the first place—it was why he had practically begged to be a shepherd, to be out in the fields and away from them. Now he had to tell his father that he'd failed his first day alone with the sheep.

He's going to kill me...

He gave a low sigh of defeat and walked across the fields toward the house, dragging his feet as he went. His father— Jesse—and two of his seven older brothers were behind the house. Eliab and Abinadab were sparring while his father stood to the side, arms crossed as he watched their every move with critical eyes. Already these two had been to war with the new king, fighting against the Amalekites. While he was jealous of their success—and more importantly, the attention they received from their father—battle wasn't something he was built for. He was smaller than his brothers, almost laughably so. Rather than interrupt their training, he stood and absentmindedly played with the sling on his belt, the only weapon he was permitted to use.

"It is all you will need to protect the sheep," his father had said.

And a fine job he'd done.

He knew how his father would look at him, with that mixture of shame and disappointment he'd become accustomed to. He leaned against the side of the home, hiding in the shadow and keeping his eyes on the ground as he listened to his brothers' sparring. As the mock battle wore on, he found himself fidgeting, rubbing his now-sweaty hands together as he waited for his father to notice him.

"What do you want, runt?"

David's head jerked up. Eliab was standing over a fallen Abinadab. "I'm not a runt," he said, though the words sounded weak even to his ears. *Better to have said nothing.*

His brother laughed and stepped up to him. David stood barely to Eliab's barrel of a chest, and he had to crane his neck to keep eye contact. "Is that so?"

Jesse stepped between them. "That's enough." Eliab smirked and turned away. His broad frame knocked David back a step. "What do you want, David?"

The annoyance in his father's voice was thick. Jesse didn't even know he had lost the sheep, and already he was unwelcome. "I"—he swallowed hard—"One of the sheep has wandered off."

Eliab laughed and looked at their father. "I told you he couldn't do it."

He met his brother's judging eyes, searching for and failing to find something to respond with. David had never been quick with words.

His father sighed, the annoyance mixed now with disappointment as he made the face David had known would come. "You said you could do it. You begged."

He couldn't take his father's expression and returned his gaze to the ground. "I'm sorry."

"Do you know when?"

"I last counted them at midday. They were all there."

"Midday?! It's nearly sundown." His father let out a long sigh and seemed to think. "I told you to count them on the hours. I should have left Ozem with you."

David flinched at the words. *He is barely a year older than me.* "Let me go and find it."

"It's nearly sundown," Jesse repeated. "It's too late to go wandering into the woods."

Eliab scoffed. "If the runt is afraid of the dark, it is."

David glared at him, though he said nothing. He turned back to his father. "Let me go. I'll find it."

His father looked down at him with one part pity and three parts doubt. "I don't know. The forest is—"

"I can do it."

"Let him," Eliab said. "He may prove himself a good shepherd if nothing else. And besides," he added with a grin, "you've got seven more sons."

His father gave Eliab an unhappy look but said nothing to him. He thought for another moment and then looked at David. "Be safe. Your mother will kill me if something happens to you."

Wouldn't want mother mad at you. David turned and left, not wanting to be among his family any longer than he had to. He stomped down the hill, by the sheep, and to the small stable at the opposite end of the fields where he kept his shepherding supplies. After packing a quick meal—it could take all night to find the lost sheep—he grabbed his shepherd's staff and made one final stop at the small creek that edged the fields. Here he ducked down and splashed some of the cool water on his face to try to clear his mind. For a moment, all was silent.

As the ripples faded, he saw the creek bed and the smooth stones he'd come for. The still water reflected a sky turning black above him. A few stars had already twinkled to life. Yet all he saw was a young shepherd, a scared boy.

Nothing more.

He sighed and dug through the creek for the stones. He found some about the size of his palm and stuffed them into the small pouch at his side, counting to be sure he had five. He hoisted his pack and set off into the woods, searching for a trail to follow.

DAVID CRESTED the small hill and stepped from the edge of the trees. Below him were rolling pastures that dipped into a low valley. The sky burned with the breaking dawn, fiery yellows and reds lighting the green grass. He saw the forest of cypress and oak resume in the distance. Even the brilliant morning sun could not penetrate the thick canopy of branches, leaving the forest covered in shadow.

He was beginning to have his doubts. It hadn't taken him long to find the sheep's rambling trail as it crushed its way through the dense foliage and underbrush of the forest. Here, however, at the relatively brush-free valley, it seemed to end. His eyes searched the valley—though now with little hope.

For a moment, he thought of turning back, of forsaking the sheep, of letting it wander lost in the forest. Yet he knew he could not. It was alone in the woods because of him, in danger because of him. He'd been entrusted with his father's sheep. Regardless of how he felt about his father—or how his father felt about him—David was a shepherd. It was his job to protect the sheep.

And it is not my sheep to lose.

David hefted his pack more securely onto his shoulder. He put his hand into the small pouch on his belt and felt the five smooth stones he'd gathered for his sling. Taking a quick drink from his skin, he gripped his staff and began the walk down into the valley.

It was still early morning when he finished his search of the valley. He'd found seven rabbits, three of which he'd killed with his sling and now hung from his pack, the used stones safely back in his pouch. He'd found an anthill that rose to his knees. He'd found the dung of a lion, an antelope that fled at the sight of him, and a flock of ibis, yet he'd found no signs of his father's sheep. No recently trampled grass, no feeding grounds, no prints.

David looked at the forest on the far side of the valley and the line of trees marking the pasture's end. He let out a low sigh and walked toward them. Perhaps the animal had wandered back into the forest. He stooped and began his search once he reached the trees. He dragged his hands through the dirt, spread the low shrubbery aside to examine the ground beneath, searched through the tall grass for signs the sheep had stopped to eat.

At least I am in the shade.

There.

He stopped and touched the blade of grass that had caught his eye. It was broken, split into two ends. Rough.

Chewed.

After another cursory search, he found a handful of blades that looked the same. The sheep was heading east, farther into the forest and farther from his father's home.

Of course it is.

He rechecked his pack, then set off into the woods,

following the now obvious trail left behind. The sheep seemed to be wandering without direction into the forest. It had trampled the foliage with such carelessness that it must have finally decided it wanted David to find it.

And then he saw it, standing and chewing absently at a small patch of grass. It paused and looked up at David, almost as if it had been expecting him.

"You've been a headache," he said. "You know that?"

The sheep bleated and then went back to its meal.

"Go ahead and eat," he said, walking toward the animal. "I'll make sure you're our next sacrifice."

There was movement in the trees behind the sheep and then a flash of brown and yellow and red fur. The sheep disappeared under the weight of a lion, its nonchalant bleating becoming a desperate scream of pain. David's sling was in his hand before he had time to think. He had a stone loaded and flying—*load, swing, aim, throw*—before he'd taken his first step. It bounced off the lion's back with enough force to push the beast off its new meal. It paused, seemed to evaluate the new threat, then rose and faced David.

He froze as the beast stared at him with evil eyes, the sheep's blood dripping staining its matted mane. For a moment, they stared at one another, a challenge hanging in the air.

Turn around...go home...it is only a sheep.

Yet, again, he knew he could not.

It is not my sheep to lose.

David moved slowly, reaching to his sack for another stone. The lion sprang forward at the movement, and David snapped into motion, his muscles working from memory: *load, swing, aim* —must be perfect this time—*throw*. The stone hurtled through the air and bounced off the lion's skull, ricocheting into the woods. The beast barely faltered. For a moment that lasted forever, David knew he was going to die. Then the lion's feet went limp, its momentum carrying it another few paces. In a flurry of fur and dirt and grass, the beast skidded to a halt a step from David.

I just killed a lion.

He let out a breath he hadn't realized he was holding. His white-knuckled hand slowly opened, and he put the sling back on his belt. He stepped around the fallen lion on shaking legs—giving the dead animal plenty of space—and then ran to the sheep.

There was a large gash in the sheep's leg, but the wound didn't look mortal. It was still bleating for its life, a healthy leg kicking at nothing as it lay on the dirt.

"You'll live."

David slipped his pack from his shoulders, dug through it for something to use as a bandage, and found the cloth he'd wrapped his own food in. Setting his pack aside, he went to work bandaging the sheep's wounded leg.

"You've ruined my day; you know that."

The sheep bleated as if in response.

"I suppose that—"

There was a roar, and David felt a mass slam into him. He tumbled away from the bleating sheep and found himself on his back, face to face with a bloodied and angry lion. He froze, his muscles refusing to move. The beast stood over him and let out a roar so concussive it knocked David back, and his head slammed into the dirt hard enough to leave a divot in the ground. Blood and saliva rained down on him. The lion went quiet, teeth bared, a low rumbling growl still rolling from its throat like thunder. Hot, sticky breath filled his face. David could see the open wound just above the lion's left eye from his previous shot and the blood running down into the beast's face.

Its jaw opened a moment before it struck; David felt paralyzed. For the second time within the span of a few minutes, he was sure he was going to die. Then he felt his arm move. It shot up of its own accord and seized the animal by the mane, halting its teeth only a finger's width from his face. He felt his muscles tense all the way down to his shoulder, an otherworldly strength filling his arm and holding the lion in place.

The movement unfroze David, and he reached into the pouch at his side with his free hand. He scooped up the three remaining stones and bashed the lion along the head, aiming for the existing wound. The beast roared in pain and lurched back, its mane ripping and tearing. Yet David's hand held firm. He struck it again and again, blood splattering his face and chest as the lion roared and jerked. Finally, the animal went silent and collapsed on top of him. Foamy blood leaked from his open jaws as the animal exhaled for the final time.

David wiggled free of the beast and stood.

I just killed a lion…again.

He looked at his hand; a lock of the lion's mane was still clutched in his throbbing fingers. His entire arm buzzed with strength not his own. He felt it aching, throbbing with unseen power and energy. Then it was gone. He felt faint and swayed on his feet before he steadied himself.

What was that?

The beast lay defeated and bleeding in the grass. David's entire torso and the side of his face were covered in the animal's blood. His gaze drifted to the sheep, bleating and still kicking its good leg out at nothing.

And then he heard a voice in his head. It was as clear as his own thoughts, and though he would at times ignore it, it was a voice he would hear for the rest of his days.

It was not your sheep to lose. But it was yours to save.

2

SAUL

"TWELVE THOUSAND."

Saul nodded in acknowledgment, but he was barely listening to his son. Battle seemed far off, thanks to Samuel's long absence. What good were reports of enemy numbers if he could do nothing about it?

"Twelve thousand Amalekites," Malki-Shua repeated.

Saul finally turned to him. His son was eager to serve, eager to prove his worth. The least Saul could do was humor him. "And us? How many do we have?" he asked.

Malki-Shua looked down at a piece of parchment. "Near three thousand." He looked older than his nineteen years, much older. He wore a leather vest and on his belt a bronze sword, sickle-shaped in the style of the Egyptian *khopesh* from which it was designed.

He is dressed for a battle that will likely never come.

Saul twirled his spear, the tip spinning and reflecting the flickering orange light from the torches around the fabric walls of his command tent. "And how many could we call up?"

Malki-Shua looked again at the parchment. "Perhaps…

perhaps another ten thousand. Maybe more depending on how far we travel and how long we wait."

"How long to muster the ten thousand?"

He thought for a moment. "One week."

"Thirteen thousand men," Saul said, letting the words hang in the tent. "Thirteen thousand Israelites against twelve thousand Amalekites." He looked off at nothing and considered the numbers. He would have preferred a more significant advantage, preferred no chance of defeat. *Not that it matters. There will likely be no battle. My men will scatter yet again, waiting on that old man.*

His oldest son, Jonathan, seemed to read his thoughts. "We should call on them," he said, stepping up beside Malki-Shua. "Call on all the fighting men of Israel and destroy these Amalekites. Numbers mean nothing when we have Yahweh behind us."

Unlike Malki-Shua, Jonathan cared less about logistics and reports. He was filled with a steadfast belief that Israel's armies were the righteous hand of Yahweh. A belief Saul shared, of course, though he had always tempered it with sensible confidence in the strength of his men, as well. What use was Yahweh at your back if you did not have an army at your front?

"We cannot do anything yet, Jonathan. Not until Samuel arrives." *Samuel, the voice of Yahweh*, he thought with a frown. *Even as king, I am subject to him.*

"He will come."

"I am sure he will." *Whenever he so desires.*

"And he will send us to destroy the Amalekites."

"I am sure he will," he repeated, though he did not believe it. Yet he wanted to be prepared on the off chance Samuel did send them. And his sons needed something to do. "Go. See to the riders. Be ready to call up the rest of the army if Samuel arrives."

They each gave a quick bow and then left. Saul followed them through the tent flaps, carrying his spear like a walking stick. His soldiers—all three thousand of them—were camped in the sprawling valley below him, where the setting sun cast long shadows from the hundreds of tents. Already fires were burning, and Saul smelled roasting lamb and goat. An old stone wall lined the edge of the valley a dozen paces to his left, crumbling in many places yet still standing higher than a man's height in others, a remnant of the Canaanites who had lived here before them. Pagans, conquered by the leader Joshua hundreds of years ago. Joshua had been second in command to Moses and had then led the Israelites as they transitioned from their time of wandering in the desert to the time of the judges—those mighty warriors who rallied the tribes in their times of need. And now Israel was in transition yet again. Samuel, the last and greatest judge of Israel, had ushered in the age of kings.

Of which I am the first.

And yet, why did it feel as if Samuel was still in control? He was a judge and a prophet, the voice of Yahweh, but not Yahweh himself. Saul was king of Israel, its first king. Why did he have to answer to a judge?

"Shalom, my king."

Saul turned and smiled at Benyamin, his armor-bearer and bodyguard. "Shalom, Beny." Together they turned and looked down at the camp.

"Can you believe how far we have come, my king?"

He sighed. "Sometimes I do not."

"Yahweh has blessed you beyond measure. I am honored to be here."

"There isn't another I would trust my life to." Benyamin had worked in Saul's father's house and been his servant since they were boys. When Saul was anointed king, he knew of no better choice to be his armor-bearer. He looked again at Benyamin. "Have you eaten?"

"I have not."

Saul nodded back toward his tent. "There is meat and cheese inside. Go. Eat."

Benyamin bowed and moved to enter the tent, then paused and looked again to Saul.

"I will survive a few moments, Beny."

He nodded again and disappeared into the tent. Saul stood at the entrance for another long while, looking down at the men mustered beneath him.

Doing nothing.

The scene reminded him of the last time he had seen Samuel. It had been at Gilgal, and then, like now, his men were simply sitting and waiting on the old man to send them on their way. There had been an enemy in reach—one he knew they could defeat—and yet no orders to go and defeat it. His men had sat, looking up at the king, watching the most powerful man in Israel wait on an old man. He had seen their doubt, could hear their whispers. Saul hated it. He hated that he was king yet could not rule. Hated that he was merely a puppet to Samuel. So he had acted on his own rather than continue waiting. He had led the nation, as he had been chosen to do.

And he had suffered for it.

Abner crested the hill. The commander of Saul's army was an older man though not yet graying. His face was hard and firm, and his body held a strength that always seemed ready to strike. He gave Saul a nod and then joined him at the entrance to the tent. For a long while, both simply stood and surveyed the army below.

"Why are we here, Abner?"

Abner did not hesitate. "We await word from Yahweh."

Saul scoffed. "We await word from Samuel."

"Is it not the same thing?"

"I suppose. But, they are restless. If we wait much longer, they may begin to scatter. Samuel seems to take joy in testing our patience."

"What do you wish, my king?"

Saul frowned, memories of Gilgal still fresh in his mind. "What I wish no longer matters, king or not. We wait for Samuel to tell us what Yahweh wills. I will not make the same mistake a second time."

Abner nodded, though he said nothing.

As if his own thoughts had summoned the prophet, Saul saw a stirring on the edge of the camp. Men moved aside as a visitor made his way through the tents, walking without haste toward Saul's tent.

Benyamin stepped out from the tent. "Has Samuel arrived?"

Saul looked at him sideways, detecting too much admiration in his armor-bearer's voice. "He has. Hopefully, to send us on our way."

"Indeed. I pray Yahweh commands us to strike at the Amalekites."

He smiled, though it felt forced. "As do I, Beny."

The three watched in silence as Samuel made his way through the camp. It was nearly nightfall when he finally arrived, leaning heavily on his cane as he stopped in front of Saul. He seemed to have aged a decade in the short time they'd been apart, and his brown robe looked even more worn than usual.

Though our last meeting was not a pleasant one.

"It is nice to see you," Saul said. "I have sorely missed our counsel."

Samual frowned. "We will not have *counsel*, Saul. I am not a counselor."

Saul felt a stab of anger at that. *Always critical. Always! I am*

Yahweh's anointed, the king of Israel, and he still speaks to me as to a child. "My apologies," he said, nearly biting his tongue to keep calm. "It was a poor choice of words."

The old man looked at him for a long moment, searching him. He was clearly hearing Yahweh's voice right now. *What is Yahweh telling you? What does he say of me?*

Finally, the old prophet sighed. "Come," he said, gesturing to Saul's tent. "I will tell you what Yahweh commands, and you will do what you will do."

Saul's fists balled at his sides. He felt like a child being chastised in front of his friends. *Not friends. In front of my armor-bearer and the commander of my army.*

Benyamin and Abner each held open a tent flap. Saul stepped aside and allowed Samuel to enter first before following him in.

"I bring you news you will like. A command you should have no trouble following this time." Samuel moved to Saul's cushion and sat, setting his cane down beside him. "This is very comfortable," he added, almost to himself.

Saul stood in front of him, hands folded at his back. He tried to ignore the jab but found himself talking anyway. "As I said at Gilgal, I did not mean to disobey. I thought that I—"

"Yahweh's commands are simple. You were to wait for me to present the sacrifice to Yahweh. Patience and faith were all you needed."

"You were later than we expected. My men were scattering. I am the king. Why could I not present the sacrifice in your stead?"

"Because you presented it with a selfish heart, out of fear. Fear of your enemies, fear of your own men. You presented the sacrifice so Yahweh would deliver you, so your men would believe they had his favor. You might as well have just burnt it for yourself."

"I was trying to do his will. To earn his favor."

Samuel met Saul's eyes. "You were trying to earn victory. He *wants* to bless you. Indeed, he has blessed you. Yet you still feel you know better than he. That as king of a nation, you are wiser than the king of kings."

"Am I not his chosen? Was it not you who anointed me?"

"Then why can you not act as such?"

Saul opened his mouth to speak, but the words fell dead on his tongue. *There is no arguing with this man.* "I will try to obey this time. What is it Yahweh commands?"

Samuel eyed him for another moment. "He sends you out to defeat the Amalekites. Yahweh wishes to punish them for what they did when Israel fled Egypt. He has heard your heart's desire, Saul, and he shares it."

A smile came to Saul's face. "He...he shares my desire?"

"Indeed, your will and his are together. But listen, Saul. Yahweh does not simply wish to defeat them; he wishes to punish them, and you shall be his righteous hand."

Saul's smile spread wider. *Finally!*

"He remembers what they did to us while Israel was still young, fleeing through the desert from Egypt with Moses. While our people were weary and worn out, they struck from the desert, murdering those who lagged behind, killing children and families. Now Yahweh wishes to turn his vengeance upon them. Listen carefully, Saul. Hear my words: Do not spare them, but kill both man and woman, child and infant, ox and sheep, camel and donkey. Nothing must be left alive. Do you understand? *Nothing.*"

Saul dropped to a knee. Finally, Yahweh was seeing things Saul's way.

"I will follow Yahweh's command, Samuel. The Amalekites will surely be destroyed."

3

DAVID

DAVID STEPPED through the trees and onto the edge of the field. The wounded sheep across his shoulders bleated once, as if in recognition of its home, and then went silent. The pastures were just as he'd left them nearly a full day ago: forty-four sheep all chewing absently at the green grass. His older brother Ozem and their younger cousin Abishai were now tending to the flock in his stead. His father's farm sat atop the hill to the west, rows of wheat and barley stretching into the horizon and melting into the setting sun behind it. He could smell the grass, the soil, even the sheep's dung that pockmarked the field.

He was home.

Yet as good as it felt to be home, his mind was elsewhere. It was stuck on the tremendous strength he had experienced, if only for a moment. Stuck on the voice he'd heard after slaying the lion.

It was not your sheep to lose. But it was yours to save.

It hadn't been his own thought, just as it hadn't been his own strength. He was sure of that, despite the fact it had come from inside his own head. Instead, it had felt like the thought of another, an intruding thought pushing its way into his mind.

Then what was it?

He was just thinking on whether to tell his father when the sheep on his shoulders bleated a reminder that they were not yet all the way home. David frowned up at the animal.

"Not enough you're alive, you wish to boss me around, as well?"

"David!"

David looked toward the voice, watched his father wade through the fields of wheat toward him. He looked happy, likely at the return of his sheep, until he saw the lion's blood on David's tunic. His face went hard as he ran the rest of the way.

His father skidded to halt before him and began to pat his chest, feeling for a wound. "What did you do?"

David frowned. *"What did you do?"* instead of *"Are you hurt?"* He laid the sheep on the soft grass, and it rolled its head over and began to eat.

"It's lion's blood." The words sounded strange, even to him. *Especially* to him. A fifteen-year-old boy slaying a lion. With rocks.

Not to mention the voice. Do I tell him?

"Lion's blood?" His father lifted his tunic to check the flesh underneath. "You're not injured?"

"No." David recounted the story, how he'd tracked the sheep and found it wounded. How he'd dropped the lion with his sling, leaving out how it had risen again. He did not tell his father of holding the lion, of the strength that had filled him in that moment. His father would likely not believe him.

I do not quite believe it myself.

"A lion," his father finally said. "And you killed it...with your sling?"

He nodded.

His father laughed, the sound echoing down the field. His

brother and cousin paused from their work and looked their way. When David didn't laugh in return, his father only grinned awkwardly. "I…I don't know if you are serious."

David only shrugged, not wanting to push the conversation any further.

His father's grin turned to a frown. "Come," he said, his voice trailing off as he eyed David. "Let's get this sheep inside and tended to."

He scooped up the sheep and followed his father to the small stable at the edge of the field. His father dug through a cabinet and came out with a small wooden box.

"There are thread and needle in here," he said, handing him the box. "As well as honey and oil to treat the wound."

David set the sheep down and opened the box. His father stood and looked at him for another few moments, still wearing that confused expression, before turning and leaving him alone. After he was gone, David looked down at the sheep. "Shall we?"

It bleated weakly and eyed the box.

"Sorry. It's going to hurt. Though not as much as a lion."

DAVID LOOKED up from the sheep and wiped his bloodied hands clean on a strip of linen. His impromptu bandage was replaced now with real stitching. Despite his threat to make the sheep the next sacrifice, he was glad to see it tended to. After trudging through the forest with the sheep across his back, he didn't want to see it die now that they returned home.

"You've been a pain, but I'm glad we're both safe now."

He stood and wiped his hands once more on the linen before throwing it aside. His eyes scanned the stable and fell upon a lyre sitting in the corner. Giving a final look to the sheep, who seemed to have already fallen asleep, David lifted the lyre and leaned into the corner. He plucked the strings, aimlessly at first, then slowly found a rhythm.

He wasn't sure why he chose the words. Perhaps the owner of this new voice put them there, or perhaps he was reciting them from a childhood memory of his mother singing him to sleep. But once his fingers were playing, he found himself speaking poetry, as well.

For you created my inmost being; you knit me together in my mother's womb. I praise you because I am fearfully and wonderfully made; your works are wonderful, I know that full well. My frame was not hidden from you when I was made in the secret place, when I was woven together in the depths of the earth. Your eyes saw my unformed body; all the days ordained for me were written in your book before one of them came to be.

"You play that very well."

He jerked upright and found a man several years older than himself looking in on him. The man wore a coat of leather armor. He had a sword at his hip, sickle-shaped like many of the weapons used by Israel's new army. David stood and set his lyre aside.

"Thank you."

The man stepped inside with an air of confidence despite his young age and surveryed the stable. His gaze finally fell on the sheep and its bandaged leg.

"You are a shepherd?"

David nodded, though his hand crept to his sling. "A shepherd's son," he corrected. "Though I have begun to tend the sheep. I am David, son of Jesse."

"I am Jonathan," he said. "Son of Saul."

The son of the king? David dropped to a knee.

"Rise, son of Jesse," he said. "I am but a man. I do not deserve a knee."

David stood. "But I have heard of you," he said, still awestruck at the warrior before him. "You struck down fifty men. By yourself."

Jonathan gave him a warm smile, and David immediately liked him. "It was closer to twenty," he said. "And I was never alone, David. My armor-bearer was with me. And always Yahweh goes before us. How else can we gain victory?"

David could think of nothing worthy to say in return and merely nodded his agreement.

Jonathan stepped forward and knelt at the sheep's side. He placed a hand on the bandage, and the sheep made a sleepy bleat that sounded halfway toward a snore.

"What happened to this one," he asked.

"He wandered. I found him the same time as a lion did."

He stood and eyed David. "A lion?"

David nodded.

"And you...you saved it?"

Another nod. "I killed the lion." He patted the sling at his side, almost absently. "With my sling." It did not sound quite as ridiculous as it had before.

They stared at one another for a long moment, then Jonathan looked at the sling and back to David. He appeared just as confused as his father had, though David felt the prince believed him.

"That is a story I would like to hear one day." He drew a breath. "But not today. Today, I am on a mission. Yahweh is sending us to battle. We are preparing to move to Hachilah to assemble an army to destroy the Amalekites. I was told Jesse had many sons, sons who would be willing to fight."

"He does," David said, keenly aware that, even if he

wanted to go, he would be asked to stay behind with the sheep. He'd opened his mouth to speak when the stable door slammed open. His father entered with Eliab following.

Jonathan turned to face them, taking a step back at the sight of Eliab, who stood almost a full head taller than Jonathan, twice that over David. His face was hard, as it always was, and expressionless. David often wondered if there was any emotion beneath the surface at all.

His father met Jonathan's eyes. A flash of recognition came over his face, and he and Eliab went to a knee. "What can we do for the son of the king?"

"You can rise, Jesse, son of Obed." As Jesse and Eliab rose, Jonathan continued. "King Saul has sent me to call upon the sons of Israel to help destroy the Amalekites. I was told at the town square that you have many."

Eliab stepped forward. "He does." He threw a glance over Jonathan's shoulder to David. "Though you will not find them among the lambs."

"I'm not a lamb," David shouted. He tried to sound firm, but the squeak in his voice only made Eliab smirk. David wanted to punch the smirk from his face, though he might need a stool to reach it.

Jonathan turned and looked at him. David felt ashamed for his outburst. He was in the presence of a prince and a warrior of Yahweh. He should act accordingly, regardless of Eliab's words. For a moment, Jonathan seemed to be in thought, his eyes drifting to the lyre in the corner. "You can never be sure where you will find something valuable," he said, almost to himself.

"I have other sons," his father said. As Jonathan turned back to him, he added, "Come, I will show you." He stepped aside and gestured for the prince to exit the stable. "Come."

The three stepped outside, his father leaving last. He

looked back at David as he left. "Keep an eye on the flock. Careful, this time. We will not be long."

"Of course, father."

Then David was alone.

Again.

4

SAUL

SAUL WRENCHED HIS SPEAR FREE. Blood sprayed up into his face, and his mouth filled with the metallic taste of it. He spat and wiped his eyes clean as he looked for his next target. Dozens of bodies blurred by before he could set up for another jab. His muscles moved from memory, aiming a bit high to compensate for the bouncing chariot, and his spear found the throat of another Amalekite. His chariot rocked. His arm jerked, and the spear snapped off in his victim's throat, leaving him with a broken stub of wood. He rammed it into the face of another Amalekite, the splintered wood crunching into bone and teeth, and dropped the ruined shaft.

Here in battle, he was at home. Here in battle, he was king. The men followed his lead, and he led them fearlessly. No more doubt about Samuel, no more worrying if his men would scatter. Here he could be himself, could be the warrior that he knew he was meant to be. And he loved it.

Benyamin stood beside him, a large shield of acacia in his hand. He protected Saul and the chariot driver, his eyes darting among the bodies for any incoming threat. The shield itself was covered in arrows, their fletching sticking up like the bristles of a porcupine. Grainy sand and the blood of his enemies filled Saul's teeth, the roar of battle filled his ears. He drew his sword, its weight comfortable in his hands, and let out a war cry of his own.

Amalekites lunged aside as his chariot plowed through their ranks. He found a target, one who stood his ground, spear and wicker shield in hand. Saul nearly felt pity for the man. *Brave he may be, but he will die all the same.* His arm arced up and down, and his chariot raced by the Amalekite, his head no longer attached to his body. Soon blood was flowing like a river from his sickle-shaped blade as he cut down his enemies.

The chariot lurched. Saul nearly fell before grabbing onto the waist-high wall and catching himself. He heard the wood grinding on stone and looked down to see one of the wheels frozen in place, dragging and scraping on the hard ground. A spear was lodged through the spokes, and its end had punched through the chariot wall only a handbreadth from his thigh.

He jabbed out with his sword, catching an Amalekite through the back, and then hacked through the spear. It cut through the shaft with ease, and the wheel began to spin again, though it wobbled precariously.

A shadow loomed over him, and he heard the telltale thud of a spear piercing wood. Benyamin was standing over him, the tip of a spear staring down at him from inside his armor-bearer's shield.

Benyamin stepped aside, and Saul sprang back up, his blade curving down and cracking along a man's collarbone. Blood sprayed up as the man went down. He raised his sword again and felt a shudder. Before he could react, the wheel spun off his chariot, and he was crashing into the dirt. He landed on his left arm and a searing pain shot through it and into his shoulder. His head swam, ringing filled his ears, dust filled his eyes. He coughed and spat sand, then rose to a knee.

His chariot clattered on, dragging on its side and bouncing

against the hard ground, still being pulled along by the pair of horses. His driver bounced along with it, the reins wrapped around his hands and his body, flopping like a dying fish. The sound of battle came back to Saul as the ringing faded into the distance. Behind him came the whistle of a blade biting through the air and—on reflex more than reaction—Saul ducked as a sword sliced through the space his head had just been. He spun and rose, his sword turning upward and entering the Amalekite through the stomach and exiting between his shoulder blades. He watched as life left the man before he slid off his blade and onto the sand.

Three more men surrounded him, creeping in closer with weapons raised. Saul gripped his sword, fear crawling up his spine. The first man lunged forward and then stopped midstep, an arrow sprouting from his throat. The other two turned and were cut down as a chariot roared past. Jonathan raised his bow from the chariot and saluted Saul. Then the chariot rumbled into the rising dust and vanished.

"Behind me!"

Saul heard Benyamin's shout, his armor-bearer moving like lightning. In a moment, he was standing over Saul and pushing him into the sand before he even realized what was happening. There were several thuds on the other side of the shield, and Benyamin faltered for just a moment. Saul wasted no time rising to his feet. He darted out from behind his cover, his blade dancing between a new trio of Amalekites. *Why do they come in threes?* Each strike found flesh and forced them back, bleeding from legs and arms. Behind them stood a dozen more, their eyes hungry with bloodlust.

He and Benyamin went back to back as the Amalekites roared in. The two of them were in constant motion. Their years of side-by-side training made their bodies move on their own. Benyamin's shield and Saul's sword moved as a pair of dancers, one deflecting oncoming blows and the other following with graceful curves that left spiraling ribbons of blood. He lost track of time as their bodies moved. Sweat and sand and blood stung his eyes, his muscles ached, still he pressed on. The corpses began to pile around them, yet the Amalekites continued to charge in like bugs to a flame.

Soon, the roar of his Israelite army joined that of the Amalekites, and his enemies fell back under the onslaught. A few heartbeats later Benyamin and Saul stood alone and breathless as Saul's army pursued the Amalekites into the distance. His muscles screamed in pain. He bent over, breathing in deep, shuddering breaths as Benyamin did the same beside him.

"Are you well, my king?"

Saul looked at his armor-bearer, his friend. Like himself, Benyamin was covered nearly head to toe in Amalekite blood and perhaps some of their own. His heavy shield was pocked and chipped and cracked, a stray sword still hanging from one particularly nasty gash.

"I am well, Beny." Saul drew a deep breath. They were standing atop a low hill, a shallow valley before them. His men were still flooding into the valley, running down the Amalekites and pursuing them up the other side. Beyond that final rise, Saul could just make out the tops of some of the homes of Shur. Smoke was already beginning to rise from the village. "Yahweh has delivered us today, my friend." He sucked another deep breath through his nose, the scent of sand and sweat filling his nostrils. *The scent of victory*. "I am well. Come," he added, walking down the low hill and toward Shur. "Let us finish this."

BY THE TIME Saul and Benyamin reached Shur, fires were raging throughout the village. Homes and shops and fields were ablaze, roaring red flames dancing fifteen cubits high and billowing black smoke into the sky. Some of the wheat fields had already burned out, leaving a charred brown stain on the earth.

The scream of his sore muscles had fallen to a dull ache as Saul walked through the destruction. The stench of charred flesh and smoke and ash was already filling the air. Saul pulled his tunic up over his mouth and nose. They were still at the edge of the village, yet they could hear the shouts—both of victory and of pain—echoing in the distance. Out of the rolling smoke came one of his men, trailing a pair of oxen behind him. Saul stepped aside as he led the beasts out of the village, sacks filled with goods hanging from their backs.

"Nothing must be left alive."

He shook Samuel's words from his head just as another Israelite appeared through the smoke. He had the lead of a goat—also laden down with goods—and was sprinting toward Saul. This time, Saul stood in his way. The man looked annoyed, angry almost, until he saw who it was. He instantly dropped to a knee, yet the annoyance remained on his face.

"My king!"

"Were my orders unclear?"

The man's eyebrows raised. "My king?"

"Leave nothing alive. Did I not say that?"

The man looked back toward the smoke, the annoyance replaced with confusion. "We...we killed everyone, my king. We're still doing it. Do you not hear the screams?"

Saul made a show of eyeing the goat.

"A sacrifice," the man said quickly. "To Yahweh. To honor him!" He stood and moved beside the goat, pulling at its coat. "See how choice it is? How very fat? It will make a wonderful sacrifice to Yahweh!"

Saul only frowned. He did not like that explanation and doubted Samuel would, either. Yet what could be said? Should he deny spoils to his people, spoils that will eventually be destroyed as Samuel commanded? And sacrificed, at that. Surely Yahweh would be pleased.

"Shall we leave with nothing," the man went on, almost reading Saul's mind. Saul was too distracted to notice the contempt in the man's voice. "Shall we return to our homes with nothing but wounds?"

Saul had no words to argue. "Be sure it is sacrificed," he said. "Within a month."

The man smiled and bowed low. "Of course, my king!" He bowed again and then pulled the goat around Saul. "Thank you!"

And then he was gone, leaving Saul with only doubt in his decision.

He and Benyamin ventured farther on through the destruction and mayhem. The screams they had heard were fading. The fires were burning themselves out. Shur was not the largest of villages. They began to pass bodies piled by the roadway, their limbs intermingled like worms and spoiled like a rotting apple. Their mouths hung open, their death screams locked on their faces forever. Saul could see the faces of both men and women, and he knew his soldiers had taken his command to heart.

At least when it came to the people.

Soon they stepped into the central square. Here two crisscrossing roads met and formed a wide-open space. A post had been dug and planted in its center, its top sharpened to a jagged point. Some of his soldiers were kicking at something on the ground, while another pair were working with makeshift scaffolding roughly the same height as the sharpened post.

The men stopped what they were doing as Saul stepped into the square and turned to him almost as one. Saul saw a body lying in the dirt behind them. The body shifted and spat blood onto the ground. He raised his eyes slowly and glared at Saul.

"Who is that," Saul asked. He understood the sharpened post now, understood the torturous mode of execution his men had chosen. To put a man on that and let him slowly slide down to his death...the thought made Saul shiver.

The Israelites all dropped to a knee. "This is Agag, king of Amalek," one of them said.

Saul looked at the post and then to the wounded king. He was bloodied nearly from head to toe, his clothes ripped from his body and hanging in tattered rags. Several of his teeth were gone, and though he was still glaring at Saul with barely contained hatred, he could see the pain in his eyes.

"You would hang him on that post," Saul asked, though he kept his eyes on Agag.

"We would, my king."

"And he would meet a slow death?"

"Excruciatingly slow, my king."

Agag snarled at him and then winced at the slight movement.

"Let him live," Saul said. "I would have him see the death we have wrought. Then you may do with him as you wish. We have posts in Israel too."

SAUL LOOKED DOWN at the valley below. All Carmel was laid out before him, the walled city standing in the shadow of the setting sun. The horizon was many leagues distant, etched by the western mountain range and the cliffs of En Gedi. He watched his army move north, toward Gilgal. Never had he seen such a force. Thousands of foot soldiers marched in the valley, flowing like a massive river. The ground shook at their march, and dust filled the sky and shrouded the already orange sun in a brown cloud.

Footsteps sounded behind him, and he turned to find Benyamin pulling a pair of horses. His armor-bearer looked good despite his many wounds. Both he and Saul had dozens of superficial cuts—though Saul did have a large gash in one bicep that had taken more than a few painful stitches.

Benyamin went to a knee. "My king."

"Rise, Beny."

He did, and they turned in unison to look at the army. After a long pause, Benyamin spoke. "Yahweh has done miraculous things."

"He has, Beny. He has."

Yet Saul felt uneasy. After many battles and many victories over his enemies, something still tugged at his heart. As he watched his army move, he spotted herds of sheep and cattle taken from the Amalekites. At the army's front, bound and stripped down to a loincloth, marched Agag, the Amalekite king. Samuel's words rang in Saul's ears.

"Nothing must be left alive. Do you understand? Nothing."

But his men had promised that these sheep and cattle would be sacrifices. Surely Yahweh would be satisfied with that. They had, after all, kept only the fattest and choicest of cattle. Only the best. Everything else they had destroyed. Then his eyes drifted once more to Agag.

And that was not even the end of it. He'd given up too early, had turned back before finishing Yahweh's commands. A dozen Amalekite cities fell after Shur, Saul conquering them all the way to Egypt. But his men grumbled after that. They begged to return home with their plunder and their new cattle and oxen and sheep. He knew he should have pressed them on, knew he should have remained in the east and moved his army south through the rest of Amalek. But a grumbling army would fail him, and he knew that, as well. So, they had turned back early, before Amalek had been completely destroyed as Yahweh had commanded.

"Nothing…"

Benyamin looked at him. "My king?"

He sighed. "Nothing, Beny. I am just eager to get to Gilgal. Samuel will be there, and my heart yearns to worship Yahweh." Yet Saul knew that was not the truth. The feeling in his heart was not yearning. It was fear.

THE RISING hill of Gilgal appeared in the distance, and a smile twitched at the edge of Saul's lips. He had fond memories of this place. Indeed, all Israel did. He could see the twelve stones stacked on the western slope where Joshua had placed them when Israel first crossed into the Promised Land.

A land that I now rule as king. Samuel himself anointed me here.

The sun was rising behind them as he and Benyamin pulled to a stop. His army flowed around him. He watched as Agag was led at the front. After he passed, Saul sat atop his horse in silence as the remainder of his army marched around the hillock that was Gilgal.

His army was smaller. Many of the men had returned to their homes, bringing their spoils with them and leaving Saul with the promise that the animals would be sacrificed to Yahweh.

It was the right thing to do, Saul reminded himself. *My men deserve some spoils, some reward for doing Yahweh's work. What better than choice sacrifices?*

He pushed his weary thoughts aside—he had thought on nothing else during their travel here—and urged his horse forward. It was late morning when Saul arrived at the center of the newly formed camp. His tent was built at the top of the hillock. Inside, he found a plate of fruits and meats atop a wooden stool. He cleaned the dust from his feet and picked at the food, brushing aside the dates and figs and instead plucking the dried meats.

"They were good battles."

Saul turned to see Abner and felt a smile go to his lips. "They were, my friend."

They embraced in the center of the tent. Despite the words, Abner looked as discontented as Saul felt. "I…I saw Agag coming in."

Saul tensed. "Yes."

"And many sheep and cattle."

"Yes…"

Abner fidgeted. "I…I thought Samuel had instructed, I mean that Yahweh had commanded…"

Saul stepped forward and placed a hand on his shoulder. "It is okay." *Is it?* "The men have given their word that their spoils will be sacrificed to Yahweh. So, they *will* be destroyed, in time."

Abner didn't look satisfied with the explanation. Indeed, it hadn't quite satisfied Saul.

"Should I tell my men no? Send them home with nothing? How would I get them to return if I sent them home empty handed?"

"I…I do not have the answer, my king. I only know what Yahweh commanded."

His tent flap snapped open. Saul spun to find Samuel stepping in. The old man wore a scowl, which wasn't much different from what Saul had become accustomed to. Saul stepped around Abner, spread his arms out, and forced a smile to his face.

"Bless you, Samuel," Saul said. "I have completed Yahweh's commands."

For a moment, Samuel held his scowl and said nothing. Then, as sudden as the dawning of the sun, he erupted in anger. "Then what is this bleating of sheep I hear?! This lowing of cattle?!"

Curse you, old man.

"The soldiers," Saul began. "My men. They brought the plunder from the Amalekites. They have spared the choicest and fattest of the cattle and sheep, the best Amalek had to offer, to *sacrifice* to Yahweh. The weakest were destroyed, the thin and—"

"Stop!"

Saul clenched his jaw and fell silent. He felt like a scolded child and was keenly aware of Abner's silent presence. Outside, the cattle and sheep seemed to quiet, as well. Indeed, even the wind stopped blowing.

Samuel drew a breath, obviously trying to steady his emotions. "Let me tell you what Yahweh said to me last night," he said, his voice even and calm despite the anger on his face.

"Tell me," Saul said through gritted teeth.

"Were you not once small in your own eyes? Yet did Yahweh not anoint you king over all Israel? Over his chosen people?"

"He did."

"You are a king, Saul, yet you allowed these men to dictate to you. Did Yahweh not give clear commands? Did I not say that nothing must live? *Nothing?*"

Saul was at least thankful Samuel said nothing of the entire cities they had not even conquered. "You did."

"Why can you not obey him? Why did you let your men pounce on this plunder?" He drew another breath, and the anger faded, replaced with a pity that caused Saul's own anger to burn all the hotter. "Why?"

"But I did obey," Saul shouted, taking an involuntary step forward. "I obeyed his commands. I destroyed the Amalekites. The women, Samuel…" Saul's voice broke. "We carried out your command and—"

"It was not *my* command, Saul."

"We obeyed Yahweh! We killed everyone. And yet I am being harassed over some cattle! Some sheep! The *soldiers* took the plunder—only the best—to *devote* to Yahweh. To *sacrifice* to him."

"Does the LORD delight in burnt offerings and sacrifices as much as in obeying the LORD? To obey is better than sacrifice, and to heed is better than the fat of rams."

He is going to ruin it. He is going to make me look weak. Me...the king of Israel. He glanced at Abner, found him looking down. *He is already shaming me in front of the commander of my army.* Saul felt his own anger surging up inside him, threatening to boil over. Yet he knew he could not lead this nation without Samuel, without the voice of Yahweh. He closed his eyes and drew a breath.

Very well, old man. You win.

"I have sinned," he said, the words tasting like filth in his mouth, perhaps because he did not mean them. "I violated Yahweh's commands and your instructions. I was...afraid. I feared losing the support of my men, my soldiers." This, at least, was truth. He dropped to his knees. "I beg you, forgive my sin. Forgive my weakness. Come out with me so that I may worship Yahweh in your presence, so my men may see us together."

There was a long silence as they stared at one another, the most powerful man in Israel brought low in front of an old man. Samuel's judging eyes looked down on him. Saul could nearly taste the contempt. Then the prophet's face broke, and Saul thought he could just catch the glint of a tear in the old man's eye.

"No."

Saul's stomach lurched to his throat. "What?"

"I cannot go with you. You have rejected the word of Yahweh. Therefore, he has rejected you as king."

Saul felt his heart beat in his head, tasted vomit in his mouth. Samuel looked at him one final time, opened his mouth as if he were going to speak, and then simply turned to leave. Saul sprang forward and caught the hem of his robe.

"No! Wait!"

The robe tore, Samuel stumbled, and Saul fell to his hands and knees, clutching the piece of fabric. Samuel spun, the anger renewed on his face. He looked at his torn robe and then down to the torn cloth in Saul's hand. "Yahweh has torn the kingdom of Israel from you. He has given it to another—one who is better than you."

The words pierced Saul's heart more sharply than any blade ever could. Fear came quickly on the tail of that pain. *The men will abandon me. If Samuel says this to them, they will leave. I will be nothing…*

"I have sinned," he said, his voice low and trembling. "But…but please at least honor me. Come out with me before the men, before my army. Let them see us together. Let us worship Yahweh together."

Samuel's face fell, the anger replaced with a deep sadness that Saul had never seen. Without a word, he turned and stepped from the tent. Saul rose and followed. Benyamin was waiting for them, holding the tent flap open like the dutiful armor-bearer he was. He averted his eyes, looking to the ground as Samuel stepped by. Saul placed a hand on his shoulder as he passed.

Did he hear us?

Benyamin's face gave little away, and Saul took a hurried pair of steps to move beside Samuel. The prophet was standing still, looking out at the men still gathering below. Saul could see his eyes drifting to the cattle and sheep, falling eventually on Agag. The former king was tied to a post, his hands bound behind him as he sat in the dirt.

"Bring him to me," he said, his eyes unmoving. Saul turned

and nodded to Benyamin, who quickly jogged off toward Agag.

Samuel and Saul stood in silence, the air between them thick with tension. Behind them, Abner finally stepped out of the tent. He fell into place beside Saul and remained silent.

When Benyamin returned, Agag was trembling. Saul recalled the last time he'd seen him, stripped down and ready to be put upon a post. No doubt, the king thought he was about to receive that very fate. In truth, however, Saul had little idea what Samuel planned to do.

The old prophet stepped up to Agag. "As your sword has made women childless, so will your mother be childless among women."

His hand shot out with a swiftness that surprised Saul. It found Benyamin's short sword, old fingers gripping the hilt with surprising strength. The next thing Saul knew, Agag's head was spinning through the air and Yahweh's prophet was holding a bloodied blade.

"I...you..." Saul stuttered.

Samuel watched in silence as Agag's body fell to the ground, twitching and filling the dirt with blood. He dropped the sword and turned to Saul. The sadness from a moment ago was replaced with a stern expression.

"Go to Gibeah. To your home. It is unlikely we will see one another again."

He turned and walked away; Saul stood, too stunned to follow.

5

DAVID

THE SLING WHISTLED over David's head, his muscles flexing as he whipped it round and round. His eyes were on the rock sitting atop a fence post more than twenty cubits away. He drew a breath, squinted in concentration, then released. The sling whipped straight, one end staying around his finger while the other shot out and threw the small stone in the pouch. The stone spiraled through the air, bending slightly to the right with the crosswind, then smashed into the rock on the fence post.

He heard Abishai give a low whistle of respect beside him. He looked over to his younger cousin, who was smiling, as he always was. They were together in the sheep fields. Since the incident with the lost sheep, David had not been left alone with them. Ozem was usually with him, but with the prophet Samuel's sudden visit—and his request to see all his father's sons—his cousin was now keeping him company.

Apparently, Samuel did not want to see all *of us.*

Not that he minded, if he was honest. It seemed that his cousin was the only one who actually wanted to be in his company.

"I bet you can't do it twice in a row," Abishai said.

David reached into his pouch and retrieved another stone. "And when I do?"

"I'll tell Eliab he smells like sheep dung."

He loaded the sling, his eyes on the rock on the next fence post. "I hope you're not overly fond of your teeth because he's going to punch them out." He swung the sling overhead and let the stone fly. It bent again to the right and clipped the rock, sending them both spinning in opposite directions.

Abishai clicked his tongue and frowned. "Let's hope he's in a good mood."

David laughed at that. "He's never in a good mood." He tucked his sling into his belt and started across the field to retrieve his stones. Abishai fell into step beside him.

"David!"

He and Abishai turned together and found Eliab and Abinadab approaching from the west. They were not quite running, but it was clear they were moving with urgency. He forgot about his stones and jogged across the field to meet his brothers. Eliab eyed him with suspicion, then glanced down at his pouch of remaining stones.

"Stop playing with your pebbles and come."

David's face reddened with anger. "They're not pebbles," he said, his voice barely above a whisper.

Eliab scoffed. "They're not a sword, either. Now come. Samuel wishes to see you."

His brothers turned and started walking away, not waiting for a response.

Samuel? To see me?

Perhaps he needs a shepherd, the voice said.

Who are you? He waited, his heart thumping in his head, but there was no answer.

Eliab stopped and turned around. "You coming?"

David shook his head clear and looked himself over. He was covered in dirt and grime, mostly from digging for the stones for his sling. His hands were calloused and his nails dirty. *No way to meet a prophet.*

"He does not care how you look," Abinadab said. David looked up and noticed both his brothers' eyes on him. "He did not care for our appearance, and you are much less to look upon. A little dirt will not make a difference."

Eliab threw a glance at Abishai. "Watch the sheep." Then they led David through the fields, around his father's home, and down the road that led into town.

"What does Samuel wish of me?"

"I don't know," Eliab said. "He has spoken with the rest of us. All of father's sons." He threw David a sideways glance. "All of his *real* sons."

David ignored the jab. "All seven of you?"

He nodded. "Perhaps he wishes to meet the smallest, as well."

Abinadab laughed at that. "I guess he needs to see the runt to appreciate the stallions."

David gritted his teeth, everything in him wanting to bash his brothers along the backs of their heads. Yet he remained silent until they came to the altar near the edge of Bethlehem. It seemed to David that the entire town had gathered, young and old, to witness Samuel's sacrifice. The heifer was already stretched out upon the altar, its blood staining the stone. His father stood near the front, and the rest of David's brothers ranged alongside him. All eyes were on David as he approached, Eliab and Abinadab now following a step behind.

As the crowd parted, Samuel finally came into view. He was unremarkable. Older, somewhat dirty himself, a bit of the heifer's blood staining his own hands. David almost smiled at that, now suddenly less self-conscious of his own appearance. He approached his father and moved to stand behind him.

His father put a hand on his back and pressed him toward

Samuel. "No, David. He is the one who wishes to speak with you."

David stepped up to the prophet. He stopped a handful of paces from him, and the prophet eyed him, searching. He paused as if he were listening to something. There was not a sound in the air. No breathing, no humming of birds or lowing of nearby cattle. The wind had even stopped. The air sat heavy on David's head.

"Very well," Samuel suddenly said, though he seemed to be talking to himself. He held a horn of oil in his hand. "David, son of Jesse, son of Obed, Yahweh has chosen you this day."

A hushed murmur went through the crowd as David's stomach lurched to his throat. "Chosen? For what?"

"Yahweh is in need of a shepherd."

"I am learning to be a shepherd," David said.

Samuel smiled. "That is convenient. Though a day will come when he will need more."

More? I can barely keep track of the sheep I have.

And yet they are alive and well, the voice said.

David shook his head clear and looked at Samuel. "I don't understand."

"You do not need to. Not yet. Just know that we are all called for something. I am called to speak his voice. Your brothers are called to wield his sword. You are called for something different."

The prophet raised the horn of oil over him, and then David felt its soothing effect as it cascaded down his face and inside his tunic. As the oil ran down his skin, he felt more than its touch. He felt a strength in his limbs, felt his heart beat faster. His skin prickled as the oil ran, the hairs on his arms and chest buzzing. His entire body felt as his arm had when he held the lion, throbbing and aching and pulsing with strength. And he knew; he finally understood whose voice he was hearing.

Yahweh?

Yes, David.

Who am I? Who am I that you speak to me?

Man after my own heart.

He fell to his knees and bent his face down to the dirt and rocks.

Whatever this is, I can't do it. Take this from me.

I need you.

How can Yahweh need any man?

You will see. Rise, David.

Yet David stayed on the ground. He had long felt unwanted, unloved, unnecessary. And now that Yahweh was speaking directly to him, telling him he needed him, he longed for the voice to go. Whatever Yahweh had chosen him for, whatever need lay beyond his sheep, David wanted nothing of it. He was the youngest of his family, the smallest of his brothers. And even among them, he was only a shepherd. In that moment, he wanted nothing more than to return to his sheep, the sheep he was only just becoming accustomed to, the job that he was only barely able to do.

Finally, he stood. He opened eyes he had not realized were closed. Samuel had not moved, though he wore a satisfied smile. All around him, onlookers stared with shock on their faces. In his fifteen years of life, David had never felt more uncomfortable, more out of place. Surely Yahweh had made a mistake, had chosen the wrong son of Jesse.

"Remember, you must always keep Yahweh before you. Do not forget that."

David had no words and could only nod.

"Very good," the old prophet said, seemingly satisfied with the day's events. He smiled at David one final time and then turned to his father. "Shall we eat?"

6

SAUL

SAUL ROCKED as the horse swayed, his legs reflexively keeping him from falling. He had no strength left, no will. At first, after Samuel had left him trembling in front of his tent with a dead king before him, he had been angry, angrier than he'd ever been. He'd screamed and kicked the dead king's body over and over again, careless of the eyes on him. Then, when his muscles ached and his head pounded, fear had taken the place of the anger. His men would discover soon enough that he was no longer Yahweh's anointed, no longer the rightful king of Israel.

"He has given it to another—one who is better than you."

The words had cut deep, deeper still because Abner had heard them. Saul's eyes drifted to the commander of his armies. The man sat tall atop his horse, surveying the men around him. He was confident, a godly man, a faithful man.

Is he the new king? Will he take Israel from me?

Another thought followed quickly behind that one: *I'll not let him.*

Deserving or not, Yahweh's anointed or not, Saul was king of Israel. *And I'll not let* anyone *take that from me.*

He sat a bit taller, projecting a confidence he did not feel, as he climbed a final hill and Gibeah came into view. High walls surrounded the city, a circle of stone protection that looked even more impressive from his high vantage point. The walls had been his first project once he became king of Israel. He had no intention of leaving his hometown undefended.

Inside the city, near the center, was his palace, his second project as king. It was smaller than he had anticipated, though it was still the most impressive structure within the city. A second set of low walls surrounded it—not quite as tall or thick as those around the entirety of Gibeah, yet nothing to scoff at, either. A large gate of acacia led through the walls, and he could see the greenery of his courtyard even from here.

The sight of his city, much improved under his kingship, brought a bit of real confidence into Saul's heart. Israel was prospering, Gibeah was prospering, his people were prospering. Saul was, by all outward signs, a successful king.

It was only ever Yahweh that held me back, he thought.

After another hour, he was riding through the gate of his courtyard with Benyamin and Abner. Olive trees and grass and stone pathways guided the way to his palace. He could see the steps ahead, radiating out from the palace doors in ever-increasing half moons, nearly ten cubits wide at the base. He dismounted, handing his reins to a waiting stablemaster and—

"My king!"

He turned to the voice, a hand reaching for his blade before he could stop it. A messenger ran through the gates and knelt. He was young, younger than Jonathan. His clothes were ragged, his face covered in sweat and grime.

"Rise, boy," Abner said. Saul felt a sudden fury rise in him.

He speaks for me now?

The boy rose. "I have come from Ephes Dammim, in the Valley of Elah," he said. "The Philistines have come!"

Saul tensed. "Explain," he said.

The boy looked at Abner and then at Saul. "They arrived five days ago. An army. Thousands!"

Saul wrung his hands together behind his back. *I have only just returned, and already an enemy is waiting for me.*

"Abner, speak to the boy. Find out as much as you can."

He turned and, with Benyamin close behind him, entered a vast hall about a dozen cubits across. Columns of hardened acacias lined the central walkway, and expansive windows let in the soft morning sun, throwing dim rectangles of light onto the woolen carpets.

He stood at the entryway and faced the hall as Benyamin stepped beside him with spear and shield. His palace was a busy place, even in his absence. Elders from the twelve tribes of Israel were always present, always politicking. Priests and Levites flowed in and out. Prophets big and small pined to have their voices heard, striving to become Samuel's successor or make some impression on the king.

He looked at his throne at the far end. He wanted to sit, wanted to relax and let his muscles finish recovering, but he was restless. His mind was already on the Philistines at Ephes Dammim. Thousands, the boy had said. When he eventually crossed the hall, the crowd's gaze followed him as the conversations dipped. He took his seat and surveyed his hall. Everyone's scrutiny lingered on him another moment before they returned to their own discussions. He felt a scowl come unbidden to his face. None seemed to be paying him any attention, and yet he feared them. Even though Samuel's words—Samuel's disowning of him—had been spoken in private, they seemed to be following Saul wherever he went.

The doors slammed open, and Jonathan stepped into the hall. Around him, the men present broke into spontaneous applause, and Saul felt a swell of pride in his son, for the moment not realizing that he had received no such praise. He rose from his throne and nearly ran across the hall to embrace him in a bear hug.

"Father," Jonathan groaned. "You're crushing me."

Saul gripped him tight one last time and then released him. "I am glad you are here, son," he said, genuine joy filling him for the first time since Samuel had made his declaration. He stepped back and looked at his son. Jonathan seemed older than when he had last seen him only a month ago during the battle. And stronger. Yet there was something else about him, something changed. He seemed more self-assured, more confident. A commander rather than a soldier.

He is...kingly. Suddenly Saul felt a distrust he had not felt before, at least not directed at his own blood. *I knew you would replace me, but I thought it would be after my death.*

Jonathan seemed to sense his discomfort. He leaned in close, his voice low in the scattered applause still filling the hall. "Are you well, father?"

Saul frowned and then raised a hand to those around him. The applause tapered off, and everyone went back to their business. "I am well," he said. "Just weary." Abner stepped in through the still open doors. "And it appears we have yet another battle to fight."

Abner stepped around Jonathan and dropped to a knee. "My king."

Saul let him stay kneeling longer than usual. After a dozen heartbeats, he finally replied. "Rise, my friend."

Abner rose, frowning with worry for the briefest of moments.

"Come," Saul said, turning and gesturing toward his throne at the back of the hall. "Let us have counsel." Abner and Jonathan followed him to the throne, then stood in front of it while Saul took his place. "Now, what did the boy have to say?"

Jonathan turned an inquisitive gaze to Abner.

"It's true," Abner said. "The Philistines are gathering to the east."

"Then we gather, as well," Jonathan said, his solution coming so quickly and confidently that Saul almost flinched. "They cannot stand before the armies of Yahweh."

Saul smiled, though only to hide the new distrust of his son. *There is no fault in this boy. I used to think that was a good thing.*

"Patience, son," he said and turned back to Abner. "Did the boy know their numbers? Their equipment?"

"I am afraid not," Abner said. "He guessed at over ten thousand but said he did not feel safe enough to stay and gather more information."

Saul reclined in his throne, his chin resting on his hand. *A chance to show them I do not need Samuel...*

He stood, hoping to elicit confidence with the motion. "I am Yahweh's anointed," he said, with all the authority he could muster. Abner's face remained stoic. "Yahweh will be with us. We will face them, and we will show them that Yahweh has not forsaken Israel."

And yet he did not believe his own words.

Abner nodded, his face unreadable. "I have no doubt, my king, though it will take some time to reassemble the army. They have all returned home." He paused, leaned in, and lowered his voice to a whisper. "Should I...send for Samuel?"

A sudden fury seized Saul, and he took a commanding step forward. "You will send for no one!" His voice echoed off the walls. The conversations throughout the hall cut short, everyone's heads jerking his direction. If he had not gained their attention with his previous expression of false confidence, he seemed to have achieved it with his childish outburst. He studied the crowd, angry and fearful at the same time. He felt himself losing control, felt Samuel's words taking hold of him.

"Leave us!" At first, no one moved. Saul stepped between

Abner and Jonathan and toward those gathered. "I said *leave us!*"

The crowd finally began to move, shuffling through the doors without urgency. Saul watched, every second heightening his anger, deepening his fear. By the time the hall cleared, he was trembling with emotion.

"I…I meant no disrespect."

Saul spun back toward Abner, embracing the rage and pushing his fear to the back. His commander's eyes were lowered; his son looked on, confused. Jonathan had not been present when Samuel disowned him. *But you were, Abner. You know what Samuel said to me.*

"You meant no disrespect?!" he shouted. "Yet you gave it! In front of everyone!" Saul balled his trembling fists. He wanted to strike Abner, to strike something. He stomped back to his throne and slapped the nearby plate of food, sending bits of bread and cheese flying. His childish reaction and the following mess only heightened his rage. He found himself kicking over his throne, sending the heavy chair crashing onto the stone floor where it split in two. "I am Yahweh's anointed," he shouted. "I do not *need* Samuel! I do not *need* that old man!"

"My king…"

Saul turned to find Abner regarding him with pity. *Pity! I do not deserve pity!*

He snatched the spear from Benyamin and took a step toward Abner. The tip shot up, ripping through his tunic and drawing blood. Abner stumbled back, falling to the ground with a superficial scratch on his chest. Jonathan leaped aside, his hand going to his sword and halting at the hilt.

You would draw on your father?!

Abner touched his wound and then looked back at Saul. The sight of the blood broke Saul's mood. A redness he had not noticed before faded from his vision. He glanced again at Jonathan and saw the dismay in his son's eyes. His rage vanished in a heartbeat, and the fear that he had pushed to the back of his mind came rushing forward. He felt like a child, felt like curling into a ball and hiding.

"I...I am sorry..." The spear fell from his hand and clattered to the floor. He dropped to his knees. "What...what am I doing, Abner?"

His friend stood, slowly, and made his way toward him. "You are being tormented, my king."

Saul looked at his hands as if they held the answer and then looked back up at Abner. Jonathan still stood to the side, his hand on his hilt and a dumbfounded expression on his face. Abner stepped forward and put a hand on Saul's shoulder.

"Something is at work here—some evil spirit. Perhaps... perhaps something to ease the king's mind? A musician? The harp and lyre are most soothing instruments."

Saul felt his hands begin to shake. He closed them into fists and pressed them into his eyes. "I don't know what I am doing. I am...I am afraid. Afraid of the Philistines, afraid of my people." He felt hot tears spread over his fists. "I am afraid of Samuel, of being found wanting. Without him, I fear that every decision I make is the wrong one." He drew a shuddering breath, his voice dropping to a whisper. "I am afraid of Yahweh."

"The fear of Yahweh is the beginning of understanding."

Saul slapped Abner's hand from his shoulder. "I do not feel in *awe* of him! I do not *revere* him! I *fear* him! I fear his judgment, his fury, his wrath. I fear him as one fears a thunderstorm. As one fears the lightning from the heavens, ready to strike us down at its whim. He is not just. He does not keep his promises. He is not fair, he has no honor. He is a god on a cloud, ready to strike us whenever he is displeased."

Abner's eyes remained calm, his face still unreadable. Benyamin, however, looked horrified. His jaw hung open, the shield in his hands sagged. "This is not Yahweh's anointed speaking," Abner said.

Saul frowned at that. Abner apparently missed the irony. "You are right, old friend...It is not."

There was a long silence in the hall. Jonathan remained frozen in place. Benyamin's shield still sagged. The only sound was Saul's heart beating in his head, thumping like a war drum.

"You are being tormented," Abner repeated. "There is an evil spirit at work. Let us send for one who can play the lyre, one whose skill can chase away the spirit that plagues you."

Saul simply stared at the ground. "It is true," he said. "I do not feel myself. I feel...split. Perhaps if there is one so skilled..."

"I know one," Jonathan finally said, though his voice was shaky. "A son of Jesse. His youngest. I saw him playing in Bethlehem when I recruited his elder brothers. He was righteous and loved Yahweh. He did not join us to fight, but he had the look of a warrior about him." Jonathan nodded quickly, almost to himself. "I will go. I will bring him, and you will be free of this spirit."

7

DAVID

FORTY-THREE, forty-four, forty-five.

David stood back and looked again at his forty-five sheep, his eyes drifting to the one that walked with a noticeable limp. It'd been months since he'd lost it in the woods, and he had not lost another since. His father had finally allowed him to stay alone in the fields, sending Abishai back to his mother, David's sister Zeruiah.

As the sun began to dip beneath the horizon, the scattered clouds suddenly shone with a mixture of oranges, blues, and purples. In the east a few stars twinkled to life, and the moon had already peeked over the trees. The scent of wet grass and the cool night air filled David's nostrils. A few random bleats punctuated the sounds of the crickets and a nearby murmuring creek.

He drew another deep breath, lay down in the grass, and crossed his arms behind his head. The damp grass seemed to wrap around him like a woolen blanket, softer than his bed of straw inside. He watched in silence as the moon continued to climb high and take the sun's place in a sky melting into black.

He found himself humming a simple tune at first. Then it changed into something new. Words soon followed.

When I look at your heavens, the work of your fingers, the moon and the stars, which you have set in place, what is man that you are mindful of him, and the son of man that you care for him?

DAVID FELL SILENT. He had not intended for the words to remind him of Samuel, to remind him of the anointing. He had not thought about that—whatever it was Yahweh wanted of him—since the day Samuel had left. And yet now he found himself wondering what it was Yahweh was calling him to do.

"It seems you are singing whenever we meet."

He looked up to find Jonathan standing over him. He rose to a knee and dropped his head in a bow.

"Stand, David, son of Jesse."

David obeyed.

"It seems there is no end to your musical talents." Jonathan was looking at him with admiration—honest admiration—something David had not seen before.

"Thank you, my prince. What brings you back to Bethlehem?"

"Jonathan will do," he said. His voice was pleasant enough, but David heard something beneath the surface, something troubling him. He stepped closer to David. "You still have yet to tell me how you overpowered a lion."

David felt his cheeks warm despite the cool night air. "It is not a story worth telling," he said. He looked out toward his sheep in a failed attempt to appear occupied.

"The slaying of a lion? By a boy?" Jonathan laughed,

though again, it seemed strained. "I believe it is the best kind of story to tell."

David felt one side of his mouth lift in a smile despite himself. He pointed to his limping sheep. "That one," he said. "That little pest wandered off just before sundown. Well, at least I did not notice until near sundown. I tracked it through the night. Yahweh had blessed me with a cloudless sky and a full moon. Without his favor, I would not have made it far."

"And you came upon the sheep during the night?"

He shook his head. "I did not find it until the following day."

"You searched that long?"

David spoke without thinking. "It was not my sheep to lose."

Jonathan seemed to consider that for a moment. "And the lion?"

"It came upon the sheep just as I found it." He patted his sling at his side. "I had my sling and a few stones. The first one got his attention; the second dropped him. I thought I'd killed him, but he came upon me again as I started to tend the sheep."

"Came upon you?"

Do I tell him? Do I tell this stranger I hear Yahweh's voice? That I felt his strength within me? Before he could answer his own questions, he found himself talking. "It tackled me to the ground, roaring and bleeding and drooling on me. I thought I was going to die. I froze. But then I…I don't know. My hand…" He looked down at his hand and remembered that buzzing strength. "It just shot up and seized the lion by the mane." He reached out and mimed grabbing the lion. "I had some stones left in my pouch. I bashed it along its head until it collapsed on me. I do not know where I got the strength or the courage, only that I have felt Yahweh on me ever since." David finished and shrugged.

Jonathan said nothing for a long while. He seemed one part confused and one part impressed. He held out his own hand out and grabbed at the imaginary lion. "You just...seized it? By the mane?"

He nodded. "I can't explain it." *He will not believe me. I hardly believe me.*

But Jonathan smiled. "I knew I chose wisely. Yahweh is surely with you, David."

Chose wisely?

Jonathan did not give him time to ask. "I will need you to come with me back to Gibeah."

"To Gibeah?"

"My father is marching out to the Valley of Elah soon to meet a new Philistine threat."

David frowned. He was no warrior. If Yahweh's calling was to put a sword in his hand, he was afraid Yahweh would be gravely disappointed with the outcome.

"But he is...tormented," Jonathan went on. "It would seem an evil spirit has come upon him in force. He is not himself."

"Will the story of my lion-slaying help?"

Jonathan smiled, though again, there was that hint of sadness beneath it. "No. I am hoping that your voice and your lyre will, though. And Yahweh is with you," he added.

David was almost excited. While he could not wield a sword, a lyre was another thing. If *this* was Yahweh's calling, this was something he could do.

Is this my calling? To play for the king?

Go to Gibeah. You will see.

And then I shall return home? Return to my sheep? And my calling is complete?

The voice remained silent, and David's moment of hope faded. He doubted this was the end of his calling. Yet what could he do? Man could no more deny Yahweh than stop the wind or sun.

"Very well," David said, more to the voice than to Jonathan. "Let's go to Gibeah."

———————

THE WALLS SURROUNDING Gibeah rose from the valley, punctuated by high stone towers and wide gates. David saw men walking these towers, the glint of their spears flashing in the rising sun. Stone and dirt roads crisscrossed the acres of farmland in the valley outside the walls, men and carts and oxen filling them like ants leaving an anthill.

At the center of Gibeah sat Saul's palace, the largest single structure in the city. The gate stood open, and David could just make out people going in and out of it. Between the palace walls and the walls of Gibeah were hundreds of buildings, some were small homes and others were large mills working at the river that ran through the city. There were open areas for markets, wells for fresh water, cisterns and pathways and blacksmiths. It was like nothing David had ever seen.

"Gibeah of Saul."

David turned to Jonathan beside him, unable to keep a smile from his face. The two of them had become close since leaving Bethlehem, closer than David had expected they would. Jonathan had told him stories of his exploits in battle against the Philistines and Amalekites, elaborating on the time he and his armor-bearer struck down twenty men by themselves. He had listened, awestruck at the young man's deeds. David himself had little in the way of adventure to share with the king's son, though that had not stopped their conversations from flowing with ease. Jonathan, it seemed, already cared for him more than his family ever had.

"It is magnificent."

"It is only the beginning of what Yahweh has in store for Israel. We will be a great nation, David. A great nation."

There was a scoff from beside them. "So great it will always need little boys who play the lyre."

David looked up and saw Eliab. He was standing beside Jonathan, a sword and spear along his back, while David himself only held his lyre. He had been excited about the journey to Gibeah until he discovered Eliab and Abinadab—even Shammah this time—were coming along. Jonathan had explained that they were about to march to battle yet again, and the king required every warrior. David's role was to ease the king's spirit while his brothers helped to supplement the army.

"We all have our duties, Eliab," Jonathan said. "And David, I think, will become a warrior before long." He smiled. "A very great one, indeed."

Eliab scoffed again but did not disagree with the king's son. His lack of respect seemed to know no bounds. He gave David another scornful look and then marched on, Abinadab and Shammah following close behind.

"I do not think he likes you," Jonathan said.

"I do not think I like him," David replied.

It was late morning when David was finally led up the palace steps and into Saul's great hall. It was empty and dark, despite the cloudless day just outside. Curtains were drawn over the many windows, shrouding it in gray, unwelcoming light. The throne lay on its side, broken in two, and David was suddenly worried.

"Where is everyone," David asked, his voice echoing off the barren walls.

"The hall has been cleared until the king is healed."

Healed, David thought. *By me and my lyre.* The thought was still beyond David, and yet the voice—*Yahweh's voice*, he reminded himself—had been clear. He was told to follow Jonathan and play for Saul, so that was what he would do.

"This way," Jonathan said, interrupting his thoughts. He gestured to a heavy oak door behind the throne.

He led David through the doorway, around a corner, and up a flight of stairs. Several halls forked off from the landing. The palace was brighter now—if only just—from fires flickering in wall-mounted sconces and throwing dancing shadows across the windowless stone walls. Jonathan guided him down one of the halls and up another flight of stairs. There was a single hallway at the top with a single door at its end. A pair of decorative braziers lit the hall—again with a muted light—and an armor-bearer stood before the door.

"This way," Jonathan said. "Let us hope he is awake."

The door opened, and a woman stepped into the hall. She was tall with long raven hair that fell to the middle of her back. Her eyes were red—from tears if he were to guess—and her face drawn. Yet she stood with an air of elegance that commanded respect. Her eyes met David's for the briefest of moments, and he could see the pain behind them. She turned her attention to Jonathan.

"Mother," Jonathan said, "this is David, the musician I spoke to you of."

She forced a smile and looked again at David. "Welcome, young man," she said, her voice strained and ragged. "I am Ahinoam, the king's wife. I pray you can soothe my husband's soul."

David dropped to a knee. "I pray the same."

She gave a short laugh, choked a bit by her sadness. "Stand, David. See to my husband."

He stood. Ahinoam gave Jonathan a quick hug, and then he and Jonathan were walking through the door.

The room was dark—darker than the main hall—and a low bed sat in its corner. David could smell the lingering stench of waste. Thin beams of gray light shone in through the curtained windows like the fingers of a ghost. An older man was sitting in a chair near the bed.

"Is this the musician," he asked. He glanced at the bed where the king was lying and stepped up to meet them halfway into the room.

"He is." Jonathan stepped aside as the other man inspected David.

"I am Abner," he said, "commander of Yahweh's armies. You are David?"

David only nodded, though his eyes drifted to the king in his bed. *What am I doing here, Yahweh? What can I do?*

Play, David. Sing.

"Then, please," Abner said, gesturing toward the bed. "Please play for our king."

David nodded again and took his pack from his shoulders. He pulled out his lyre and stepped toward the bed. The king looked haggard, unshaven and unkempt. His lips moved though he said no words, and his eyes were open and staring at nothing.

"He has gotten worse," Jonathan said.

David glanced back. "Is…is there something my king wishes to hear?"

Abner only shrugged. "I am told Yahweh is with you. Play what you will."

He drew a breath and plucked at the strings, playing a simple melody from memory. *Give me something, Yahweh. Fill me with your words. Let me say what is right; what is comforting to this man who is tormented. Let me give your anointed peace.* He opened his mouth and let the words come:

The cords of death entangled me; the torrents of destruction overwhelmed me. The cords of the grave coiled around me; the snares of death confronted me. In my distress I called to the LORD; I cried to my God for help. From his temple he heard my voice; my cry came before him, into his ears. He reached down from on high and took hold of me; he drew me out of deep waters. He rescued me from my powerful enemy, from my foes, who were too strong for me.

HE FELL silent and let his fingers drift along the strings for another moment before stilling them, as well. The final note hung in the air and filled the room for a handful of heartbeats. Then the king jerked, only an arm at first. He stretched, as if working sore muscles. His eyes came into focus, and David found the king's gaze directly on him.

"That was…that was nice, boy."

8

SAUL

SAUL LAY STILL in his bed, a fog over his eyes. He knew there were figures nearby, and he could almost hear the muffled sounds of speech. He felt dimly aware that his wife had just left. There was even a spot on his cheek that felt warm from her lips. All else was gone; the fog was too thick. He was not asleep, and yet he knew he was not awake, either. Darkness had crept over him, and every waking moment stretched slowly into the next, each breath feeling like his last.

In this fog, two emotions reigned supreme. Anger burned from within, a simmering rage directed at his once-loved god. Yahweh had sent this fog, Yahweh had un-chosen him as king. He felt ashamed and powerless and small under the judging gaze of an all-powerful god who had chosen to humiliate him. And Saul hated him for it.

Stronger than the anger, more potent than the hate, fear gripped his heart with icy fingers, squeezing ever tighter with each breath. He was the king of Israel, but for how much longer he did not know. He knew Yahweh had chosen another —*one who is better than you.* He did not know when this other would arrive, when this other would come for his throne.

He will have to kill me, Saul thought. He would remain vigilant, remain steadfast. No warrior would come near him unbidden, no threat to his throne would live. When he saw this one—this man sent by Yahweh to steal what was rightfully his —he would know.

And he would kill him.

Suddenly, from a very great distance, came the sound of music. The fog shifted as if moved by the sound. Another moment passed, and he thought he heard singing. The voice was like the sound of angels. Though he could not hear the words, it spoke to him nonetheless. It told him he would be okay, that he did not need to fear. A calmness drifted over him. The fog cleared enough for him to see a figure, a small and insubstantial thing. A boy, it would seem. He held a lyre, and Saul knew that the singing was not coming from angels but from this child. As the fog fully cleared, he realized he was opening closed eyes. His vision sharpened into focus. He found his eyes locked on a boy of maybe fifteen. The boy looked shocked, his eyes wide and mouth hanging open as the last sound of the lyre tapered off.

"That was…that was nice, boy," was all he could say.

Abner's eyes widened, and the hint of a smile came to his face. "My king? How…how do you feel?"

Saul pushed himself up and turned so his bare feet hung off the bed. He pressed his toes down, feeling the wool carpet on the floor. "I feel…relief." He turned again to the boy. "What is your name?"

"I am David, my king."

Saul smiled, the first genuine one in some time. "Thank you, David." He looked at Abner and was reminded of the Philistines gathering somewhere in the north, reminded that he must quickly act the king. "Has the army gathered?"

Abner could not contain his excitement. "It has, my king. We merely await your command to march."

"Have Benyamin prepare my chariot." He drew a breath. "And the command is given. Let us march at once."

Abner gave a quick bow and then practically sprinted from the room. Saul watched him go as his strength returned. Fresh, clean air filled his lungs. He put some weight on his legs and stood to his full height once they felt strong enough. Then he turned and looked at the boy standing beside Jonathan. "Thank you, child, for calming my soul." The boy bowed low, placing the lyre on the wool carpet.

"It is my honor to serve Yahweh's anointed."

Despite Saul's improved mood, the words stung. He was no longer Yahweh's anointed, if Samuel's words were to be trusted. He pushed the thoughts away and turned to his son. "Find a suitable mount for him. Send him back to his father well rewarded for his talent."

Jonathan nodded his agreement, a broad smile beaming on his face. Saul stepped forward and embraced his son, pulling him tight and pressing him into his chest. "Thank you, Jonathan."

His son's arms wrapped around him, and he felt a warmth fill his body. He wanted to stay in the embrace—to savor this moment for as long as he could—but he knew Abner was already organizing the march and that they would expect their king to be at the head. He stepped back and held his son by the shoulders. They eyed each other in silence for another moment.

"Get the boy mounted and returned home. Then see to Malki-Shua. Join the army."

Jonathan smiled once more and then turned, placing a hand on David's back to guide him out of the room. Then, for the first time, Saul looked down at his attire. His clothes were ragged and dirty, his collar lined with his own drool and bits of food likely fed to him in his stupor. He was recently bathed, but his skin still felt unclean and rough. He once again felt that burning hatred for Yahweh, the cause of all his pain.

How many saw me like this?

Shedding his clothes, he cleaned his face and oiled his hair and beard. The door creaked open just as he slipped on the last of his battle gear. He turned to see Ahinoam standing in the doorway, her shadow cast into the room. She was smiling, fresh tears on her face, and Saul stepped to her and wrapped her in a heavy embrace as her head dropped onto his chest.

"I am happy to see you well," she said, her voice low and hoarse.

He squeezed her tighter. "As am I."

They separated and stared at one another in silence for a handful of heartbeats, each one thudding in his head like a war drum. "You must go to battle again," she said.

"I must go to battle again," he repeated.

She smiled a sad smile. Reaching up, she straightened a lock of his hair that had fallen into his face, stood on her tiptoes and kissed his cheek, then ran a hand through his beard. She stepped around him and grabbed his crown from a chest against the wall.

"The king must have his crown."

He smiled as she slipped it onto his head, her hands lingering again and touching his hair and face. He grabbed her hands in his.

"I'll return," he said. "I promise."

Her smile broadened by a fraction. "I know. You go with Yahweh at your back. You cannot fail."

His heart fluttered in his chest. *I go alone this time.*

"Yes," he lied. "With Yahweh." He pulled her again into a tight embrace, though this time there was a distance between them that wasn't physical. "I must go."

"I know." They inched apart, Ahinoam's gaze on her own

hands as she took a long, deep breath. "Do you...do you want to talk about it?"

Saul tensed. "About...what?"

She gestured to the bed. "About what happened to you? About...perhaps...why?"

"Why? I don't care why," he lied.

"Will it happen again?"

Saul said nothing and stepped away from her.

"Why would it happen to Yahweh's chosen?"

He spun back to her. "What are you saying? Who have you spoken to?" He'd raised his voice; the words were harsher than he intended.

But I will not have my wife know of Samuel's words.

"Nothing. No one. I...I am only concerned. Concerned for you. For us."

For your place as queen, likely. Yet he knew that was not true. Ahinoam had loved him long before he became king.

He grunted again. "I am fine." He stepped by her. "And I will *be* fine." And then he was walking alone through his palace, his wife left standing in his room. As he stepped outside, he saw that Abner already had the army marching. He watched as the procession moved through the city gates, thousands of Israelites moving in unison and discipline under their commander. The ground shook from their footfalls, and Saul felt the familiar swell of pride he always did when he looked upon his men. This time, however, guilt and shame swept over the pride.

"He has given it to another—one who is better than you."

Samuel's words had not changed simply because some boy with a lyre brought him out of his stupor. *A stupor Yahweh sent. Already he is trying to belittle me.* He knew his men felt the same, even if they were unaware of Samuel's words and Saul's condition. They knew he was being replaced, knew he would not be king for long. *I'll not lose Israel to another.* He drew himself up. *I am still the king.* Saul went to the stable and found his horses and chariot waiting for him. Benyamin and his driver were each petting one of the steeds. Benyamin smiled when he saw him.

"My king."

Saul embraced his armor-bearer. "Let us join the army," he said, stepping up onto the chariot. With one hand, he took hold of the crossbar and rested the other on the hilt of his sword. The driver and Benyamin joined him in the chariot, and they were soon rumbling through Gibeah in a rush to join the army.

The chariot rounded the rearguard and sped alongside the marching army. They rattled by rank upon rank of Israelites, all eyes turning to look at Saul, if only for a moment. He drew his sword and held it high.

"For Yahweh," he shouted, his voice carrying far and kingly among the troops. They raised their weapons and shields into the air and echoed the cry.

"For Yahweh!"

Saul pumped his sword in the air, drawing more shouts of encouragement until they drove by the forward ranks and joined the commanders at the front. He sheathed his sword as his driver found Abner—who himself was on horseback—and guided the chariot beside him.

"I am glad you are better, my king," he shouted over the rumble of the army.

"As am I," Saul said, though he knew he was not.

———

THE ROLLING green hills of the Valley of Elah stretched into the distance, fading under a distant fog. As Saul looked around at the northern hills that sloped gently into the valley, he could smell the nearby pines, the crisp air, and the pastoral scents of the valley below. A river, sluggish in the fall, rumbled from the east to cut a swath through the center of the valley, adding the music of flowing water. The early morning sounds of his camp also came to his ears, that of cooking and cleaning and preparations that accompanied every morning.

Then his eyes drifted across the valley to the southern hill, to the thousands of tents stretched out on the far slope, to the smoke rising from the hundreds of firepits. He could hear the blacksmith hammers of the Philistines ringing loud across the valley, the clinking and clanking of thousands of troops securing their armor.

Saul turned to Abner and Jonathan standing beside him. "Do you think he will come again?" Saul asked, hoping his fear did not come through in his voice. His breath made mist in the air and reminded him that fall was well under way.

"If he does, it will be forty days without rest," Abner said.

He watched as the Philistine camp began moving, its soldiers filing out and making their battle lines ready in the middle of the southern slope. He could feel the ground shaking beneath his feet.

"Move the men," Saul said, though he genuinely hoped battle did not come today. As much as the waiting was killing him—over a month now—he did not wish to see his men slaughtered under the heavy hand of the Philistines.

Abner nodded and disappeared into the Israelite camp. Jonathan turned to follow him. "Stay with me, son," Saul said. This time, even he heard the fear in his voice.

"As you wish, father," Jonathan said, returning to Saul's side.

His battle lines formed on the northern slope as the fog cleared. He hoped his men could not see it, but the difference in numbers was clear from Saul's vantage point. They were outnumbered nearly two to one.

"What do I do, Jonathan? How do we face such a force?"

He felt his son's eyes on him, felt his disappointment. "With Yahweh, numbers do not matter."

Saul nodded in agreement though it lacked genuineness. "Indeed. But how do I know Yahweh is with us?"

"Why would he not be?"

He drew a breath and looked at his son. He did not have an answer, at least not one he was willing to share. Eventually, he turned and looked back out at the Philistine army, that familiar fear taking hold of him.

I wish Samuel were here.

Saul immediately regretted the thought. *I do not need that old man.* Yet he knew he did. Perhaps not Samuel himself, but he needed Yahweh's help. He did not know what to do, how to handle his men. Every decision tortured him, froze him with fear. The chance of death and defeat that hung forever before him had kept him looking down into this valley for over a month.

I wish Samuel were here...

The Philistine battle lines parted. Saul watched as their champion stepped forward.

9

DAVID

T HE PATH NARROWED AHEAD—IF it could get any narrower—
and David looked over the edge, not for the first time. The
drop looked close to a hundred cubits, not straight down but
near enough. Now that the morning fog had cleared, he could
see the slow-moving river that flowed west out of the Valley of
Elah. As if placed as a trap, loose dirt and gravel littered the
walkway's outer edge. He braced himself on the high rock wall
on the opposite side, reassured by the solid stone. It was cool to
the touch now that fall was underway. The donkey brayed
behind him to remind David that he was still there.

Like I could forget you with your constant complaining.

Nevertheless, he set a reassuring hand on its nose. "Just a
bit farther," he said, trying and failing to keep his voice calm.
The animal had been a menace in the days since David had
left his father's house, braying and snorting and doing anything
a donkey could to express its annoyance. It was an annoyance
David himself shared. Once he had completed his calling from
Yahweh and healed the king with his music—something he was
still having trouble believing—he had hoped to return to his
fields and spend his days with the sheep he had come to love.

He had, after all, not heard Yahweh's voice since then. Yet his father had barely let him rest before sending him on his way again. And so here he was, leading a stubborn donkey loaded down with bread and meat for his brothers in the army.

He sighed and turned back to the donkey. "Let's go," he said. He gave the lead a gentle tug, and the donkey began to follow. He moved with careful and deliberate steps, looking back to watch that the donkey did the same. For all the headaches it brought, he did not want the beast to tumble over the side of a cliff.

Its hooves scraped against a patch of loose gravel and threw a handful of small stones over the edge. It gave a panicked snort and scrambled to get its footing, then froze in place, its ears shooting up in a refusal to move.

He petted the animal between its ears and gripped the bridle, as much to comfort it as to give himself something to hold. The beast brayed again—hot breath steaming from its nose in the cold—and David brushed his scraggly mane. "Just a bit further," he said, his teeth gritted with frustration. "Around this bend, and we will be able to see the valley."

He tugged at the bridle, yet the donkey refused to move. David turned and seized the bridle with two hands. "Let's… go…" he grunted, jerking and pulling to little effect. The beast just stared at him, ears still pointed straight up, and snorted. Hot breath and spit sprayed into David's face. He stumbled back and released the bridle. After wiping his face clean, he pointed down the path. It curved hard to the right after another dozen paces, the other end of the sharp turn out of sight beyond the rock wall. "You're going that way." He pointed over the cliff. "Or *that* way. Your choice."

The beast followed his hand, looked over the cliff, and then turned once more and looked toward the bend ahead. It snorted again, but it seemed a more compliant snort, if there was such a thing.

"Thank you." He took hold of the bridle. "Now, let's go."

They moved together, slinking toward the bend. The path narrowed even further, and David guided the beast against the hard stone on their right. The goods strapped to the donkey rattled and clanked against the stone, but David ignored them and continued.

David peeked forward and around the bend. The path widened dramatically as it descended toward the Valley of Elah. He could see the Israelite encampment on the northern slope and could nearly make out the rough shapes of the armies arrayed in the valley beyond.

"Just a bit farther," he said, more to himself this time. He drew a breath and eased himself around the bend, his arm stretched back and holding the donkey's bridle. "Let's go…"

His arm jerked to a stop as the beast again refused to move. *I'm gonna kill this donkey.*

He pulled harder, clicking his tongue in encouragement, and the animal finally took a cautious pair of steps, stones flying over the edge with each hoof fall. The donkey snorted and took another few steps, its upper half around the bend now. "Good boy…just a bit farther. Good bo—"

A chunk of the path crumbled away, taking the donkey's rear legs with it. The animal brayed furiously, foaming and spitting and snapping at David as its backside began to slide down the cliff. Its legs jerked and kicked and struggled to stay on the path, more stone and dirt flying off with each movement.

"Easy! Easy!" David gripped the bridle and pulled, putting a foot on the stone cliff wall for support. His other foot kicked at the dirt and stones, throwing more gravel as the donkey slid backward. "Come on!"

He finally found solid footing on the edge and managed to slow their descent. He grunted and strained and pulled, but the donkey was still sliding back. The donkey's eyes were wild and desperate, its legs pumping behind it like a warhorse and kicking up a spray of dirt and gravel.

Then David felt a set of invisible hands lie on top of his. With a strength that he hadn't thought possible, the hands pulled on the bridle, and the donkey jerked forward and onto solid ground. Once it had its footing, it ran over David, hooves pounding dangerously close to his face, and sprinted another hundred paces down the path until it was well beyond the sharp drop of the cliff and in relative safety.

David lay still and looked down at his hands. The now-broken bridle still hung from his fingers.

What was that?

I have plans for you, David.

The voice's sudden return left him momentarily speechless. He drew a breath and stood, unsure of what to think. He'd hoped his calling was complete, that Yahweh had only needed him to heal his anointed. Yet now Yahweh was back and—to David's dismay—clearly not done with him.

But what does that mean?

I will show you.

He looked down the path and saw the donkey, seeming to have already forgotten their near-death experience as it munched casually on a patch of brown grass. He sighed and began to walk down the path. "Why do all animals hate me?"

David had collected the animal and fashioned the bridle back in place when he realized he was no longer alone on the path. Dozens of men were walking in his direction, some armed with spears and shields. His first reaction was to reach for his sling, but as the men came closer, he saw that, though armed, they were not marching for battle. Their weapons were dragging behind them, their shields sagging in their hands. David released his sling and watched as the first man trudged by, his dragging spear leaving a long trail in the path behind him. He watched the man pass in silence, his hand still gripping the bridle of his donkey. Three more passed him by, no sound but that of their sandals padding on the soft dirt, their heads down and eyes fixed on nothing. One had no weapon, only a small basket with a few loaves and dried meats inside.

"What happened," David finally asked, not directing his question to anyone in particular. Most only glanced his way and then fixed their eyes back on the dirt as they continued to shuffle by. "Is the battle over?"

One of them finally stopped beside him. "It will be soon." The man looked haggard, eyes surrounded by dark rings, beard unkempt. His hair was matted to his pale face, sweat glistening in the rising sun despite the cool air.

"Have...have we won?" Yet he suspected the answer to the question before he even asked it.

"We cannot fight him."

"Him? Who?"

His eyes went wide as he looked at David. "Goliath. He is no man, no Philistine. If Yahweh exists, he surely built Goliath to punish us."

David felt anger bubble up inside. "*If* he exists!? Are you mad?"

"The king will not even fight. Yahweh's supposed chosen stands frozen with fear. What are *we* to do?"

He drew a breath to steady himself. "You have not even fought the battle? And you are running?"

The man scoffed, and David was reminded of the donkey's snort a few moments ago. "He is twice the size of a man, teeth jagged like daggers." He shook his spear. "His spear makes my own look like a child's toy, a stick from a shepherd's field. His armor alone weighs as much as you do, boy."

"What does that matter," David shot back. "You have the Living God of Israel at your back. His anointed should lead you into battle!"

That is what I healed him for, he thought. *To fight. To do Yahweh's will. Not to stand in fear.*

David was keenly aware of his reluctance to follow his own calling, but reluctance and retreat were two different things. He did not want to be here; he had not wanted to leave his sheep, and yet here he stood nonetheless.

"This man could *kill* a god, boy! He is a warrior like I have never seen!"

More defeated warriors shuffled by. Defeated not in battle but in mind. He could see their faces, drawn and afraid, eyes fixed on the ground in their shame.

"So, you run," David asked. "Abandon your king *and* Yahweh? Over one man?"

The fear had returned to the man's face, his already pale color fading even further. "He is no man," he whispered. "He is a giant."

And with that, he turned and trudged on with the rest of them. After a few moments, they were all around the bend and out of sight. David renewed his grip on the donkey's bridle and continued down the path, dumbfounded that the armies of Israel had so little faith.

By midday, he climbed a low ridge and finally took in the entire valley before him. The Israelites were camped on the valley's northern slope, their tents stretching out into the horizon in numbers he had never seen. The soldiers were moving through the camp and forming orderly battle lines. Despite the fear he had just witnessed, the sight brought a swell of pride to his chest.

Not all have abandoned Yahweh.

Then he looked at the southern slope and witnessed the fullness of the Philistine camp. It stretched endlessly in either direction, more tents than Israel had warriors. Their soldiers moved like ants at this distance, but David could still see their far superior numbers. A fear of his own began to creep up.

What possible use could you have of me here? Let me deliver the food and return.

Go to your brothers. I will show you what to do.

Part of him wanted to argue with the voice, to plead to be sent home. Yet he knew he could not. And after all, had he not just challenged that very same attitude? Had he not just lectured soldiers about faith in Yahweh? If Yahweh had brought him here, Yahweh would bring him out.

He stood with renewed determination. He knew not what Yahweh wanted of him, but he suspected he would be shown soon. After a quick check of the donkey's pack, he walked into the Israelite camp. Finally he found the keeper of supplies, surrounded by cabinets and makeshift shelving stocked with stale bread and hard cheese. Toward the top of one shelf sat a basket of fruits. The keeper was an older man with a long gray beard and worn-through clothing. To David, he looked like a poorly cared for prophet.

"These are from Jesse of Bethlehem," David said, patting the donkey. "For Eliab, Abinadab, and Shammah."

The man looked up. He looked the donkey over and gave a low grunt in his throat. "That *might* replace the supplies stolen this morning."

"Stolen?"

He spat off into the camp and adjusted his tunic. "Near fifty men made off this morning with baskets of supplies. Afraid of Goliath, I hear."

David's ears perked up. "Goliath. Have you seen him?"

He nodded. "I have."

"Is he as fearsome as I have been told?"

"I don't know what you've been told, boy, but odds are they didn't do him justice. The man's no man at all, more than likely. Something fashioned together by the gods of the Philistines to challenge the God of Israel."

David gritted his teeth. Did everyone in Israel have such

doubt? "There are no gods of the Philistines. They worship false gods and idols, things made by man."

He grunted again. "You're more than welcome to go and tell that to him."

David handed the donkey's lead to the old man and said nothing.

Armed with only his staff and sling, he ran through the camp toward the battle lines, eyes on the lookout for his brothers. By the time he reached the battle lines, he found them already drawn on both sides of the valley. He slowed to a jog as he saw the army of the Philistines lined up to the south. They stretched beyond sight, nearly twice the number of the Israelites. Now that he was closer, he could see their armor and weapons glinting in the sun. Again, he felt that familiar pang of fear, and this time he forced it down.

Yahweh is the stronghold of my life—of whom shall I be afraid?

He ignored the Philistines and turned instead down each rank of the Israelite army in search of his brothers.

There.

Eliab was in the vanguard, the very front. David sprinted his way and was nearly there when he saw the army across the valley begin to move. He halted, the pang of fear almost becoming full-blown terror. He had no desire to be between two armies clashing in battle. But they had moved very little, only parting enough to let a man through.

David's eyes went wide as he saw the man, the Goliath. He was indeed nearly twice as tall as David and at least half a man taller than Eliab. He was covered from shoulders to feet with thick scales of bronze armor, and he held a spear that looked like a small tree with a tip that was at least as big as David's head.

"He *is* a giant," David mumbled to himself.

The man stepped out in front of the Philistines' ranks and jabbed his spear into the grass with such force that David felt the ground tremble beneath him. David's heart pounded in his chest as Goliath removed his helmet and handed it to his shield-bearer, who drooped under the weight.

"Why do you even come out and line up for battle," the giant shouted, his deep voice rumbling like thunder. "You cower in fear! Are you not warriors? Is your god so small that you fear a man? Fight me!"

David felt an anger swell inside unlike anything he had ever felt, red and hot and scorching like the fires of a forge. The fear fell away beneath its force, snuffed out of existence like a candle. It was replaced with a burning rage toward this giant— this *man*—who would denounce Yahweh.

"Who is this man," he said aloud.

"He is Goliath."

David turned to find an Israelite soldier speaking to him. "I know his name," he snapped. "Why has no one silenced him?"

The man made a sound somewhere between a snort and a laugh. "Do you not see him?" The man pointed. "He is a monster, a giant from the times of Abraham."

A moment ago, David had thought the same thing, though now the anger was so intense that it left no room for fear. Yahweh was God of all, not only of the Israelites. He was the creator of the earth, the creator of every man. To ignore your creator was expected, for man is selfish at heart. Yet to insult him was another. And to let it go unpunished was unthinkable.

"Why does that matter? Do we not have the Living God of Israel at our backs? What can man do to us?"

A new voice spoke up. "Why are you even here?"

David recognized his brother's voice instantly. He looked at Eliab, only a few paces away, who was now standing out from the ranks and glaring at him.

"Haven't you sheep to watch?"

David stepped toward his brother, his patience with Eliab reaching its limit. "What have I done? Can I not even speak?"

"David?"

An older man stepped through the ranks. David recognized him as Abner, the commander of Israel's armies, who had been in the room with Saul when David had played.

"David, what are you doing here?"

What am *I doing here?* He looked back toward Goliath, a sudden and almost violent realization hitting him. *Goliath? Is he why I am here?*

You have been a faithful shepherd, a faithful musician. Now, however, I need a warrior.

David felt the fear make an attempt to rise back up within him, yet he shoved it aside. He had spent the morning chastising men for their lack of faith, had just declared that they had the Living God of Israel at their backs. He would not cower now.

Yahweh is the stronghold of my life.

"I've come to answer this Philistine's challenge," David said, his eyes still on Goliath.

There was a long silence, followed by Eliab's laugh.

Abner silenced him with a look, then turned to David. "You wish to fight him?"

Goliath shouted, repeating his challenge, repeating his insults of Yahweh. The anger burned deeper, and David felt it ignite that otherworldly strength. His entire body began to hum with energy, to throb with power.

Of whom shall I be afraid?

"I do. He cannot be allowed to speak of Yahweh like this."

Abner looked from David to Goliath and back to David again. "Come with me," he finally said. David followed Abner through the ranks and back up the slope, aware of the eyes on him and caring little. Soon he could see Saul standing at the top of the valley slope, Jonathan beside him. The worry on the king's face was unmistakable.

Saul looked down at David and almost smiled, the worry fading for a moment. "What have you found here, Abner?"

"It seems your musician wishes to be a warrior."

Saul's brow furrowed, and he looked again at David. "Is that so?"

David dropped to a knee. "My king, do not lose heart because of this Philistine. Your servant will go and fight him."

There was a silence among them for a long while. Only the distant screaming of Goliath was heard, each word stoking the anger within him.

"But...but you are a boy," Saul finally said, his voice laced with confusion. "This Philistine has been a fighting man since his youth. He's more than twice your size. You're a shepherd and...and a *musician*." He gave a nervous laugh. "You cannot fight him."

David rose and looked at the king. A few moments ago, he would have agreed with him. He would have said that there was no way for a shepherd—David least of all—to defeat a giant. Yet as the power throbbed within him now, he knew he had already won the battle. He thought of the lion, of how he had faced death before and how Yahweh had delivered him.

"It's true. I'm only a shepherd," he said, his voice firm. "And I have only ever kept my father's sheep. Yet when one wandered off, I followed it. As I found it, a lion did, as well. I struck the lion and rescued the sheep. When the lion turned on me again, I seized it by its mane and struck it dead. I killed the lion, and this Philistine will be the same." He turned and looked at Goliath. "He has defied Yahweh. Just as he delivered me from the paw of the lion, Yahweh will deliver me from the hand of this Philistine. I *can* fight him. And I *will* beat him."

Jonathan was smiling. As was Abner. But the king remained confused. He looked at David and then over his shoulder to Goliath in the distance. The silence was punctuated by

Goliath's continued shouts. "Then…you will go," Saul finally said, saying each word slowly, as if they were foreign to him.

Before anyone could respond, David turned and marched toward Goliath. He held his staff firm in one hand and pulled his sling out with the other. The comforting weight of his pouch of stones bounced against his hip as he walked down into the Valley of Elah. He passed the army lines and continued walking. Though he didn't look, he could feel Eliab's scornful gaze. But he no longer cared. None of them mattered. All that mattered was the Philistine ahead of him, the enemy of Yahweh.

When Goliath saw David walk beyond the front lines and head straight toward him, he laughed loud and long, his voice nearly shaking the entire valley. "Am I a dog that you come at me with sticks?" His voice was like a drum, echoing in David's head and rattling his skull. He grinned at David and waved him forward. "Come here, boy, and I'll give your flesh to the birds of the air and the beasts of the field."

David stopped a hundred paces from the Philistine. His hand was gripping his sling so hard his knuckles popped. The power within nearly shook him, humming and throbbing with an intensity he could not contain. He felt it on his skin, craving to get out, begging to be released. His vision tunneled down to the Philistine, to Goliath.

"You come against me with sword and spear and javelin," David shouted, his voice roaring like the lion he had slain. "But I come against you in the name of Yahweh, the God of the armies of Israel. The God whom *you* defy. It will be your flesh that the birds of the air and beasts of the field feast on. Your flesh and the flesh of your army behind you. Then the whole world will know that it is not by the sword or the spear or the javelin that the battle is won, for the battle is Yahweh's."

Goliath was silent for a moment, doubtful almost. The valley fell into a silence. Then he smiled.

"Very well," he said. He pulled his spear from where he had planted it in the grass. He took a pair of steps—the ground shaking with each one—and then broke into a run, charging toward David and neglecting to collect his helmet from his armor-bearer. David pulled out a stone and loaded his sling. He charged the Philistine, that pulsing power from within exploding free and filling his limbs with strength. He felt as large as Goliath. Stronger, faster, more focused than he had ever been.

His muscles worked from memory—*load, swing, aim, throw*—and he let the stone fly. It whistled through the air and struck Goliath between the eyes, the stone itself disappearing into his skull. The giant continued on, just as the lion had, then faltered. He took another pair of fumbling steps forward and then crashed to the ground, skidding another dozen paces until finally coming to a halt in a cloud of grass and dust.

David did not drop his guard as he had with the lion. Beasts often fall only to rise again, fiercer and stronger. Goliath would get no chance. David continued his run, came upon the giant and reached for his sword. It was large, the blade almost as long as one of David's legs, and for the briefest of moments he didn't think he'd be able to lift it. But that strength from within easily overcame it, and the massive blade pulled free. He held it aloft for both armies to see, the bronze glinting in the sun and burning like fire. Then it swung down in a swooping arc and sliced through Goliath's neck like a scythe through wheat. Blood splattered, and the giant's ruined head was rolling into the grass. It came to a stop and seemed to stare up at the heavens with wide eyes. In the end, it seemed, he would acknowledge his creator.

Silence filled the valley as both armies looked on in dismay. David felt his heart pounding in his head as he looked down at the dead Philistine. He turned to the Philistine army, saw their dumbfounded faces. The strength from within blasted free one final time, and he let out a war cry that echoed across the valley, thundering through the hills and trees, seeming to shake the very foundations of the earth. The Philistines faltered at the sight of their dead champion and the small shepherd boy standing on his corpse. Then the shofar sounded from behind him. Like a flood, the Israelite army descended into the valley, bodies rushing by David and breaking into the Philistine ranks.

SAUL

SAUL WATCHED his young musician marching down the frozen ranks of the Israelite army. He walked with confidence, a familiarity about him Saul could not identify. Surely, he was marching to his death, despite his faith and Saul's own blessing to go to battle. But what else could he have done? Told him no? After his foolish little speech about Yahweh saving him from a lion?

I'm sure it was his own kitten that he was thinking of.

Saul scoffed. Grabbing the mane of a lion. It was ridiculous. And now he was walking off to slay a giant? He hadn't even taken any armor or weapons, leaving with only his staff and sling.

Saul turned to Abner. "Whose son is that?"

Abner only glanced his way, not wanting to take his eyes off David. "I...I don't know."

David had reached Goliath now. The Philistine laughed and began to taunt him.

"I would like to know," Saul said. *I would like to know who to apologize to for the death of his son.* Then David and Goliath were charging at one another. Saul nearly looked away. He did not wish to see his musician split open, did not wish to witness the massacre that was about to happen. However, just as he was turning, Goliath stumbled and fell to the ground, skidding another dozen paces before coming to a halt in a cloud of dust.

"How did…"

David rushed on, then drew Goliath's massive sword and held it high. It glinted in the sun, suspended in the air for a handful of breaths, and then it was swinging down. Blood arced like a crimson ribbon, and Goliath's head rolled away. For a long moment, not a sound was heard in the valley. Saul's own heart was beating in his head. Then David turned to the Philistine army and let loose a mighty cry, cleaving into Saul's own ears even from a distance. The cry echoed into the valley, bouncing against the hills and trees like a mighty war drum, and then everything faded to silence.

"Sound the shofar," he said, his voice just above a whisper.

"My king?"

"Sound the attack! Go! Now!"

The shofar rang out through the valley, and the ground trembled with the rush of his army's feet. They surged by David, who still stood atop the dead giant, and into the Philistine army ranks, breaking over them like the waves on a shore. Within moments, the Philistines were retreating, and their dead lined the valley's slope.

"That was…that was amazing," Jonathan said.

Saul had still not fully processed what had happened. "Yes. Yes, it was. I would like to meet this David. I wish to know him as more than a musician." *Someone so talented, so brave and godly. This David is a threat. Perhaps even the one…* He turned to Abner. "Bring him to me."

Abner nodded and walked down into the valley. David was still standing by Goliath, the rest of the army fading over the hill as they ran down the Philistines. Saul felt an urge to climb upon his chariot and charge into battle alongside his men, but he could see the rout would be over in short time. With the death of Goliath, the Philistines were utterly defeated.

"What do you think, Beny?"

His armor-bearer took a step forward and stood beside Saul. "My king?"

"What do you think? About our David?" Abner had reached David.

"I think...I believe he was sent by Yahweh, sent to free us of this threat."

Saul nodded his agreement. Though there was a twist to it in Saul's own mind, Samuel's words distorting his every thought. He allowed himself to finish the idea he had started earlier. *Perhaps this boy is the one who is better than me. Perhaps he was sent to free them of me, as well.* "Maybe he was, Beny..."

Abner and David stepped up to Saul, and David went to a knee. Goliath's blood stained his tunic. "Rise, David." He did. "Who is your father?"

"I am the son of Jesse of Bethlehem."

Saul knew the name. "Eliab? Abinadab? Shammah? These are your brothers?" David only nodded. "It would seem Jesse of Bethlehem did not send me his best sons right away." David's mouth twisted into a smile for the smallest of moments.

Jonathan suddenly stepped forward. "I feel a calling from Yahweh, son of Jesse." He removed his belt, and the scabbard of his sword scraped along the ground as he held it out to David. He took it carefully, glancing up to Saul. "You may have my sword." Jonathan reached behind him and grabbed his bow. "And my bow." He laid it at David's feet and then stepped back, a light on his face that Saul had not seen in years.

This is too much...

"I would like you to remain with me," Saul said, more to interrupt the moment than anything. "Perhaps you can be more than a musician."

"My king?"

He waved toward the soldiers still fading into the distance. "I have soldiers, men who can fight, men who will die for Yahweh. I need more men like you, men who can inspire, men who can lead."

"My king is too kind," David said.

No, Saul thought. *Your king merely wishes to keep you close.*

PART II

Once more war broke out, and David went out and fought the Philistines. He struck them with such force that they fled before him.

11

DAVID

DAVID RAN his hands through the brook, splashing the cool water on his face and neck. It ran down his beard and into his tunic, soaking it through so it to clung to his chest. He dug back into the creek, this time eyeing the stones under the flowing water. He flicked a few aside until he found one with the right smoothness and texture.

"There you are," he said to himself, lifting it to examine it closer. He closed his fist around it and looked around the Valley of Elah. It was midspring, and the sun shone hot and bright. The smell of wet grass, wildflowers, and lilies filled his nostrils. He couldn't help but smile as a cooling breeze blew through the valley.

"Must you always gather your stones?"

He turned to Jonathan. He looked much the same as he had five years ago.

David, however, had changed a great deal. He was no longer a child, but a man. He'd grown in strength if not in height, and his once smooth chin was covered in a thick beard. His hair was longer now, hanging nearly down to his shoulders, though he had it tied at the nape of his neck with a thin cord.

David pocketed the stone. "They have yet to fail me," he said with a smile.

"This is true." Jonathan turned his gaze toward the southern slope. "Do you think they will come today?"

David followed his gaze and looked at the Philistines standing in a neat and uniform line. Near seven hundred, if he guessed right. Nowhere near the numbers he'd faced five years ago, though it seemed the days of massive armies had passed. As of late, there had been little aside from these skirmishes. Their numbers had been the same for nearly three days now. He had initially feared that they were waiting for reinforcements even though they outnumbered David's own men two to one.

Or so they think.

"I hope so," David answered. "I am not overly fond of this valley."

"And will you give them your speech?"

"Always."

Three Philistines stepped through the line and began the slow walk down the slope.

"I guess we have our answer," Jonathan said.

David closed his eyes and drew a deep breath.

The Lord is my light and my salvation—whom shall I fear? The Lord is the stronghold of my life—of whom shall I be afraid? When evil men advance against me to devour my flesh, when my enemies and my foes attack me, they will stumble and fall.

"You are a brave man, David!"

He opened his eyes and found the three men standing only a dozen paces out. Far behind them, the rest of the army had not moved. Jonathan still stood beside him, his hand now resting on the hilt of his sword.

"Why do you say so?" David called back.

The one who had spoken stepped forward. He was tall, though still a great deal smaller than Goliath had been. One side of his face was a jumbled mass of recently burned flesh, and the other a spider web of crisscrossing scars. His left eye was a milky white, and the right was a vibrant blue that would have been beautiful on a less ragged face. He was armed with sword and shield and javelin.

"You come against my army with such few numbers."

David looked over his shoulder. Lined up just as neatly as the Philistine army were David's four hundred men. He looked back at the Philistine and smiled. "Numbers do not matter. Yahweh always goes before me. And I do not come against you at all. Rather you come against me. This land rightfully belongs to Saul, king of Israel and Yahweh's anointed."

The Philistine smiled wide and revealed a row of darkened gums and few teeth. "Your king does not scare me, and neither does your god."

"Then you do not know my God."

"I know him well enough."

"Then you know what he said to Moses many years ago?"

The Philistine was silent. David heard Jonathan mumble under his breath beside him. "Here we go again…"

"He said that the stranger who resides with you shall be to you as the native among you, and you shall love him as yourself." David opened his arms wide. "So, I give you an opportunity, Philistine. Though I give only *one* chance. I am less merciful than Yahweh. Circumcise your people, consecrate yourself before the Living God of Israel, the one true god, and I will welcome you into my land. Think quick, however, for I am not as patient as Yahweh, either."

The Philistine scowled in return. "You insult me, David, son of Jesse. You insult my men, you insult my country, and you insult my gods."

"Your gods do not exist to be insulted."

The man snarled and drew his sword. "You will die for your words, dog."

The three Philistines charged in together, splashing as they stomped through the creek. David pulled his sword free and heard the scrape of Jonathan drawing his blade beside him. He felt that familiar strength fill his limbs as the weight of the weapon filled his hand. His vision tunneled down to his adversary, and all else faded away. Soon it was just him and the Philistines, him and the enemies of Yahweh. This was not battle fever—though he did feel that, as well, that surge of blood through the body, that rush of emotion, of fear and excitement and pure joy that came with fighting for his life. No, it was not battle fever that brought the strength and the focus. It was Yahweh. Ever since his calling—a calling that seemed to change every time Yahweh spoke to him—he had felt the Living God of Israel join with him whenever his sword was in his hand.

Perhaps this is *my calling.*

The scarred Philistine and one of the others came at David as the third charged in toward Jonathan. David caught the first strike on the edge of his sword and sent the Philistine with the scarred face stumbling into the grass. He pivoted, dodging the blade of the next man and bringing his sword in a looping arc that sliced him open along his spine. The man fell hard to the ground and spasmed once before going still.

The Philistine army broke into a run and came charging down the hill toward David. The man with the scarred face stood, threw his shield aside, and pulled the javelin off his back. "Hear that? That is the sound of seven hundred Philistine warriors bearing down on you."

Seven hundred…I was right, David thought with a smile.

"Why are you smiling?"

"Because numbers do not matter," he repeated. On the northern slope, David's men gave a mighty war cry and charged down the hill and into the valley. Then, from the thick forest to the east, another war cry joined the first, and four hundred additional men charged from the cover of the trees, flanking the Philistine forces. David shrugged. "Or maybe they do."

He darted forward, and the Philistine parried his first attack. David twisted around a javelin thrust and positioned himself closer to his own charging forces. The javelin came again. David backpedaled and parried, his sword a blur of motion as it deflected blow after blow. The Philistine was relentless as he alternated between jabs with the javelin and sideways strikes with his sword. But David was fast. And he was not alone. He could almost feel the hands of Yahweh guiding him, pushing him out of the way of danger.

He blocked a low strike and leaped forward. The Philistine wheezed as David's knee struck him in the chest, and he collapsed onto the wet grass. David paused over him, still smiling.

"Stop smiling," the Philistine snarled, his javelin darting up.

David caught the shaft of the javelin in his free hand. He jerked it free and spun it, jamming it back down. The Philistine rolled aside as the weapon dug into the grass beside him. He sprang to his feet, looked at David, then turned and ran.

"You're going to let him go?"

David looked at Jonathan beside him, his own sword bloody. "No," he said. He gripped the javelin and pulled it from the grass. He held it aloft, felt the weight of it. Then he stepped forward and hurled the javelin with all his—and Yahweh's—strength. The weapon whistled through the air, peaking for a heartbeat in the midday sun, then plunged down and into the back of the fleeing Philistine.

"Nice throw," Jonathan said.

A few moments later, the two armies came crashing together around them. David and Jonathan wasted no time joining the fight. The once quiet valley was filled with the sounds of battle: men screaming and grunting with effort, iron and bronze scraping against each other, bows twanging and arrows whistling by overhead. Blood and sweat and dirt filled his eyes and face, soaking into his beard and running down his chest. His tunic clung to his body. His sword hung heavy in his aching arm, yet that familiar otherworldly strength kept him going. He could smell the stench of blood and death as men, both ally and enemy, were cut down around him.

A Philistine dashed before him. His aching arm rose and parried and struck, and the man fell dead in the grass. David stepped over his newest casualty and faced off against yet another. It seemed endless. For every one he struck down, another three took his place.

A spear darted out of the mayhem and jabbed toward him. His arm moved on its own, slashing at the spear and sending the tip spinning off into the battle. He closed the distance with its owner in a single step, as his sword flowed in a loop and crashed down on the spearman's helmet with a resounding clang. The helmet caved in and crushed the man's skull; David's arm rattled from the impact.

A sharp pain lanced up his leg, and David fell to a knee. Blood ran down his calf and into the grass beside him from the unseen blow. He looked up in time to see a Philistine turning a spear and driving it down. He twisted, and it glanced off his leather vest, the tip catching on the seams that held it in place. The spearman fell awkwardly, and the shaft of the spear splintered. David stood, pain spiking in his calf, and drove his sword into the Philistine's back. The two of them collapsed into the grass together. His heart raced, his arm ached, his leg throbbed in pain, yet that strength never left him. He rose to a knee and looked out at the battle.

David's men, the best trained in all Israel, were pushing back the Philistines. He could see his now-grown cousin Abishai—also his second in command—leading a charge on the left flank. Jonathan was rallying men on the right. He stood, ignoring the pain in his leg. His leather vest nearly fell from his body, hanging on now by only a thin string. He gripped the shoulder of it and tore it off.

Yahweh shall be my armor.

"To me," he shouted, his voice filling the battlefield. To his sides, the flanks closed in, drawing a single new battle line as the warriors piled around him. Fresh men from the back rushed to the front, replacing the injured and the tired. David raised his sword high, ignoring the sore muscles and aching wounds. "Forward!"

The Israelites charged forward, plowing through the faltering Philistines. His own sword painted a portrait of blood and death as the enemy dropped all around him. Within a few more moments, they were in full retreat, his Israelites charging forward and cutting them down as they fled.

DAVID SQUATTED BY THE BROOK, lifted a handful of cool water, and splashed it into his face. He felt the dirt and grime and blood run off with the water. Wounds he wasn't even aware of screamed out as the water ran over them. He ignored the pain and splashed another handful down his back and then into his face before standing up straight.

The brook traced the Valley of Elah east to west before curving north and disappearing around a hill. The valley still looked the same as it had five years ago when David had first seen it, though now there were hundreds of bodies strewn about. There had been blood back then, as well. He looked down at his hands and the dried blood in his nails and the crevices of his fingers. It seemed a lot of the last five years had blood in it.

David looked down the creek. Jonathan was walking among the men, checking on the wounded, and ensuring everyone was tended to. Most of the others were washing in the water, though there was no one close to him. He dropped to a knee and closed his eyes.

I will give thanks to you, LORD, with all my heart; I will tell of all your wonderful deeds. I will be glad and rejoice in you; I will sing the praises of your name, O Most High. My enemies turn back; they stumble and perish before you. For you have upheld my right and my cause, sitting enthroned as the righteous judge.

He rose—his muscles groaning in protest now that the battle was over—and watched the afternoon sun burned in the bright sky. *I have met with only success these last years. And I am grateful. But who am I, Lord, that you have chosen to bless me so?*

You will see, David.

"So, a man buys a horse."

David looked to his right and found Abishai. He looked only a little better than David felt; his hair's copper color turned black from blood and dirt. Even though he was younger, he was much taller than David. He still held his spear, the wood smooth from years of use.

"A man buys a horse?"

"Yes. A man buys a horse." He dropped his spear in the grass and pulled his tunic off, revealing a crisscrossing network of scars. Soon he was splashing the cool water over himself, as well. "The owner tells him the horse only knows two commands: Praise Yahweh and Serve the Lord. 'Serve the Lord' is the command of stop, and 'Praise Yahweh' makes this horse run."

David rinsed off once more and then stepped back, letting the sun dry his skin. "Strange commands."

Abishai chuckled then dunked his head into the creek. He whipped his head out and sent up a fountain of water. "I agree. Not exactly the ones I would have chosen, but it was not my horse. Anyway, the man takes the horse for a ride. They near a cliff, and the horse does not slow. The man pulls on the reins, kicks, and shouts at the horse, but the proper command escapes him. He yells, 'Stop!' and 'Halt!' and 'No!' yet the horse charges on."

"If only the horse had been taught regular instructions."

"Of course, but it had not. Finally, just as they are nearly over the cliff, the man remembers and shouts, 'Serve the Lord!' and the beast stops."

"Lucky man."

"Lucky, indeed. The man is so happy he raises his hands toward the heavens and shouts, 'Praise Yahweh.'"

David said nothing for a moment as Abishai's attempt at a joke sank in. "Praise Yahweh?"

Abishai nodded, then his smile faded as David did not laugh. He gestured with his hands, miming a horse running over the cliff. "Then the horse...it ran."

"I get the joke, Abishai. Yahweh has blessed you with abundant talent, cousin, but humor is not one of them."

"Jonathan thought it was funny."

David chuckled. "I find that unlikely."

Abishai stared off at the rest of the men for a moment. "Will we be returning to Gibeah?"

"You will, yes."

"You are going to Nob again?"

He nodded.

Abishai sighed, long and deliberate. "I guess *I* will lead the men back to Gibeah."

"I will not be long. There is no reason I cannot rejoin you before you reach the city."

"So, help me understand. I will lead them in the long march, and you will arrive just in time to lead them into the city? To bask in the admiration of the women of Gibeah?" He smiled. "Sounds fair."

"If you prefer, I can not show up at all, and *you* can speak to the king once you arrive."

"Me? Before the king?" He laughed. "I think not."

"As I thought. How are the men?"

A new voice answered him. "They are well."

Abishai and David turned and watched Jonathan approach.

"Good," David said. "They did good work today. Your father will be happy."

Jonathan looked out at the valley. "You have spent years fighting the Philistines, David, and have only ever met with success. With you, my father is always happy."

Yet every time I see him, he seems displeased.

"I am merely a tool of Yahweh, serving his anointed king."

Jonathan nodded in agreement. "As are we all. But it will be nice to return to Gibeah."

"Yes," David said. "It will." His thoughts, however, spoke differently. While the comfort of his own home and the absence of the constant threat of death would be welcome, he had found little joy in being in the king's presence as of late. There was something about Saul that nagged at David.

"David?"

He shook the thoughts away and looked at Abishai.

"Are you well?" Abishai asked.

David forced a smile. "Just thinking about your horse."

His cousin smiled. "Praise Yahweh."

DAVID CRESTED THE HILL, and the tabernacle came into full view. Its curtained walls formed a long rectangle in the plains of Nob, smoke rising from the altar within. From his vantage point above, he could see the temple tent near the back wall and the numerous tables used for sacrifices dotting the court in front of the temple. Priests meandered throughout the court, offering burnt sacrifices and inquiring of Yahweh for all who came. Everything threw long shadows in the light of the setting sun.

Far beyond the tabernacle sat the town of Nob. Dozens of homes and farms covered the landscape. The inhabitants were nothing more than dots from a distance, though he could hear the faint ringing of a blacksmith's hammer.

He approached the tabernacle, then turned wide of the entrance and walked down the side of one of the long curtains. He could smell the burning meat within. Part of him wanted to enter, if only to be closer to the presence of Yahweh. But he had no business inside today and instead wished to speak with Ahimelech, the head priest, who he knew resided in Nob.

Nob was like so many other towns in the new nation of Israel, though small even by David's standards. It was only a little larger than his hometown of Bethlehem, and he felt he knew every inhabitant of his hometown. After more than a dozen visits to Nob, he was beginning to know the men and women here, as well.

"David," someone shouted, as if in response to his thoughts.

He turned and found Abiathar, Ahimelech's son. Abiathar was not much younger than David and still training to take his father's place one day.

"Shalom," David said, embracing the younger man.

"Shalom! It is good to see you again," he said once they parted.

"It is good to be back. Is your father near? I wished to visit him before I returned to Gibeah."

Abiathar smiled. "Back from battle?"

"I am."

"Would you tell me about it?"

David looked at the priest in training. He had the yearning of a man who had never seen battle, the curiosity of a man who had never taken a life. He saw a younger version of himself in him, a glimpse back to David the shepherd, and was hesitant to ruin that image with tales of blood and battle.

"You do not want to hear of my battle with the Philistines."

"I do!"

He frowned. He hoped that the young man could be deterred, but it didn't appear to be possible. Indeed, it was never possible when he visited Nob. As the two began to walk toward Ahimelech's home, David recounted some of the battle. He told the younger man how he and Jonathan had offered the Philistines peace before.

"They do not deserve it," Abiathar said.

David chuckled at that. "I do not disagree."

"Then why offer them peace?"

"Who am I to deny Yahweh's mercy?"

The priest in training said nothing to that, and they continued through the town in silence. Ahimelech was sitting outside his home and sipping at a cup of wine as David and Abiathar approached. His face lit up at the sight of David, and David himself felt a joy swell within him. He may hear the voice of Yahweh on his own, but there was something about receiving instruction from this aging priest that brought him a comfort he could not describe.

The old man stood with a groan, leaning heavily on a staff, and the two of them embraced. "I was hoping to see you again," Ahimelech said.

David stepped back and held Ahimelech by the shoulders. "You say that every time we meet."

"I am getting old. Every time you part could be our last meeting."

He frowned at that. "You still have plenty of time, old friend."

Ahimelech looked over David's shoulder to Abiathar. "Could you see to the tabernacle? I will be that way shortly."

Abiathar nodded and then was gone. Ahimelech gestured to a seat. "Please, sit."

He offered David a cup of wine as he sat. David sipped at the drink and watched the rest of Nob scurry about him, finishing errands or walking home from the small market, some even returning from the tabernacle. They sat for a long while in pleasant silence.

"Not that I do not like these visits," Ahimelech finally said. "But I am sure you have something you wish to speak about."

David turned to the priest. "I am just in no hurry to return to Gibeah."

Ahimelech gave a nod. "The king. I understand."

"He did not take kindly to my declining his offer of marriage to his daughter."

"What king would? And what kind of man says to no to marrying a princess?" He smiled. "And one as beautiful as Merab."

Nearly a year ago, the king had offered David the hand of Merab, his oldest daughter. She was beautiful. Kind, as well. A woman who seemed to share his zeal for Yahweh. Yet the thought of becoming Saul's son-in-law had been enough to make him decline.

"Indeed," David finally said. "What kind of man does that? What kind of man am I?"

Ahimelech looked at him in silence for another moment. "Have you heard the story of Gideon, David?"

He looked up from his wine. "Gideon? He was a judge."

"Yes, he was. Do you know his story? Why we still speak of his name?"

"I know he won a great battle."

The old priest smiled. "Something like that. Did you know he led some thirty thousand men against over one hundred thousand Midianites?"

David's eyes widened. He had fought for over five years.

And despite having heard of the times of the judges, the thought of an army of that size felt ludicrous to him. "Over one hundred thousand? With only thirty thousand?"

"He *started* with thirty thousand, yes. But Yahweh told him he had too many men and should let anyone afraid to fight return to his home. Twenty thousand men left."

David set his wine down and gave his full attention to Ahimelech. He'd heard pieces of the story before, but never the details. "Yahweh let Gideon face one hundred thousand men with only ten thousand?"

The older man shook his head. "No. He did not. Yahweh told Gideon that he still had too many men. He eventually whittled Gideon's army down to three hundred."

"Wha…three *hundred*?"

Ahimelech went on as if David had said nothing. "Gideon armed each man with a trumpet and a torch covered with an empty clay jar. They approached the camp at night and smashed the jars, revealing the three hundred torches. Together, they blew three hundred trumpets. The Midianite army feared a larger force and devoured itself in fear."

"But…why? Would thirty thousand men with thirty thousand torches and thirty thousand trumpets not have worked better?"

"Perhaps," he said. "But then Gideon would have thought it was he who had won the battle. He would have boasted of his own strength and would not have seen that it was Yahweh who delivered them. Yahweh who delivers us all. You see, David, Yahweh does not work as you or I do. His ways are not our ways." The old priest shifted in his seat. "Look at you. You are a shepherd, the youngest of your family. You are not from a great town with a great name. Eliab, your brother, is twice your size. You are brash on the rare occasion. You do not seek glory." He grinned. "You are actually quite unimpressive. Yet Yahweh has blessed you greatly. You lead men fearlessly into battle. You have risen high in the ranks of Saul's growing army."

David sighed. "But why? What you say makes sense, doesn't it? I *am* a shepherd and the youngest of my family. I am brash on more than the rare occasion. Though I have little good to say of Eliab, he would appear to be a better warrior than me. Why has Yahweh chosen me? And what is it he even wants of me? First, I was a shepherd, then a musician and a warrior. Now I lead men into battle. My calling seems to change by the day."

"Who can speak the mind of Yahweh? All we can do is what Gideon did: trust him. Send home your thirty thousand men, David, and face what comes with only Yahweh to go before you."

12

SAUL

Saul slouched in his throne, one hand absently clutching his spear while the other drummed on the arm of his throne with a steady *tap tap tap*. Jagged squares of white light from the high windows dotted the hall. The tall acacia pillars—reinforced now with bronze strappings that Saul hoped made his palace appear more substantial—lined the center of the great hall. Long dining tables were piled against the outer walls behind the pillars, stowed for now but ready to be pulled out tomorrow. Benyamin stood at his side, a spear of his own in one hand and a shield in the other.

Men of import, or so they claimed to be, filled the spaces between the great pillars. They paid him no mind, each involved in his own business. Their speech filled the air, a dozen individual conversations all droning together to make one steady hum so he could not discern any words.

I do not need to discern them, he thought. *They are talking of David.*

Occasionally someone would glance his way. Saul would feel his heart quicken, and his palms become sweaty. He would feel their stares, his mind reeling as he wondered what they thought of him. Did they fear him or laugh at him? Was he king only by title, or did he still have their respect? Then they would look away, returning to whatever it was they were discussing, and he would let out a breath.

They may not have heard what Samuel said all those years ago...but they know.

Shouts came from outside, and Saul jerked. The conversations faltered for a moment. There was silence as the shouting faded into the distance. Then the men turned back to one another, and the hall was again filled with the droning of speech.

A few minutes later, the cedar doors creaked open, and Rimmon of Beeroth stepped inside. He was a short man—Saul was nearly as tall as he was while sitting—though he had not let that slow him down. One of the elders of Gibeah and of the tribe of Benjamin, he wore a robe of imported silk, notable due to the difficulty of obtaining the material, thanks to the Philistines and their constant aggression.

Saul stood as his favorite counselor made his way down the hall. "Greetings, friend," he said, a genuine smile on his face.

"Greetings, my king," Rimmon said, going to a knee as he and Saul met in the center of the hall.

"Stand. Stand, please." He bent and helped Rimmon to his feet. "What brings you here?"

"Your son has returned," he said. "David with him. They are just beyond the city walls. The women and children are rushing to the streets to celebrate."

Again, we celebrate David.

Saul's smile became strained. "Then we shall join them." He addressed the men of the hall. "Come! Let us see Israel's sons!"

Saul turned to leave. He stopped, a strange longing filling him. He turned back and eyed the spear he had left by the throne, then walked back to his throne, lifted his spear, and took it with him as he followed Rimmon from the hall. Benyamin followed a few steps behind them.

Women and children were indeed rushing through the streets, the former yelling for the latter to slow down. He watched with a mixture of annoyance and jealousy as the people of Gibeah joyfully paraded to the city gates.

"They act as if it had been David rather than Moses who led Israel through the desert for forty years," Rimmon said, a hint of disdain in his voice.

Saul gave a rough scoff. "It is a wonder they have not built him a monument within the very tabernacle."

Rimmon laughed at that. "Could you imagine? A monument to a shepherd."

"Armed with sling and staff with little sheep in tow."

He snorted more laughter. "They will forget him in a few years."

Saul frowned. *Sooner, one can hope.* He led Rimmon down the palace steps and joined the crowd, despite every urge pulling him back to the security of his throne. Out here among the people, he felt hundreds of eyes on him. He knew their thoughts; like the jackals of his hall, they would rather see David on the throne than him.

Every step through the city was agony. Saul was thankful when they finally arrived at the city gate. He and Rimmon mounted the steps built into the walls and were soon standing on the top of the gate. In the near distance, he saw Jonathan and David's men approaching Gibeah from the west. He sought out his son among them. When Jonathan had heard of the size of the Philistine threat, he had begged to go. Saul had chosen David instead, as he nearly always did. From the moment David had entered his service, Saul had sent him on as many life-threatening missions as he could in the hopes that the Philistines—or the Amalekites or the Edomites—would handle his problem for him. They never did. However,

Jonathan had not given in, and so Saul had to let him go, sending an additional four hundred soldiers for protection. He was not yet willing to trade Jonathan's life for David's.

His son was leading the vanguard with David at his side. Saul watched in silence as they approached the outer wall. From his vantage point, he could clearly see that most of the men he had sent were returning. Either the Philistines were routed in their entirety, or David had not even met with battle.

Let us hope for the latter. He has fame enough.

But Saul could soon see the extra cattle and lambs, both piled high with plunder. The people of Gibeah were already cheering, their voices rising high into the afternoon sky and filling the city with joy, reaching an ear-piercing crescendo as David stepped through the city gate. Saul looked down on his most courageous captain, his most successful warrior, and felt nothing but raw hate and hot jealousy.

He is the one. He is the one who is better than me.

"Saul has slain his thousands," someone shouted, his voice carrying over the din. For a moment, Saul smiled, his spirits rising.

Do they credit me with his victory?

"Saul has slain his thousands," the crowd repeated. Saul began to turn to wave.

"And David his tens of thousands," the voice cried out.

"And David his tens of thousands," the crowd echoed.

Saul's hand clenched around his spear as Samuel's words echoed in his mind. The crowd repeated the chant, growing louder and more joyous each time. "Saul has slain his thousands and David his tens of thousands!"

"Such foolish words," Rimmon said. "Do they not realize *you* sent him? That *you* decided where to attack? And when? That it was *your* soldiers in the battle?"

"They see only his handsome face and swoon." Saul gnashed his teeth, trying to control his anger.

"They see only what they want to see."

"They do not know what they want."

Yes, they do, he corrected himself. *They want to see David on the throne. But they will never see it. I will make sure of it.*

He leaned in close to Rimmon, his patience with this shepherd reaching its limit. "We must ensure David never sits on the throne," he said, his voice barely above a whisper. Not that anyone could hear him over the shouts of the crowd.

Rimmon glanced at Benyamin, who was paying too much attention to the returning army to notice. "What do you mean?"

"What do you think I mean?"

For a moment, Rimmon seemed taken aback, but Saul could almost see the gears turning in his mind. Rimmon was his friend, and he valued wealth and esteem above all else. He would understand the need to rid Israel of David, both for Saul's sake and his own. "You are suggesting…an accident?"

"I have been hoping he would die in battle, but the Philistines have been uncooperative." Saul held his old friend's gaze for a handful of heartbeats. "It seems we must help them."

Rimmon said nothing, though he no longer looked to be in doubt.

"Will you help me with this?" Saul asked.

"I will do what needs doing."

Saul nodded. "Good. Meet me tomorrow in my council chambers. Early, before the sun rises. Bring only whom you trust."

Then Saul turned from the wall and stomped down the stone stairs beside the gate. He'd had enough of this show and was ready to be back in his palace. Benyamin hesitated before following. He found his palace empty and, for a moment, simply stood in the doorway and stared at his darkening hall. The jagged blocks of light had crawled their way up the eastern wall and taken on an orange hue as the sun neared the horizon.

"Fetch Adriel," Saul said over his shoulder to Benyamin. He heard his armor-bearer turn and walk away, leaving him standing alone.

Alone...

Saul plodded to his throne and sat. He twirled his spear and watched as the bronze tip gleamed like fire in the orange light. For the first time in a long while, Saul was alone with himself—the worst company he could imagine. His mind was filled with competing thoughts—fears and worries and angry shouts—each coming in louder than the previous in an attempt to drown each other out. The result was a chaotic storm in his mind, an indiscernable tempest of noise and fog and mayhem. He turned his focus on the spinning spear and attempted to silence the voices, but he was able to achieve only a dull aching in his mind instead. After a long while, Benyamin entered the hall with Adriel in step beside him.

Adriel was near the same age as David. He was roughly the same height and build. A strong man from a strong family. He was not, however, a military commander.

And therefore not a threat to my throne. A perfect husband for Merab.

Saul had initially offered his oldest daughter to David on the condition that David continued to fight for him. David had refused the marriage and went to battle nonetheless. Saul should have been happy—he had gotten what he wanted without giving up anything. And yet he felt rejected. He knew David was not rejecting Merab; she was far too beautiful. No, David was rejecting Saul. He was rejecting the king of Israel the same way Samuel had, the same way his wife was beginning to, the same way *everyone* was beginning to.

Adriel knelt before the throne as Benyamin took his place beside it. "My king," he said.

"Rise, my friend."

The young man complied, swiftly and properly.

He will make a good son-in-law.

Saul turned to Benyamin. "Be sure David is brought to me as soon as he is able." The armor-bearer gave a curt bow and left again. Saul turned his attention back to Adriel. "You are prepared? For tomorrow?"

"Yes, my king. Everything is in order."

"That is good. Merab has talked of nothing since the arrangements were made. She is in the market this very moment." Saul gave a joyless smile. Everything was joyless lately. "It seems months of preparation were not enough for her wedding."

"I have my work cut out for me. But no worries, my king. She will be well loved."

"Not until tomorrow, of course." Adriel laughed at Saul's lousy attempt at humor. For a moment, Saul felt a spike of anger at the pitiful attempt to curry favor, but he heard so little laughter that he let it go. "She is anxious to get to Abel Meholah."

"Our house is in order," Adriel said, his eyes drifting to the spear in Saul's hand.

Do you think I am dangerous, Adriel?

The hall doors groaned open, and Benyamin led David inside. Adriel took a step to the side to make room for him as Benyamin resumed his post at Saul's side. David went to a knee. Saul was silent, letting him kneel until even Adriel fidgeted with discomfort.

"Rise, David."

He did, his eyes darting to Adriel. "My king. I bring news of victory from the Valley of Elah."

Saul reclined in his throne. "That valley has been good to you, my son."

It was slight, but he saw David wince just a fraction at the word *son*. "So long as Yahweh leads us into battle, we will succeed."

So pious. So irritating. "Have you met Adriel?"

"I have not." He turned and offered a hand. "I am David, son of Jesse of Bethlehem."

Adriel took his hand. "I am Adriel, son of Barzillai of Meholah."

"He is to be wed to Merab tomorrow," Saul put in.

David's face flushed for a moment at Merab's name. "Congratulations," he said. "Merab is a fine woman."

"That she is."

Saul cut in again. "David was to be wed to her before he declined the offer."

David winced, and this time Adriel blushed. "Well…" Adriel stammered. He straightened a bit and gathered himself. *How pathetic.* "Well, I am very thankful you did. It has made me a very happy man."

"I'm glad for that," David said. "Yahweh guides all."

Saul felt his grip tighten on his spear. *I could kill him now. No one would know but those here, and they could be bought.* His grip tightened further until he felt his knuckles pop.

David turned to him. "If my king has no further need of me, I would see to my men."

Not today. But soon. Saul waved him away. "You may go. Both of you. And please send in my son as you leave."

13

DAVID

David and Adriel strode down the wide palace steps together. It was nearing nightfall, and David was anxious to be away from the palace. He turned to Adriel and found the man looking at him, as well.

"I apologize," David said. "He seems to thrive on making me uncomfortable. I'm sorry you were a victim, as well."

Adriel only smiled. "All is well." He offered his hand, and David shook it. "The king is prone to his moods. You would know that better than most."

"This is true. And Merab is truly a fine woman. Congratulations."

"Thank you, David." He gave a short bow. "Now I must prepare for tomorrow. I will see you there?"

"You will."

As Adriel walked away, David turned toward Abishai and Jonathan, who were both standing at the bottom of the steps. The rest of his men were already returning to their homes. There was a third man—or boy, by the looks of it—that David did not recognize standing a step behind Abishai.

David looked first to the king's son. "Your father wishes to see you," he said.

"I hope you did not steal all our glory," Jonathan replied with a smile as he walked by David and toward the palace.

"Trust me, friend, there is much left over." David then turned to Abishai. He gave a long sigh once Jonathan had disappeared into the palace. "I'm glad that's over." He nodded to the boy. "And who is this?"

Abishai stepped aside and guided him in front of David. "This is Ira of Tekoa."

David offered him his hand. "Greetings, Ira of Tekoa. I am—"

"David, son of Jesse of Bethlehem," Ira cut in. "A great warrior, a great leader." He dropped suddenly to a knee. "And I offer you my sword."

He glanced to Abishai, who only shrugged. "He is a friend of a friend."

David frowned. "Stand, Ira of Tekoa. I am no king." Ira stood, though the admiration in his eyes was fierce. "And you have no sword," he pointed out.

Ira patted his hip where his sword would have hung. "My father is a blacksmith," he said, turning and looking off into the city. "I will have one by morning."

He looked him over. "You are a boy."

"I am no younger than you were when you defeated Goliath."

Abishai snorted a laugh and then covered his mouth.

"That was different," David said. "I was…called to do what I did."

"And *I* am called," Ira countered. "I pray to Yahweh every night and every morning. I follow his commands. I serve him with all my heart and mind and soul and strength." He started to kneel again and then caught himself. "I *must* serve you, David. He has told me so."

Abishai snorted another laugh, and even David smiled. "Yahweh has told you?"

Ira nodded fiercely.

Perhaps I am not the only one to hear his voice.

You are not, David.

David paused at the voice. He had not expected a response. *Does he speak true?*

He does. You will need him.

"Very well," he said, more to the voice than to Ira. "Meet me in my courtyard the morning after tomorrow."

Ira beamed. "Thank you! You will not regret it, I promise."

He nodded toward Abishai. "See that he gets a sword."

Abishai stepped forward and clamped a hand down on Ira's shoulder. "Come with me, child." David watched the two of them turn and walk down the steps and into the city.

And where do I go?

He found his feet walking, taking him nowhere in particular. The prosperous and well-built households of Gibeah were squashed together like a beehive. Most were smaller than his father's home, though obviously of a much more refined crafts-manship, with stone walls and wooden rooftops covered in clay to produce a sleek look. The men and women walking in and out of the courtyards—every house had one, no matter how small— wore thick and colorful tunics and robes. They were well groomed, and their skin gleamed with oil and fragrance. David was suddenly aware of his own worn tunic and the sword at his hip.

He eventually found himself in the market. In sharp contrast to the pushed-together homes, the market was a large clearing, yet the area felt even more crowded. Dozens of stalls dotted the market edge, hundreds of men and women filling the spaces between them. Goats pulled carts, their bleating filling the air. People shouted over the goats and bartered for goods. The stench of too many people in too small a space caused him to gag suddenly. He covered his mouth with an arm and took an involuntary step back.

"For a man known for battle, you seem easily overwhelmed."

David turned to the voice and found a woman holding the lead of a young lamb. She wore a simple white dress the same color as the lamb's wool and stood nearly as tall as him, though that was not a difficult task. Raven-dark hair fell around azure eyes that reminded him of the freshwater springs in the hills of Judea. She was slender, standing with an elegance that David was unused to in his time of constant war. She seemed a sculpture made from a craftsman's hands rather than something of flesh and bones.

"I-I…" he stuttered. "Uh…"

"And not much of a talker," she added. When he said nothing still, she smiled, and David felt his heart stop for an instant.

What is this?

"I…"

Her smile turned to a playful frown. "Is this David, slayer of Goliath?"

He tried to smile and managed something closer to a grimace, his face drawing a laugh from her. "I-I am."

"Well, it is a good thing you are more fearless in battle than in banter." She stepped by him and pulled the lamb toward the market. "Or Goliath would be running through these very streets."

He cleared his throat. *Say something!* "I am unused to such beauty and found myself without my voice." He gave a low bow. "And for that, I am sorry."

Her smile returned in full, and David's heart skipped another beat. From that moment on, his only desire was to see her smile. "He speaks! And his words are sweet as honey. I didn't know David the slayer of giants was also so adept with his words, even if he is a slow starter."

"Yahweh has blessed me with many talents. Before I was a warrior, my first love was the lyre."

"I am sure you had a captive audience."

David barked a laugh before he could stop himself. "Yes, my sheep were most intrigued by my music."

The woman leaned back and raised an eyebrow. "I had forgotten that David the warrior was once David the shepherd."

"In fact, David the warrior still sounds odd to my ears. I find myself longing for my sheep more every day."

"Hmm. David the shepherd." She gave a coy smile. "I like it."

His heart fluttered in his chest. "May I ask your name?"

"You may ask," she answered, the smile still lingering on one corner of her mouth.

David returned the smile. "Then I will. What is your—"

"Abigail!"

They turned in unison to the voice rising above the din of the market. Merab, Saul's oldest daughter, stood not far off. She held a bundle of flowers and was waving toward them. "Abigail!"

David looked back to the woman—to Abigail. *A maidservant to Merab?* She was waving to Merab. "Coming, Merab." She turned to David. "I am afraid I must go. I have a wedding to help with." She gave a short bow. "It was a pleasant talk, David the shepherd."

He watched in stunned silence as she walked away.

14

SAUL

SAUL STOOD by the window and watched the stars dim and the eastern sky lose its black-blue hue. The cool breeze of night blew in on his bare chest, and he could feel goose bumps forming on his skin. He looked down at Gibeah, at the great city where he had been born. It had exploded since his anointing so many years ago. Since then, he had single-handedly raised it up from the little village it had once been to the bustling city it had become. From his high vantage point, he could even see the distant line of caravans making their way toward the city—*his* city—from the south, bringing silk and spices.

I have made Israel great, he thought. *And the people still look to my replacement.*

He scowled down at the ungrateful city and turned back into his room. His bed lay empty; it had been almost a year since anyone had shared it with him. Ahinoam had long since sought her own quarters, and Saul had no interest in concubines. He had turned them away at first out of love for his wife. Now, however, it was from a lack of desire of any kind.

He dressed in silence, the night sky slowly gaining light as the hint of sunrise approached. He took up his spear and left his room. The palace halls were empty but for the odd servant cleaning or preparing the morning meals. He passed the massive oak door to his throne room and instead descended to the basement and into his council chambers. It was a single room with windows sitting high on the walls and level with the ground outside. The small room smelled of dust and stale air, even though his garden was just beyond its sandstone walls. Only flickering torchlight lit the room.

There was a large, round table occupying the center of the room, a dozen or so chairs and stools pressed up against it. He took his seat at the table and waited, his spear twirling at his side. Rimmon would be along soon and would likely have his sons with him. Baanah, the oldest, was not the wisest of men, but he was a warrior and as selfish as his father. Saul knew he could be bought. Recab was Rimmon's youngest son. He was even less wise and by no means a warrior. Saul knew little of him. Other than the two of them, he did not know who Rimmon would bring, who he trusted.

Luckily, he did not have to wait long.

The chamber door creaked open, and Rimmon stepped inside. Behind him came his sons, as Saul had expected, but then another man entered the room. Saul himself was a big man, near a head taller than most of his own warriors. Rimmon was nearly as a child beside him, both in height and weight. Though much of Saul's muscle had gone soft in the last few years, he was still a powerful man. And though he feared many things—indeed, it seemed he feared nearly *all* things—a fight was not usually one of them.

Yet the man who entered behind Rimmon and his sons would have put Saul on his back foot had he been standing. He was nearly as tall and decidedly larger, yet his bulk had a lean-ness to it that was frightening. He walked with an aura of confidence that edged on cockiness. Yet Saul had no doubt the man could back it up.

Rimmon and his sons sat across the table from Saul. The other man moved to stand behind Rimmon as if he were a bodyguard.

"Greetings," Saul said, taking his eyes off the behemoth of a man and looking to Rimmon. "Your sons, I know. Who is this man?"

Rimmon glanced up at him. "This is Doeg of Edom."

Saul eyed the man, sizing him up. He did not like the idea of an Edomite sharing in their scheme. "And what services does an Edomite offer?"

Doeg smiled, and Saul felt a chill run up his spine. "What services does the king require?" His words seemed to scratch their way out as if his throat were full of sand.

"That is yet to be decided," Saul replied.

"There is not a task you can ask of me that I cannot do." He paused. "For the right reward."

A selfish man, then. This, Saul could work with. "And if it was to take a life?"

"Then I will take it."

"And if it is a person you have never met?"

"I don't make it a point of meeting my victims before I rid them of their heads."

Saul thought on that for a moment and then merely nodded. He dragged his eyes from Doeg and looked at Rimmon's sons. He eyed Baanah first. "You know why you are here?"

"To protect my king's interests," he said, "in whatever form that takes."

"Good." He turned to Recab. "And you?"

"To do as my king commands."

"We shall see." He leaned back and looked again at

Rimmon. "David has grown strong, powerful. He is loved by the people and, it pains me to say, a great leader."

He is, after all, the one who is better than me.

He physically shook Samuel's words from his head. "And he is ambitious and grasping. A jackal. I can see it in his eyes. He seeks my throne, and I will not let that happen. He came to me a thorn in my side. Now that pain has grown more than I can take. I would see him dead."

"Point me in the right direction," Doeg said. "And I will end him."

"I would rather he fell at the hands of our enemies."

Doeg scoffed. "Your enemies are weak."

"Then we must even the odds."

"How do we do that?" Rimmon asked.

Saul spread his arms wide. "That is what you are here to tell me."

15

DAVID

THE NOISE of the banquet hall never fell below a dull roar. There were two women in the corner of the hall, one with a tambourine and one with a lyre, their attempts at music doing little to penetrate the din of conversation coming from the dozens of tables. The pleasant scent of meat cooking over a fire mixed with perfume, sweat, and burning torches created a unique aroma. Soft late afternoon light fell in through the windows.

David's eyes were fixed on the servants as they darted between the tables with platters of fruits and cheeses and cups of wine. He searched their faces for Abigail's, hoping beyond hope that a maidservant would be needed to help serve the food.

She is likely still upstairs with Merab helping the new bride dress.

"Do you know the fastest way to a man's heart?"

David rolled his eyes and looked over to Abishai. "Why did I bring you?"

He grinned. "Because you had no woman to bring."

"That will not last forever."

Abishai shrugged and took a long drink from his cup of

wine. He eyed a food plate as it passed by. "So, the fastest way to a man's heart?"

"Is it food, Abishai?"

"No." He made a knife hand and jabbed David in the ribs. "It's between his ribs with a sharp knife."

David slapped his hand away. "You are special."

"Thanks."

The heavy cedar doors at the back of the hall groaned open, and the conversations fell dead as all eyes turned to the open doors. David sat up a bit straighter and watched with curious eyes as Merab and Adriel entered the banquet. They entered alone, much to his disappointment, and waved to the crowd. Cheers and congratulations filled the air as the newly-weds took their seats beside King Saul and Ahinoam at the head of the hall.

"You should have married her."

David looked back at Abishai. "And become a son to the king?" He sat back on his stool. "No, thank you."

"Would it be so bad? To have a chance at the throne?"

David was so shocked by the words he nearly choked on the air he was breathing. "The throne?"

His friend downed the wine. "Why do I feel you fight against understanding?" He leaned in close and dropped his voice, unnecessary now that the hall had filled with the roar of conversation again. "Why do you think the king continually sends you against the Philistines instead of sending any of his other captains?"

He tried to placate his friend with a smile. "Because I am the best?"

Abishai chuckled. "You have the best men with you; that at least is true. Do you not see his jealousy, David? Do you not see the way he looks at you?"

"Of course, I see it," he snapped. "I see it every time we speak."

"You are a threat to him. He wants you dead."

"He wants his most successful captain dead? I do not think his jealousy runs that deep. Why offer me his daughter?"

Abishai was not deterred. "Do you remember his request when he offered her to you? 'Serve me bravely and fight the battles of Yahweh.' He was basically asking you to die for him."

"I fight for him anyway."

"He did not know you would. He does not know your heart." Abishai reached back and took a fresh cup of wine from a servant. "There are few of us who do."

David frowned at his cousin. Abishai was loyal, a good man. He may be rough at times, but he had a good heart. "I'm sorry," he said. "I know it's not easy following me."

Abishai leaned in again with an intense look in his eyes. "That's what you don't understand: it *is* easy following you. It's not safe, but it *is* easy. You are a leader. Your men love you; they would die for you. You should be king, not that jealous little fool." He downed his wine in one gulp. "You should have married her."

"Jonathan is next in line for the throne. Did you forget that? And he is a good man, a man of Yahweh. Men follow him as they follow me. I would not take what is rightfully his."

Abishai only frowned. "I did not suggest you would."

David turned away from his friend. In part, Abishai was right. Saul's jealousy may indeed run deep enough to threaten his life. Yet he didn't want to think on that now. He didn't want to think on that ever, in fact. He shook the thought away and resumed his search of the servants. Once Merab emerged without Abigail at her side, he realized he had little hopes of seeing her. It was mostly men serving the food, though the occasional female servant did arrive to refill a cup of wine or take a plate away. He sighed, and his eyes drifted toward Merab and Adriel. Adriel leaned in and whispered into his new bride's ear, drawing a giggle as she slapped his shoulder.

"David the shepherd."

David and Abishai turned together and found Abigail standing behind them. She was dressed modestly, a simple blue dress the same color as her eyes and a beige shawl draped over her shoulders.

"Abigail," he said. "It is…it is nice to see you again."

"And you."

"You look beautiful," he said. Abishai started to laugh and choked on a hunk of bread. He broke into a coughing fit, wheezing and hacking and pounding his chest until he finally cleared it with some wine.

"Sorry," he muttered, turning back to the table and picking at the bread and cheese.

Abigail grinned at Abishai and then looked back to David. "Thank you," she said, smiling and melting David's heart. "You look very handsome, as well."

I'm going to marry this woman, he thought.

She looked about the room and eventually at the pair of women playing the tambourine and lyre. A few of the revelers had begun to dance, mostly unorganized and clearly drunk. Abigail grinned. "Would you like to dance, David the shepherd?"

"Yes," he squeaked, standing a bit faster than he would have liked and probably looking much too eager. Abishai chuckled again beside him. David ignored him and cleared his throat. "Yes. I would like that."

He held out his hand. As she took it, he guided her through the tables and toward the musicians, catching a grin from Abishai as he did. By the time they reached the somewhat open area in front of the two women, the small band of dancing revelers had grown to more than a dozen, crowding the small space, yet David barely saw them, so lost was he in Abigail's presence. The music was a lively song, one he recognized from his childhood, and he and Abigail fell in with the rest of the dancers.

Time seemed a distant thing as they danced, the changing music the only sign of its passing. It went from upbeat and memorable to frantic and desperate, and their dancing changed to match it. His feet pounded the floor as his heart pounded in his chest. Abigail disappeared into the crowd, surrounded by the other women of the hall, as David slipped in with the men, then they both emerged, wide smiles and joyous faces as they found one another again, hands clasping together as they spun. His vision tunneled as it did in battle, and he began to have the feeling that *this* was where he belonged. Not with a bloodied sword in his hand as he had often thought, but rather with Abigail's soft fingers there instead. They twirled and danced and laughed, and he prayed a prayer of thanksgiving to Yahweh.

The music faded to silence. They stopped, standing there in the middle of a wedding, surrounded by revelers and exhausted dancers, eyes locked on one another. David's heart beat as much from effort as from the feel of her touch. He was vaguely aware of the men and women around him, of something happening at the front of the room, but he could not take his eyes off Abigail. He felt himself leaning in, leaning toward this woman he'd only just met. Every inch of his skin tingled with goose bumps. She stood on her tiptoes, their faces inching closer together…

"Honored guests," a voice boomed from the front of the hall.

David opened eyes he hadn't realized were closed and saw Abigail do the same. He stared at her, wanting nothing more than to close the little space between them. From her eyes, he could see she wanted the same.

"Next time, David the Shepherd," she whispered. She turned to the voice, and David reluctantly followed.

It was Saul speaking, standing at the front of the hall with his arms spread wide. David had never been more disappointed to see the king, and the king had disappointed him more than once.

"Honored guests," he repeated. "Evening is upon us. Let us now bring this party to the courtyard." He waved his hands toward the front of the hall, and the doors groaned open. As the doors opened, David saw that the sky was indeed a deep orange in the west. The courtyard itself was alight with torches and threw flickering shadows into the hall.

"Shall we," David said, turning and gesturing outside even as the other guests made their way through the now-open doors. She smiled and took his offered hand, and he guided her out. The cool, evening air was a welcome relief after what he hadn't realized had been a sweltering hall. His sweat dried almost immediately as he led her away from the crowds and to a lone olive tree at the edge of the courtyard.

They sat in the well-manicured grass at the foot of the tree. He leaned against the tree, and she leaned against him, her back resting on his chest. They sat in silence like old lovers, and he felt a comfort that he'd never felt before. The sun finished its slow crawl beneath the horizon; the lengthening shadows disappeared, and the moon took the sun's place in the sky.

"Tell me about yourself, David the shepherd."

He looked down at her. "What do you wish to know?"

"How does David the shepherd become David the warrior?"

"That is a story everyone knows."

She shifted in his arms. "But is it not a story worth telling? How a young shepherd defeated a giant? Were you not afraid?"

His mind returned to that day. He remembered the fear,

first from the retreating men and then from himself as he laid eyes on Goliath. But then he thought of the giant, standing above the armies of Israel and cursing Yahweh. The memory of the fear was replaced with the much more vivid memory of his anger.

"I was too angry to be afraid."

"Angry?"

"Goliath did not speak overly fondly of Yahweh," he said. "He blasphemed the Living God of Israel and therefore blasphemed all that is sacred."

She seemed to think on that. "I have heard Yahweh speaks to you," she finally said. "Is this true?"

He shifted, uncomfortable with where this conversation was going. "He speaks to us all," he said, avoiding a direct answer to the question. "All we must do is listen."

"A very diplomatic answer. I pray to Yahweh daily, observe the festivals, sacrifice what I should. I would say I feel his presence, but I have never heard his voice. Do you suggest I listen harder?"

"I am not a prophet," he said. "I cannot know why he speaks to some and not others."

She smiled wide. "So, you do hear him?"

David sighed. "At times, yes."

"And what does he say?"

"It depends."

"What did he say about Goliath?"

David again felt himself remembering that day, twice now in as many minutes. He could see the grass, see the armies of Israel and of Philistia facing one another. He could hear Goliath scream his curses, see the king too afraid to answer them. And he could hear Yahweh's voice.

"He told me he needed a warrior."

"A warrior with no training and a sling to fight with?"

He shrugged. "I won, didn't I?"

"I suppose you did."

"And what of you," he said. "What's your story?"

She laughed. "Now *that* is a story not worth the telling."

"I shall be the judge of that."

The din of conversation fell off. David watched as King Saul stood at the head of the crowd.

Again...

"I suppose it is a story that will have to wait," she said, standing and making him feel like a piece of him was leaving. "It seems the party is over."

SAUL

SAUL STOOD on the city walls and watched the small procession lead away from Gibeah. There were oxen pulling carts, donkeys laden with the many wedding gifts, and servants and soldiers surrounding the new pair of lovers at the center. His daughter was his no longer, instead riding off to Meholah with Adriel.

It had been a trying week for Saul, having to watch his oldest daughter marry and prepare to leave him. He still had Michal, his younger daughter, as well as his sons, but watching Merab go tugged at his heart. She was his first girl and his most cherished little one.

And yet, now that she was leaving, he felt anger instead of sadness. Merab was not leaving because she was wed and that was what married women did. No. In Saul's twisted and fear-laden mind, Merab was abandoning him like the rest of Israel had. Not for David, but for another. She was *choosing* Adriel over Saul, *choosing* to leave him.

Deep down, he knew it was foolish thinking. He had himself offered her to David before pairing her with Adriel. But he couldn't help it. He could only watch her leave with anger simmering just beneath the surface. He stayed until near midday when the last vestiges of the procession were no longer visible. By the time he turned to leave, even Benyamin, his faithful sentinel, was twitching uncomfortably at his side.

"You'll not leave me, right, Beny?"

His armor-bearer did not even hesitate. "Never, my king."

Saul smiled. "That is good," he said, patting Benyamin on the shoulder. "That is good."

When he arrived back at his palace, he found a man standing at the base of the steps. He had a long and unkempt beard and disheveled hair that looked like dirty sheep's wool, yet he wore a fine tunic that looked to be silk and stood with a confidence that belied his appearance.

The man dropped to a knee as Saul approached, yet with a reluctance and casualness that Saul found irritating.

"You may rise," he said. Benyamin took up his place behind him, though even Saul could sense the tension in his armor-bearer. His own hand drifted toward his hilt.

"I am Nabal," the man said as he stood. "From Maon." He paused. "Maon is south of—"

"This is my nation, Nabal. I know where Maon is."

"Then why is it left to the lawless and the bandits? Why does it feel we are forgotten?"

Saul stepped forward, his hand doing more than drifting toward his sword now. *Now is not the time, stranger.*

"What did you say?"

Nabal frowned, quickly realizing his mistake. "Apologies, king," he said, though he sounded far from apologetic. "I have traveled through the night to see you and have lost some of my manners in the journey."

"You should look to find them," Saul said. "And quickly."

"I will do just that." He gave an overly extravagant bow. "I have come to seek aid, my king."

"You would do better to lead without insults in the future."

"More wise advice."

Saul felt his anger subside—if only just. This man was coming to seek aid from bandits and lawless men. *A perfect task for David.*

"Fetch me David," he said, leaning back toward Benyamin, who nodded and walked away. Saul turned again to Nabal, the thought of sending that shepherd back to battle quickly raising his spirits. "Come," he said, gesturing to his palace doors. "Let us take counsel."

Nabal bowed low and stepped aside to allow Saul to walk by him. As Saul entered the palace, he was assaulted by that constant noise of conversation and politicking that always filled his hall. He lowered his head and marched down the center, feeling the eyes of prophets and elders and other men of Israel as they watched him. Soon he was seated on his throne, and Nabal stood before him. He could not help but let his eyes drift among the dozens of men in the hall.

Jackals...

He forced his eyes back to Nabal. "Tell me of these bandits," he said. "Where do these lawless men come from?"

"From the forest," he said. "My king," he quickly added.

"How many?"

"I know not their numbers, only that they grow every day."

"And why have you drawn their attention? You are obviously a wealthy man, but not the only one in Israel. Why have they targeted you?"

"I am indeed a wealthy man, my king. Wealthy because I am careful with my goods. I do not throw wealth away to men who can perform no work. These men resent me for my...prudence."

"So, you are uncharitable," Saul said, not unkindly. "And the poor and hungry try to steal from you as recompense. Is that it?"

Nabal could not help but smile. "I am not fond of funding

the poor, no. They are like wild dogs. A bit of meat, and they will follow you forever."

Saul chuckled at that. "You are not wrong."

The palace doors opened, and Benyamin led David in. Saul saw the immediate change in the men of the hall, all eyes turning to the young shepherd turned warrior. There was admiration there that no longer came in his direction. He swallowed the anger bubbling inside him and stood.

"Just the man I needed to see," he announced. He was suddenly happy for the audience in the hall. Not that he would, but there was no chance David would refuse a battle in front of so many. "I trust I am not disturbing you with my summons."

David stepped around Nabal and knelt. "Never, my king. I was training with my men, but they are skilled with or without me. I am here to serve Yahweh's anointed."

Again, Saul saw the admiration at David's feigned piety. "Good, my son," he said, watching with grim satisfaction as David flinched at the word. "It seems I require your services yet again. This is Nabal."

David turned to Nabal and offered his hand. "I am David, son of Jesse."

He looked at David's outstretched hand and then back to Saul. "You would send the shepherd?"

David's hand hung out awkwardly for another moment before he pulled it back. Saul looked again to the room and saw the admiration fade, replaced now with apprehension.

"Israel's greatest captain is not good enough?"

Nabal scoffed loud enough for the entire hall to hear. Suddenly, Saul was very thankful for this man's excessive rudeness.

"I would prefer a man of renown and not a shepherd's son. I have shepherds of my own." He looked David over and eyed him as if he were one of his sheep. "He does not seem overly impressive."

David stiffened, and Saul had to bite his lip to stop from laughing. "He has won a great many battles. He has only just returned this month from the Valley of Elah, where he defeated a Philistine army of near a thousand."

Nabal was still frowning. "I am told Jonathan accompanied him. Should not be praising your son rather than your servant?"

David's face reddened, though he said nothing. Sending David to battle had been Saul's preference, but this public shame would have to suffice. "Very well," Saul said, raising his voice to be sure everyone heard him. "If David is below you, I will send another to defend your land." He glanced as casually as he could at David. "It seems I do not need you after all, son of Jesse. You are dismissed."

17

DAVID

DAVID WALKED down Saul's palace steps more frustrated than he'd been in a long while. He was feeling emotions that he hadn't felt since his childhood. Nabal had dismissed him so completely, more completely than he had ever been dismissed, even by his own father. It bothered him more—and he knew it shouldn't—that nearly everyone of import in Gibeah had seen it, as well. He tried to shake the thought, but it had taken root. He was having flashbacks to his youth, to the days of Eliab and Abinadab mocking him endlessly. He felt for the briefest of moments like the slighted child he had been. Useless and insignificant and small. Like a shepherd and not a warrior.

And he hated it.

He tried to push the thoughts and insecurities from his mind as he stepped through the gate from Saul's courtyard and into Gibeah. The sun was slowly crawling toward the horizon as the crowds bustled around him, more than a few people dipping their heads in an acknowledgment to him. He waved back, yet the esteem he felt at the recognition of men and women he hadn't met—and likely never would—only served to remind him that it was fueling his pride. He felt that splinter of haughtiness digging deeper into his being, threatening to infect him wholly.

He guides the humble in what is right and teaches them his way.

The words came to him like an old friend, words he'd heard his mother repeat more than once.

Guide me, Yahweh. Teach me your way.

He drew a breath to calm his nerves and continued his walk through Gibeah. He heard the sounds of mock battle long before he reached his courtyard. The clacking of wooden practice blades bouncing off one another, the shouts of effort and pain and frustration, the thuds of arrows sinking into hay targets. Then he was around the final bend and standing at the entrance of his courtyard.

He surveyed the elaborate arena, dirt packed and lined by cedar and acacia pillars that supported the wooden and clay-brick overhang surrounding it. To his left was the balcony of his own home, built into the colonnade's roof and enclosed with acacia rails. The arena was filled with his men, those warriors under his command who lived within the city. It smelled of dust and blood and sweat, and he couldn't help but smile. This was where he belonged, among his fellow warriors. He quickly forgot about Nabal and Saul and his wounded pride.

Abishai was in the center of the arena with a pair of men holding wooden practice blades. One of them was Eleazar, the son of Dodo. Dodo was a kind man, and his son was no different. Eleazar had been with David since near the beginning. Not as long as Abishai, but for nearly all the five years of David's service, Eleazar had been nearby. He was a good man and a good warrior, a born leader.

Standing opposite Eleazar with eyes fixed on Abishai was Ira, the young boy David had met on Saul's steps not a week ago. He'd acquired a sword, as David had instructed him to, and had trained every day since here in the arena. David watched as Abishai stepped back and Ira turned to face Eleazar.

He has no chance.

Their blades came together slowly at first, as Eleazar probed Ira's abilities. Ira blocked the first pair of strikes with relative ease. Eleazar pivoted and struck a bit faster. Ira stepped back in response, his sword moving with more finesse than David had expected. He could see the confidence build on Ira's face as he blocked strike after strike, deftly parrying Eleazar's sword each time it came.

Yet David knew Eleazar well. And he knew the art of war even better. He watched with a thin smile as Ira, full of confidence now, stepped in and struck at an apparently defenseless Eleazar. The older and somewhat larger Eleazar sidestepped the strike and, dropping his own sword, caught the hilt of Ira's. He twisted it hard, eliciting a shout from the unsuspecting—and no longer confident—Ira, and pulled the weapon from his failing grip. Ira tumbled to the ground, drawing a laugh from both Eleazar and Abishai.

"Well fought, child," David said, his voice loud and carrying in the arena. He walked between battling warriors and toward the three men. "Still some way to go, but well fought."

Ira spat dirt from his mouth and turned to David. "And yet, I am in the dirt."

"But you are alive." David offered him a hand and helped him to his feet. "Better to be in the dirt in the arena than on the battlefield." Ira nodded his agreement, and David turned to Abishai.

"What did the king want," his cousin asked.

David frowned, that splinter of pride digging in just a little bit more. "Nothing worthwhile. Have the men return to their families," he said. "It is nearly nightfall."

Abishai nodded an acknowledgment and walked among the men.

"I had him."

David turned to Ira. "Did you?"

"I could feel it. I was close."

Eleazar laughed at that, loud and long. "You were never close, my little cub."

Ira frowned at the name, though David could sense he liked it. Despite the insult the nickname implied, it meant he had been accepted, meant he belonged. And David knew better than most how good it felt to belong somewhere.

"Eleazar is right," David said. "He was toying with you, tiring you out. Often an enemy will choose the safer, smarter way to beat you. He will feign exhaustion, feign a lack of skill, and simply wait for his opening. And you gave Eleazar his."

"How am I to know the difference?"

"Practice," he answered. "And a lot of it."

He turned back to the men and saw that they were cleaning up. Wooden swords were being washed—some of blood—and put back into small barrels under the overhang. Arrows were being plucked from hay and examined for reusability, the good ones put into quivers beside the swords. Even Ira and Eleazar stepped away to wash. Soon, the sun had set, and David was left with only Abishai in the courtyard as the rest of the men filed out into the city.

"You're going to see her again, aren't you?"

David looked at his cousin and smiled. "A quick bath first."

"Can you not see her during the day?"

"She was a maidservant to Merab," he said. "Saul did not take it well when I chose not to wed his daughter. And now I would court her maidservant?" He shook his head. "He cannot know. Not yet."

"What would he do? Send you back to battle? That's going to happen either way."

David only shrugged. "I don't know. I'm only glad that Abigail did not accompany Merab to Meholah."

They bid their farewells, and Abishai left the arena to go wherever it was he went when he was not at David's side. David went upstairs to his home and, after a quick wash with a basin of cold water and a change of clothes, he was again on the streets of Gibeah. He walked directly to the city gates, the moon casting enough of its pale light to guide his path.

He found her—alone, as she had been for three nights now—leaning on a pillar near the city gate. She was dressed modestly in a gray dress with a light blue shawl, the latter pulled up and over her hair in a makeshift hood. He couldn't help but smile.

They embraced in the shadows of the city gate. He delighted in her warmth and the feel of her body against his. He pulled her closer, never wanting to be free of that embrace.

"David the shepherd," she said, her breath soft on his chest.

The shepherd...

The term had stung only a few hours earlier and yet, coming from her lips, it sounded sweet.

They parted, and he looked down at her. Her vivid blue eyes reflected the pale moonlight and shone all the brighter. He knew he was in love; it was now only a matter of wedding this woman.

"Did you have trouble getting out," he asked.

She frowned. "Out of where?"

"The palace. Did the guards see you? Or Saul?"

"The palace? Merab is gone and I am no longer her servant. I do not stay in the palace."

"Where do you stay?"

"A little hovel near the palace wall." She waved her hand as if it did not matter. "It is a nowhere place, a temporary home until I am wed." She grinned at that last word, and

David's heart fluttered. "And where do *you* stay, David the shepherd?"

"It is no palace," he said, though he was eager to impress her. "Yet it is no hovel, either. Shall I show you?"

She gave a showy bow. "Lead on, my lord."

He offered his arm, then he guided her through Gibeah and back toward his home. "You never told me your story," he said as they walked. "I know not where you come from, what tribe you belong to, how you came to be in Saul's service."

"All good questions," she said. "Which one would you hear first?"

"That is up to you. It is your story to tell."

"And I am afraid it is not as exciting as yours. I fought no giants and slew no lions."

"And I would hear it nonetheless. I would know everything about you."

That drew a subtle smile. "Very well. I am of the tribe of Judah, from a small town of little import. My mother died in childbirth, and my father when I was a bit older. Upon his death, I was sold to the family of Saul as a slave."

David frowned at that, at a life summed up in three sentences. "How old were you?"

"A child, maybe ten. Saul has always treated me kindly, however. I grew up with Merab, received the same education as she, little as it was."

"Why did you not accompany her to Meholah?" He smiled. "Not that I am complaining, of course."

She returned the smile, though there was a hint of sadness behind it. "Adriel had maidservants enough for her. It was a bitter parting, I will admit. She has been like a sister to me for many years." She threw him a sideways glance. "And she was most unhappy when you chose not to wed her."

David felt his face flush and said nothing.

"Why didn't you?"

"I was waiting for you," he replied.

She laughed and elbowed him in the ribs. "I would hear the real story."

"Would you hear the truth?"

"Always. You shall never lie to me, David."

"I did not wish to be Saul's son-in-law. It is as simple as that."

Abigail chuckled softly. "He is not overly fond of you, I will admit. I know not why."

"Neither do I."

"He was not always so angry, so bitter. When I was growing up, he was a gentler, kinder man. He tried to do the right thing, though I suspect he has always struggled with it. It was not until several years ago that this change in him happened."

David did not wish to continue this discussion of Saul and so was happy when he rounded a building and saw the outline of his courtyard not far in the distance. "My home," he said, spreading a hand before him.

Abigail's eyes widened slightly as she looked at the courtyard and his home attached to the side of it. David had spent much of the last five years here and had become accustomed to its size. Looking at it now with Abigail and seeing the admiration on her face, he felt that splinter of pride pinch at him. He ignored it and led her into the courtyard, into the arena where he and his men trained. She looked at the cedar and acacia pillars, at his balcony jutting out above it all. She was unable to keep the awe from her face.

"It is wonderful," she said. "And so...so large."

David smiled, this time not feeling as the splinter burrowed just a bit deeper. "It does not feel so big when full of training men. Often there is little room to walk."

"How many men do you lead?"

This number he did not need to think about. "Three hundred and forty-two, though they do not all live in the city."

She turned to him, surprised at the speed with which he responded. "You know them all?"

"Of course," he said. In his mind, he could see their faces, as well. "I lead these men to battle, often to their death. They are closer to me than my own brothers."

She looked at him for a long while, her eyes focused and clearly in thought. It seemed to him that it was the first time she viewed him as David the warrior and not David the shepherd, despite the stories she'd heard. He was not sure how he felt about it.

But then she smiled, and her face lightened. "What else have you to show me?"

18

SAUL

"I DON'T CARE about the Amalekites," Saul shouted, pounding the table hard enough to shake the map askew and cause the six men around it to flinch. He was in his council chambers, the same chambers where he had sat just weeks ago to discuss the fate of David. But today, the topic was the growing strength of the many nations that surrounded them.

"Amalek is no threat! We have Edom to the east and Philistia to the west!"

The men all stared in silence. The outburst had shocked them. Indeed, it had taken Saul himself aback. As time went on, he found that he was losing more and more control over his emotions, especially when his mistakes were plain to see. This trouble with Amalek was only reminding him of those failures, reminding him of that day Samuel had disowned him. After all, it had come as a result of his failure to follow Yahweh's commands about the Amalekites.

It was Abner who finally leaned forward. "My king," he said, calmly and evenly. His passive tone only served to annoy Saul more. "Edom is no threat; it's been no threat for years."

He knew it was true that Edom was nothing. He also knew

that Amalek had grown strong in the last five years. True, not quite strong enough to challenge them, but strong enough to become something of a threat. His attention *should* be to the south, *should* be focused on their growing strength, on stopping it before it became more than a thorn in his side. Abner had requested this council for that very reason.

Yet Saul did not want to focus on the Amalekites. He wanted to ignore them, to put them out of his mind along with Samuel and the words the prophet spoke five years ago. He wanted Amalek to mean nothing to him, though he knew that could never be.

"And Philistia," Saul said, refusing to give up his line of thought. "They are stronger than Amalek. More organized. Five kings united against us!"

"Philistia is powerful, yes, but David and his men—"

Saul punched the table again. This time he felt his knuckle split from the force. He ignored it. "I don't care about David!"

Abner drew a long breath and exchanged a glance with Jonathan. "I understand, my king," he continued in that calm, emotionless voice. "But Philistia is being held at bay, at least for the moment."

"He is right," Baanah said. "Philistia *is* a threat, but Amalek is one we can easily crush."

Saul turned his gaze on Rimmon's oldest son. "Can *we*?"

Baanah sat up taller. "I have men under my command. Strong men, fighting men." He nodded, more to reassure himself than anything else. "We can give Amalek more than a little trouble."

Saul scowled yet said nothing.

Baanah paused and seemed to think on his next words carefully. "I only wish to remove this problem from the king's mind, so he can focus more clearly on more…pressing issues."

His scowl faded, if only just. "Very well. Take your men," he said and then nodded to Recab. "And your brother. Remove this thorn from my side so that I may focus on real threats to my kingdom."

Like David.

Jonathan finally leaned forward. "If Philistia still worries you, let me accompany David on another expedition. We can secure our borders, press our advantage."

Saul looked at his oldest son. *You would like that. Another chance to fight by your friend's side, to leave me and serve your future king. No. You two will never fight together again.*

And with that thought came an idea.

"I have different plans for you," he said. "You will go to Maon, with Nabal."

And far away from David.

"Maon? What threat is in Maon?"

"Unruly Israelites. Bandits. Thieves."

Jonathan frowned. "And this is a danger? More than Philistia or Amalek or even Edom?"

"If we cannot control our own lands, how can we defend our borders?"

His frown deepened, though he said nothing.

Saul was about to speak when the door slammed opened and Doeg entered. Abner, Jonathan, and Malki-Shua turned to the newcomer, alarmed. Benyamin shuffled behind him and drew his sword. Saul stood and raised a hand. "He is a friend," he said. "A servant of Rimmon's." Abner and Jonathan relaxed, if only just, and Benyamin sheathed his weapon, though his hand did not leave his hilt. Saul turned to Jonathan. "Go prepare your men," he said. Then he looked at Abner and Malki-Shua. "Both of you. Go with him." Then one last look at Jonathan. "You leave in two days. Do not fail me."

The three men exchanged a cautious glance as they stood, doubt evident in their eyes, although they said nothing as they filed by Doeg and out of the room. The Edomite watched them leave, paying particular attention to Abner as if he'd heard what was said about his homeland. He bore a scowl that Abner chose to ignore. It wasn't until the door was secure and they were gone that Doeg moved to sit.

"Who's the old one," he asked, picking at his teeth with a nail.

"He is the commander of my armies," Saul said, more than a little annoyed at his quick disrespect for his longtime friend. "And he has more than earned my respect."

"Then why is he not in here with us?"

Saul stiffened and said nothing.

Doeg examined his nail and flicked something off to the side. "It doesn't matter," Doeg said. "I have news."

Saul looked over his shoulder to Benyamin. "I am afraid I need you outside, old friend."

Benyamin's hand finally left the hilt of his sword. His expression of distrust deepened, yet he said nothing as he went. Saul could almost feel him standing on the other side of the door, his vigilance not diminished in the slightest. Saul had no doubt that if he sensed danger, that door would do little to hold him back.

Saul turned back to Doeg. "News?"

"About the shepherd."

"Something useful, I assume?"

He shrugged. "Maybe. David's got himself a girlfriend."

"Have you come to brag on him? All the women of Gibeah fawn over that jackal."

He grinned. "*He* fawns over one. Merab's little servant. They were together at the wedding."

"Abigail?"

"I saw the two of them walking around his courtyard."

Saul shook his head. "You're mistaken. Abigail is like a daughter to me. I would have known."

Doeg scoffed. "A daughter? Did you not remove her from your palace the moment Merab was away with Adriel?"

Saul was taken aback by the comment, but he could not argue the point. "Perhaps not as a daughter, but I still would have known."

"Did you not see them dancing at Merab's wedding?"

He thought back and could not recall. *How much did I drink that night?* "As friends, surely."

Doeg went back to picking at his teeth. "If you say so. I know what I saw."

"David has nerve," Rimmon said. "I will grant him that."

"Nerve?"

"There's a good reason no one knew of this," he said. "David knew what he was doing. Turning down marriage to Merab herself and then pursuing her maidservant?" He scoffed. "He's a brave man. Foolish, but brave."

Saul had not even made that connection. *The jackal! He would turn down my daughter and then pursue her slave? Does he see me so far beneath him? The arrogant little rat!* The wound at his knuckle seemed to pulse along with his now-racing heart. "He is a snake," Saul said, his voice low and trembling.

"But what good does this do us?" Baanah asked. "Why do we care who he courts?"

"You've got to be creative," Doeg said. "Use it against him. Abigail's a fine woman. I'm sure it would crush the little shepherd if something were to happen to her."

Saul's rising anger stopped short.

"Like what?" Recab asked, speaking for the first time.

Doeg shrugged. "Whatever makes her disappear the fastest. It would unnerve him, at least."

Recab's eyes went wide, and his mouth dropped. "You're talking of killing an innocent woman," he said, "merely to *unnerve* David?"

"I've done worse."

The room fell into an uncomfortable silence, a silence Saul judged carefully. He was unsure how he felt about it himself, yet he wished to get an idea of his council's thoughts first. He would not condemn a woman to death if it were to lose him support among these few, key men. So, he watched, refusing to blink, refusing to breathe in the thick tension hanging over the room. Indeed, only Doeg seemed at ease.

If it were to rid me of David…

"Surely, you jest," Recab finally said, breaking the tense silence. "We cannot simply kill Abigail."

Saul let out a breath, and Doeg shrugged.

"Recab is right," Saul said, though, again, he was unsure.

"We cannot kill her," Rimmon agreed, leaning forward as he spoke. "Though I may have an idea."

19

DAVID

EVEN FROM A DISTANCE, David could hear the arrow thud into its mark. The bale of hay was nearly fifty cubits away, and it looked as if the arrow had punctured the center of the target.

"Fine shot," David said, taking the bow from Jonathan.

"Good luck matching it."

David grabbed one of the arrows from the wicker basket between them. The target looked a little bigger than a fig from a distance. He drew, closed an eye, held his breath, and released. The fletching of the arrow dragged across his cheek and forearm, and the arrow took flight, sailed high into the morning sky, and thudded in the grass a few cubits from the target.

Jonathan laughed. "Still a fine shot."

They were outside the walls of Gibeah, near the western forest that stood an hour's walk from the city. It was peaceful, quiet, only the two of them for some distance. Jonathan practiced with the bow as much as David did with the sword and, as he had already demonstrated, was an excellent shot.

"Give me a sword over a bow any day," David said, patting the blade at his hip.

"Better for your enemy to never know you are there."

David watched as Jonathan fired another arrow, this one sinking only a hand's width from his previous shot. "I have a sling for that," David said, taking the bow. He aimed longer this time. Despite his jest, he did not like how much better Jonathan was with a bow. He let the shot go and watched as the arrow sailed clean by the target and flittered amongst the trees behind it. He frowned, annoyed.

"I lose more arrows in a day with you than a month on my own."

David forced a laugh and handed the bow back as the two started to walk toward the target to retrieve their arrows. "My apologies, your highness."

"You can't please everyone, my friend."

He frowned. "I know it; trust me. Like that boor, Nabal. I can't say I'm sad that you go to Maon and not me."

"I don't know many who could please that man."

He scoffed and felt that splinter of pride twist inside him. "A man who can't protect his flock thinks *I* am beneath him? He is a fool."

Jonathan laughed at that, though it was an unsteady laugh. "Does this man bother you that much?"

David felt a warning go off in his head and knew what he was about to say was wrong. Arrogant. But he found himself speaking before he had time to heed the warning. "I've seen more success in my five years of service than that little man will see in his entire lifetime. He does not deserve to have his flock protected."

Jonathan's eyes widened a fraction. "When pride comes, then comes disgrace," he said, quoting an old proverb. "But with humility comes wisdom."

David felt a rush of shame as the words sank in. *Why am I bothered so?* Yet he knew the answer, even as Eliab's mocking voice filled his head. He let out a long sigh. Best to forget

Nabal even existed. After all, he would never see the man again. "You're right. When will you leave?"

"Tomorrow at first light. As soon as my men are assembled." Jonathan sighed. "Enough of me. I saw you at Merab's wedding, dancing with Abigail. How long has *that* been going on?"

David's face reddened against his will. "I don't know what you're talking about."

"I'm sure you don't."

They reached the bale of hay. David glanced at Jonathan's arrows sticking from the target as he circled the hay to find his own.

"Don't tell your father," he said, bending and grabbing an arrow. "I'm not sure how he would take it."

Jonathan thought on that, likely remembering David's refusal to wed Merab. "I suppose I should be offended too. Big brother and all. You are going to have to speak with him eventually if you ever plan to do more than dance with her."

"I'm waiting," he said.

"Is David afraid?"

"For Abigail, yes. Saul will not hurt me."

"He will not hurt Abigail, either. She grew up almost alongside Merab."

"Then what do you suggest? Your father already dislikes me. This will only worsen things."

"And yet you cannot court her without speaking to him. She is his slave. You *must* speak to him. For her sake."

David sighed, loud and long and overly dramatic. He knew his friend was right, knew it would be worse if Saul found out on his own. Both for him and Abigail. "You are right," he said. "Tomorrow. I will talk to your father after you leave."

DAVID WAS in mixed spirits as he walked the streets of Gibeah the following day. His mind was on Abigail; she was as a storm in his head. He wanted nothing more than to wed her, to spend his life with her. Yet he knew Jonathan was right. Speaking to Saul was the only way to make that happen. And so, he saw them both: Abigail, smiling and glowing, her brilliant blue eyes lighting up her face, and Saul, scowling and glaring at him with fierce, unfounded jealousy.

I lived my childhood in obscurity and was constantly berated by my father and brothers for it. Now that I have achieved something, I am hounded by jealousy. Is there no middle ground?

He shook the thoughts from his mind as he trekked through the city. His talk with Saul would come, but for now, he was on his way to see Jonathan off, to watch his friend go defend the flocks of Nabal.

David climbed the stone steps that led up to the city walls beside the gate. A hundred men were lined up in ten rows of ten, forming a perfect square in the fields beyond Gibeah. He could clearly see Jonathan mounted at their head. A pair of figures stood beside him, one of which was clearly Nabal. The other was a woman, though David could not see her face.

The boor's unfortunate wife, more than likely.

"Here to see off the king's son?"

David turned and saw Rimmon of Beeroth move beside him. Rimmon was one of Saul's counselors and, if the word could be used of anyone, his friend. David was not overly fond of him.

"I am," he said, then turned his eyes back to the army.

"Odd that the king sent him off with a wife when all he asked for was protection."

David's ears perked at that, and he looked again at the woman beside Nabal. "A wife?"

"Nabal comes as a single man asking for help against

raiders. He leaves with an army at his back and a maidservant of Merab as his wife."

David's heart skipped a beat. *Maidservant of Merab...*

"Abigail?"

Rimmon's eyebrows rose in surprise, though David knew the man well enough to be certain it was an act. "You know her?"

A wave of anger unlike anything he'd felt before rose inside him, strong enough to rival the joy that he'd felt in Abigail's arms. His wounded pride returned, swollen now with jealousy.

"Did the king say why he would send such a beautiful woman with such a boor of a man?"

"I wouldn't know." With that, Rimmon flashed a smile and climbed from the wall.

David watched him leave and then turned back toward Nabal and Abigail. She was standing at his side, her head bowed, as Jonathan prepared the men to move around her. He could feel her pain, for he shared it himself. His heart cried out to her in that moment, longing to be near. He would never see her again, never hold her again. Yet he knew it was his fault. He had pursued her, had shown an interest—no, a love. And now she was suffering for his feelings; she was being sent to a land she did not know with a man she would likely never love.

He turned from the sight, no longer able to watch, and stomped down the stairs. He stormed through Gibeah, the the surge of anger reaching blood-boiling intensity. He knew Saul had done it intentionally, had sent Abigail off with Nabal to punish him.

Soon the sounds of wooden practice blades clacking together brought his attention from his mind to the men around him. He was near the courtyard of his home, within sight of that large dirt arena where he'd stood with Abigail less than two days ago. It was full, just as he'd told her it would be, as his men practiced and trained for battle.

Perhaps some training of his own would help release his anger. Yet he knew it wouldn't and found himself wishing for real battle, wanting to spill actual blood. He felt foolish to think that he could ever be anything besides a weapon. Abigail had made him believe he'd found a purpose that did not involve blood and battle, but Saul had taken it from him, given her away to Nabal as if she were a sack of grain. He'd known since Goliath that he was called by Yahweh to shed blood, but he had hoped there would be something more.

Is this all, Yahweh? Am I nothing but your weapon against the pagans? Nothing but your vengeance against the unholy? Vindicate me, O Lord, for I have led a blameless life; I have trusted in you without wavering. Tell me this is not all.

This is not all.

David's heart stopped. *Then what? What else is there?*

In time, David. In time.

Not the answer he'd wanted. Not one he was willing to take. Shrugging the voice away, he stepped into his courtyard. There was a ring of warriors in the center. Within them were Ira and Abishai, dancing around each other and snapping quick blows with their practice swords. David tried and failed to push aside his own anger—anger at Saul, at Nabal, at himself, and indeed, even at Yahweh—and then joined the ring of warriors, his eyes on the two men sparring in the middle. They came together in a flurry of blows—the smaller Ira looking substantially more exhausted than larger Abishai. Their blades bounced and rapped off one another, a dozen strikes within a few heartbeats, as Ira slowly fell back under the assault.

This will be over in a moment, he thought as he saw Ira's arm begin to sag. Another handful of blows came down hard on his wooden sword, the tip dipping lower with each strike. Then he ducked a final overhead blow and rose up inside Abishai's guard. Their heads came together with a sickening crunch.

Then Ira was standing over Abishai, the latter's nose covered in blood.

Cheers and taunts came from the surrounding warriors as Ira helped his defeated opponent back to his feet.

"Well done," David said, silencing the rest of the warriors as he stepped out into the center of the courtyard. He tried and failed a second time to push aside his anger and felt it leaking out into his words. "Not a fair move, though the world is unfair." He looked at Abishai's bloodied face. Despite the wound, his cousin sensed his mood and gave him an inquisitive look. David ignored it. "That will heal nicely, Abishai. Soon you'll be as pretty as me."

Abishai smiled, though his eyes were still cautious. He spat a mouthful of blood onto the dirt. "Yahweh forbid. With two of us that pretty, there wouldn't be enough ladies in Gibeah to go around."

A few of the men laughed. David did not. There was only one woman he wanted, and she was no longer in Gibeah. He snatched the wooden sword from his cousin. "Clean yourself up while I defend your honor."

There was another round of taunts as Abishai wiped the blood from his face. "After what I saw of your dancing, I should be defending yours."

David winced at the thought of that night. He flashed Abishai a look that silenced him and then turned his attention to Ira, his hand clenching the wooden sword a bit harder than he would have liked.

"I do not even get to rest?" Ira asked with a cautious smile.

"You will get no rest on the battlefield," David snapped. He saw a moment of fear in Ira's face and forced himself into a small bow. "Though we are not on the battlefield," he said, more to himself than to Ira. "Take as much time as you need."

"Thank you," he said, breathing deeply and bending at the waist. "I will—"

Ira lunged forward midsentence with a quick jab. David whipped his sword around and knocked the blow wide. As Ira's momentum carried him forward a pair of stumbling steps, David kept his own sword moving and cracked Ira on the back of the head—more than a bit too hard—and the boy fell to the ground.

"I tried to be fair," David barked.

Ira grunted and rolled over, his hand on the back of his head, eyes tight in pain. "I see that."

David felt suddenly ashamed and leaned down to offer his hand.

"Are we picking on children now, David," a voice bellowed into the training grounds.

David's momentary shame vanished in a heartbeat, and a sudden resurgance of anger left him feeling cold. He turned to face Saul as the rest of his men dropped to a knee before the king. David hesitated, his eyes on Saul as the king strolled into the training grounds. He clenched the wooden practice sword hard enough to make his knuckles pop, his face tense with anger that he knew he was doing a poor job of hiding. Finally, he joined his men in bowing.

Saul was not alone; the ever-present Benyamin stood at his side. Rimmon of Beeroth was also there, and David felt a particular vein of anger directed at him for the show he put on earlier at the gate. He had been sent by Saul to ensure David knew Abigail was gone; of that, he had no doubt. There was another man with them that David did not recognize. He was large with heavily muscled arms coiling out of a thick leather vest. He looked ready for training himself, tightly wound sandals on his feet and a wooden practice sword already in hand. There was a confidence about him that reminded David of Eliab and not in a good way. Almost as an afterthought, Michal, Saul's younger daughter, walked in behind them.

"Merely training our newest recruit, my king," David said through gritted teeth.

Saul stopped and looked around the training grounds as if he were inspecting it. He had an air of assurance that David found unnerving. Saul lacked many things, and confidence was usually at the top of the list. "You may rise. Perhaps you would like to show me what Israel's greatest captain considers training."

David and his men stood. "If the king desires," he said.

Saul smiled. "He does." He turned to the man David did not recognize. "Doeg?"

The big man gave a curt bow. "As you wish." He stepped into the center of the grounds with David and gave a smug smile. "Do you need a rest?"

"I will get no rest on the battlefield."

Doeg thought on that for a moment and then gave a nod of respect. "You will not."

Then he was charging in. His practice sword came down hard. David angled his sword to parry, catching the wooden blade on the edge of his own. Their swords came together with a thunderous clack, and David felt the blow all the way up his arm and into his shoulder. He stepped back as they both recovered, swords held ready between them.

"You are fast, David of Bethlehem."

David tightened his grip. "And you are strong, Doeg of…"

"Edom." His sword came again in a flurry of strikes, each of which David caught on the edge of his. Every blow made his shoulder throb. Doeg followed David's retreating steps with large steps of his own and was soon nearly on top of him. David ducked a high strike and twisted around him, striking low at his calf. His blade met with only air, and then a foot hit his chest, and he was tumbling into the dirt.

He rose to a knee and gasped for breath, his vision fuzzy. A warning went off in his mind, and he rolled aside just as

Doeg's blade sank into the dirt. David rolled again, putting distance between the two of them, and then stood to his feet. He wobbled once, drew a breath, and steadied himself.

David put a hand on his chest, his ribs already tender to the touch.

"You are not fast enough, David of Bethlehem," Doeg said with a grin.

The man's smug smile fueled his anger, and David charged in. Strength filled his limbs, though this time from the rage and not from Yahweh. His strikes were slower than they should be, clumsier than they should be, and his opponent was soon on the offensive. David moved to parry Doeg's counter, his sword a moment too slow, and Doeg's strike nearly knocked the practice weapon from his hand. His anger-fueled strength was already fading, something he was unaccustomed to, and he was forced to backpedal as the bigger man continued to press his advantage.

Doeg feigned an attack high. David fell for it, raising his sword to block, realizing his mistake a moment too late. The first blow hit his wrist, and his sword clattered to the dirt. The second blow hit his already bruised ribs with the flat of the wooden sword and knocked the air from him with such force he nearly vomited as he dropped to his knees.

He was dimly aware of the king's laughter filling the courtyard as Abishai appeared at his side.

"Are you okay," his friend asked.

David tried to reply but only managed a breathless squeak. Abishai laughed before he could stop himself and then pulled him to his feet. David slowly became aware of clapping.

"Well done, Doeg," Saul said. David turned to the king, who was smiling so hard it seemed his face would split. "That was an impressive showing."

David sucked in a mouthful of air. "It was indeed," he said, gasping the words more than saying them. He drew another deep breath and stood under his own weight.

"Though it was not for a show that I came." Saul stepped aside and gestured to Michal. She stepped forward, brushing her dark brown hair from her blushing face. "It seems my daughter has taken a liking to you, David."

David barely saw her. Abigail still dominated his mind, despite the fact that she was at that very moment marching toward Maon to marry Nabal. He forced her from his thoughts and looked again at Michal.

"And I am always weak when it comes to my daughters' wants," Saul continued.

Not again…

"I am only a shepherd," David began, repeating much of what he'd said when Saul had offered him Merab. "I have only been brought high by you, Yahweh's anointed. You have already given me more than I deserve." He gestured to the training grounds around him. Then he knelt again, bowing low. "And it is no small thing to become the king's son-in-law."

"Stand, David." His voice changed, became firmer. David's defeat, it seemed, was only fueling the king's confidence. "You have done great things for me, for Yahweh. You are right; it is no small thing to become the king's son-in-law. But it is something you deserve."

It is not something I want.

"My king…"

"Let me finish." He looked at Michal, and David followed his gaze. "I will give you a second chance." Saul turned back to David. He took Michal's hand and offered it to him. "I make you an offer today, David, son of Jesse. I offer you my daughter's hand in marriage for the price of one hundred Philistines. Defeat the enemies of Yahweh and receive my daughter's hand."

His protests had been enough last time, enough to change Saul's mind. This time was different.

"You honor me, my king. But I cannot—"

"I am not asking," Saul said, his voice as hard as David had ever heard it.

David looked at Michal and then back to Saul, his thoughts racing. He had no desire to become Saul's son-in-law, to be forced into his presence more than he already was.

"Surely, you would not reject me twice," Saul said, the threat more than apparent in his tone.

He drew a breath and looked at Saul's smiling daughter. David forced a smile of his own, but it felt fake even to him. She was beautiful, there was no doubt of that, but David could still not get Abigail from his mind. And there was something about Michal that nagged at David, something just beneath the surface. She was dangerous, just like her father, though he could not say why.

Yet it appeared he had little choice in the matter.

"I will not. If it pleases Yahweh's anointed, it pleases his servant." He bowed again. "I will return with the prize or not at all."

THE SUN SET SLOWLY, creeping below the western horizon like sap down a tree. The village of Nob was settling down, as well. David sat in silence and watched, a cup of warm wine in his hands. Everything he saw—indeed, everything he *thought*—reminded him of Abigail. Women were returning from the well, laughing as they walked with wooden buckets filled to the brim to last them through the night and into the morning. Each of them looked like Abigail, walked like her, laughed like her. He tried to shake the thoughts—physically shaking his head as if the movement would help.

It didn't. It felt as if nothing ever would.

David sipped at his wine and watched as a pair of oxen pulled a cart by, the wooden wheels rattling as a man guided the animals to a nearby stable. Children screamed and laughed, running circles around their mothers—Abigail, every one of them—who were trying desperately to rein them in for the night. He could smell the night's first fire as it crackled to life in the distance.

"And you brought only fifty men?"

He turned to see Ahimelech sitting beside him. The old priest was eyeing him, obviously sensing the turmoil in David's mind.

"I am like Gideon," David replied.

Ahimelech smiled. "This is true, though Gideon's was a mission from Yahweh. Yours is a mission from a king."

"Also true. Yet I am lucky to have even fifty."

"Do you not command hundreds?"

David sighed, thankful that a conversation would help clear his mind.

Even if the conversation is on my mission to win the hand of Saul's daughter.

"I could not exactly command my men to go to battle for a bride price. I asked for volunteers only. And even then, I asked only those who have fought with me for some time."

"And yet you brought Ira."

David couldn't help but smile. The boy had not left David's side for the entire journey to Nob, always asking questions of battle and weapons and Philistines. He had been thankful at the time, if a little annoyed, since the boy's incessant talk had been enough to keep Abigail from his mind.

"He will not fight," David finally said. "Only watch."

Ahimelech sipped his wine. "Have you got a plan?"

"Something like that."

"So, you have your men and something of a plan. Have you an enemy to fight?"

"There is always an enemy to fight," he said. "It is just finding the right one that is sometimes difficult."

Ahimelech had opened his mouth to reply when the sound of running footsteps interrupted him. Abishai and Ira ran around a corner and skidded to a halt in front of them.

"We've...we've found them..." Ira said, gasping for air between words.

David looked from Ira to Abishai. "How many?"

"They were on the move. I could not be sure." Abishai gave a shrug. "Likely under three hundred."

He looked at Ahimelech. "I think we found our Philistines."

DAVID POINTED over the cliff's edge and down toward the Philistine camp. "Count the tents," he said, gesturing to the neatly aligned rows of tents in the valley below. Ira looked down, his gaze fierce as he tried to count them.

"Seventy...eighty...there are too many."

David pointed to one corner of the camp. "See how they are arrayed? Perfect rows? Count the rows, not the individual tents."

He nodded, and David saw his lips moving as he counted. "Five rows...twenty in each. So...one hundred tents."

"As well as the large command tent near the center," David added, pointing again at the camp. "And that's why we don't camp like that. We form loose circles, no pattern, no rhythm. It may be less organized, but it's harder to scout." David pulled back from the cliff's edge. "So how many Philistines are down there?"

"Two to a tent, plus ten in the command tent makes two hundred and ten."

"Right, though that's an estimate. Often a particularly stubborn Philistine will get his own tent or a close-knit scouting group may share one."

"But…but we are only fifty…"

"But they are Philistines." He smiled. "I will take fifty Israelites against two hundred Philistines any day." He rose to a knee. "Stay here and watch them. See their movements, watch for the changing of the guard. Come get me when that happens."

Ira nodded an acknowledgment, and David slid carefully down the hill. Abishai was leaning against a boulder and picking at his teeth with a dagger. His white teeth stood out in stark contrast to the painted black skin of his face. Like David and Ira, he had used coal dust to blacken his face. A bit further back were the eight others that Abishai and David had chosen to join them on this side of the camp, each of their faces dark with coal, as well. The other forty men were on the opposite side of the camp, hiding in the shadows and awaiting the same changing of the guard that David was.

"You're going to cut your tongue out," David whispered as he settled down beside his friend.

Abishai smiled without removing the dagger from his teeth. "I have fairly good aim," he said, finally pulling it back and examining a bit of food sitting on its tip. He flung it from the dagger with a flick of his wrist, then went back to picking his teeth. "As many Philistines would attest to, were they still drawing breath."

David couldn't help but laugh. "You've been known to slip. Though I suppose I would be rid of your constant badgering if you did succeed at slicing out your tongue."

Abishai turned his eyes to David without turning his head. "Then who would tell you such fine jokes?"

"Ira will have to develop a sense of humor."

Abishai snorted and removed the dagger to laugh.

"This will never work if they hear you cackling from here."

He wiped his mouth and smiled, a bit of coal dust now on the sleeve of his tunic. "This is not going to work anyway."

David shrugged. "It worked for Gideon."

He rolled his eyes and slipped his dagger back into the sheath on his hip. "Again, with Gideon."

"He had only three hundred men, Abishai, and he defeated the Midianites. An army of them."

"And we have fifty." Abishai nodded back toward the Philistine camp. "These men are Philistines. A nation of Goliaths. A few jars filled with torches will not scare them off."

He grinned. "I'm planning on it."

There was the scattering of rocks, and Ira slid down beside them. "The guards are changing," he said, his voice an excited whisper.

David and Abishai exchanged a glance and then climbed back up the hill. Below he could see a small group of Philistines speaking to one another on the camp's outskirts. They passed a torch between them, and then two of them began to march back.

"Why attack at the changing of the guard?"

David looked back at Ira, who had apparently followed them up.

"The fresh guards will not be adjusted to the night for some time," David explained. "They have just awoken and are tired. The previous guards are settling down for a well-deserved rest and will be equally lax." He nodded down the hill. "Fetch the rest of the men."

Ira slid back down the hill. "He is learning fast," Abishai said once he was out of earshot. "Not as fast as I did, of course," he added with a smile.

"He will make a good scout. In time."

There was rustling behind them, and the eight men crawled up beside him. At the rear came Ira.

"No," David whispered. He pointed to Ira. "Back down. You will watch, not fight."

The kid looked broken. He frowned heavily but did not argue as he slid back down the hill.

Shouting erupted and drew David's attention back to the Philistines. Points of light like fireflies appeared on the camp's far side, accompanied by war cries and rattling weapons. Even from up here, David's forty men and their torches looked like a fearsome army appearing out of nowhere. They descended on the camp with speed, setting fire to tents and slaying unprepared Philistines. To their credit, the Philistines responded quickly, despite the chaos David's men were creating. It was as if they had been present hundreds of years ago when Gideon had tried this same trick of attacking a superior force at night.

Not the same *trick, to be fair.*

David and Abishai watched in silence as the torches rampaged through the camp. Soon, the sounds of battle came to his ears: bronze and iron clashing together, the twang of bows and thudding of slung stones, the shouts of effort and pain and death. Already his heartbeat quickened, the anticipation of battle causing his muscles to tense and his senses to heighten.

He forced himself to wait as the battle raged. His men halted their assault on the camp, though they had done significant damage. Tents were burning, and David could see dozens of dead Philistines. Soon the torches were fading slowly into the distance as his men retreated and the Philistines gave pursuit. Then, as the last point of light disappeared beyond sight, he turned to his men. He pulled his sword free, and that tingling of anticipation exploded into full-blown battle fever. He welcomed that familiar strength to his body, the focus and oneness of mind that he knew would keep him alive. Beside him, his men followed suit, their swords covered in black tar and appearing almost invisible in the starless sky. Abishai lifted his spear from the dirt.

"Ready?"

He bared his teeth. "Always."

David rose and sprinted over the hill, his men following behind him. They stayed low and in the shadows; their cloth-wrapped feet made almost no sound. The first tents whipped by, empty now, and they continued until they met their first adversary: A Philistine with a blanket trying desperately to put out a fire. David's sword shot out and sliced across the man's throat. He fell into the fire and lay still. David's men spread out around him, forming a line as they tore through the camp. They killed in silence, unaware Philistines falling dead beside their still burning tents as they made their way deeper.

They slowed as they neared the center of the camp and the large tent that sat there. Here the fires were few and spread apart. David took the lead, leaning around one of the smaller tents to look at the larger one. There were no guards, all the Philistines either dead or in pursuit of the other forty men. He motioned for his men to surround the tent. They spread out, always staying low and in the shadows, and he made his way to the tent's entrance. Abishai joined him. David held up three fingers and began counting down. *Three, two, one...*

Together they ripped into the tent. He held his sword in one hand and his loaded sling in another. Abishai two-handed his spear. They had hoped to find the Philistine commander, and they were not disappointed. The commander leaned on the edge of a large, oval table with his open palms resting on a map. He was, however, far from alone. Seven others stood beside him. They looked up from their map in unison and stared at David and Abishai. For a long moment, no one moved as the confused commanders eyed the Israelites.

"Israelites!"

The shout came from outside and was quickly joined by others. Then battle erupted, both inside the tent and outside. David let his stone fly, and one of the commander's men fell back from the table with blood running from his head. Abishai grabbed his dagger and flicked it at another. It buried itself down to the hilt into his chest.

The remaining five pulled out swords and charged at them. David ducked a blow and parried another. He stepped inside the third strike and head-butted the Philistine. He stumbled back with a bloodied nose, and David followed with an upward strike that opened the man's stomach and spilled his insides onto the map. He felt himself twist, those unseen hands physically spinning him just as another sword came down and crashed into the dying man's innards. Blood and bile sprayed up into David's face. As he coughed the filth clear, another blade was jabbing in at him. He jerked aside, and the tapered end of the Philistine's long sword ripped the shoulder of his tunic. David reached out with his free hand and grabbed the man by the back of the head. He brought his knee up and the head down, bones shattering with a sickening crunch. He tossed the man aside and looked for the next foe.

Abishai was backpedaling under the assault of the two remaining Philistines while the commander shouted something from his place at the end of the table. David held his sword like a spear and threw it into a Philistine's back. The other faltered for just a moment, and Abishai dropped him with a swipe of his spear. David turned to the commander.

"What do you want, giant slayer?"

Abishai smiled while David frowned. "So, you know who I am?"

The commander spat into the dirt beside him. "Every Philistine knows the face of David."

Outside, the sounds of battle began to dim. "Do you hear that commander? I think the battle outside is ending."

"Your men must be dying."

"I think not. My men are well trained. And we fight on the side of the Living God of Israel." He pulled his sword free from the back of the dead Philistine. "A God you may fight for if you wish. I have said the words of Moses to your men before, and now I say them to you, though I am already confident in your answer. Yahweh has declared that the stranger who resides with you shall be to you as the native among you, and you shall love him as yourself."

The commander spat again. "I spit on your Moses, and I spit on your god!"

David frowned. "I figured you would. I think you know what I must do. I fear I will enjoy it more than you."

The commander's knuckles turned white as he gripped the table harder. The map curled between his fingers. "I will not go easy, giant slayer."

David wiped his sword clean on his tunic. "You never do."

DAVID WATCHED as the Philistines returned to the camp. Even from a distance, he could see how ragged they looked from their night of battle. He counted them at nearly ten across and five or six deep.

At least fifty men. Better than I had hoped.

The army stopped within earshot of the Philistine camp—now the Israelite camp. David stepped forward, his line of seven remaining men standing tall behind him with Abishai at their head. The Philistines began to form up for battle yet again. David could not help but admire their resolve. These men had fought throughout the night, pursuing an always fleeing foe, only to return and find their camp in the hands of their enemy.

"Welcome back, Philistines," David shouted.

One of the men stepped forward. He looked worn and disheveled from his night of battle, plus perhaps the haste with which he donned it. Feathers jutted up from his helmet and distinguished him from the men standing behind him.

"I thought you a coward, giant slayer, attacking in the night. Now I know you are a fool, as well, standing before my army with fewer than ten warriors."

David smiled. "I would not call your fifty men an army, Philistine. And my warriors are *Israelite* warriors, each worth ten of your own."

"Then why did you not meet me in open battle?"

"I did not want to sweat in the desert as we fought. It is much cooler at dawn." He could hear Abishai chuckling behind him.

The Philistine grinned and then drew his sword and hefted his shield. "All you have achieved is that you will die in the morning sun." He shouted a command, and the small army began a slow march forward.

David raised his sword high. "Ready!" He thrust his sword forward. "Fire!"

Arrows and stones came sailing from the tents, coming from the thirty-two men who had survived the night assault and circled back around. They rose high over David, peaked for a moment in the brightening sky, then crashed into the charging Philistines. A handful fell dead or injured, though their places in the approaching army quickly filled.

"Again!"

Another volley of arrows and stones went by overhead. More Philistines fell dead into the desert sand.

"Fall back!"

David and his seven men backpedaled to spread out among the tents and join the rest of the men. The Philistine army tore into the camp, the tents and firepits causing their lines to break and the battle to dissolve into individual skirmishes. David chose a small cluster of men and charged in, that otherworldly strength wiping away all his fatigue. He feigned a strike and baited a parry from one of them, then flicked his wrist, and the Philistine was suddenly disarmed. A lunge and a thrust put his sword through the man's chest. He pulled it free and caught the throat of another in one motion.

Abishai charged by David, his spear thrusting and piercing and finding holes in the Philistines' defenses. David was right beside him, his sword performing a bloody dance and throwing crimson ribbons into the air. Together the two became an unstoppable whirlwind of bronze and blood.

After what felt like hours but was likely less than five minutes, David lifted his sword and found no target. He spun full circle and spied nothing but Israelites—albeit far fewer than when he had started. David thrust his sword into the air and gave out a battle cry, one his men quickly echoed, and the Philistine camp was filled with the roar of Israelite pride.

20

SAUL

SAUL PARRIED THE JAB, the wooden blades clacking together. The move put Jonathan off balance, and Saul stepped in for the killing strike to the chest. His son was fast, however, and Saul's sword met with air. He pivoted on the ball of his foot and parried Jonathan's next blow. They both parted and stared at each other.

"You are getting faster, son."

Jonathan grinned. "Perhaps you are getting older, father."

The words were said in love, a friendly jest between father and son, yet they struck deep at Saul and stabbed at his already brewing jealousy. *Jealousy toward my own son?*

Jonathan eliminated the chance for any future thoughts with an overhead slice that Saul caught on the edge of his blade. He turned his wrist and sent his son's wooden sword slamming into the ground beside him. Jonathan twisted around Saul's first follow-up and ducked the next as he scooped his sword back up. He barely parried another blow and leaped back.

"Old, you say?" Saul growled the words with more venom

than he anticipated, and he immediately saw the disappointment on Jonathan's face. *Why? Why am I so angry?*

Because they do not respect you. Saul's eyes flashed to the men watching the fight.

Jonathan dove back in, and they came together in a flurry of blows, Saul's rage mounting uncontrollably with each strike. His limbs grew weak, his muscles ached, and his anger boiled hotter. He felt his arm moving slower, each blow coming closer and closer to striking his flesh rather than his sword. *My son is going to beat me.* His eyes drifted again toward the spectators. Abner and Benyamin and several dozen of Gibeah's wealthiest inhabitants all looked on. He could see them whispering to one another. Rimmon stood among them with Doeg not far off. *He is going to embarrass me.*

Saul parried a blow and tried to step out of range, but his son was too fast. The sword came down inside Saul's guard, and he was sure he was going to be struck down. But Jonathan's blow struck wide—unusually wide—and left him open for an easy counter. Saul hesitated, his eyes meeting his son's for the briefest of moments. He saw pity in them and felt that rage rise inside. His sword flashed, much harder than necessary, and Jonathan grunted in stunned pain and fell face first onto the stone courtyard.

Do not pity me. Do not let me win.

His knuckles turned white as he clutched his wooden sword. Saul scowled down at Jonathan as he rolled over and revealed a bloodied nose and bruised eye. He felt the rage roil even harder. *Look what you made me do. Pitying me. I do not need your pity. I need your obedience.*

But as his son looked up at him, that same pitying expression on his now-wounded face, Saul felt such a shame as he had never felt. His scowl softened, only briefly, then applause broke out from amongst the spectators.

"Well done, my king!" Saul turned to find Rimmon

standing close by with the rest of the elders of Gibeah not far behind. He had moved as close to Saul as he could while still remaining in the shade of the olive trees that lined the stone courtyard. "You are truly a master swordsman."

Saul smiled and bowed his head.

"It was a bit rough for a training bout." Rimmon moved to sit on one of the many stone benches that dotted the courtyard, placed in the shade of the trees. "Though I guess a father is always roughest with his son."

Saul glanced at Jonathan and found him now kneeling, the front of his tunic stained with blood as he dabbed at his still bleeding nose. Abner was helping to clean his wound. "Learning to be the future king is a cruel task," he said, joining Rimmon at the bench. Benyamin moved in silence and took up his place behind Saul like a sentinel, Doeg mirroring his movements behind Rimmon.

"It certainly is. And yet, I hear he did well in Maon."

"He did," Saul said. "Nabal sent him back with much praise. And quickly, at that."

"He will make a mighty king when it is his time."

He gritted his teeth at the words. "When it is his time," he repeated, almost to himself. He forced a smile. "For my own sake, I hope that is a long way off."

Rimmon laughed. "Yes," he said. "A long way off. Israel is happy with Yahweh's anointed."

A sudden cheer from outside the courtyard cut off any reply Saul may have had. He and Rimmon stood together. "What do you thin—"

He was interrupted by a cry from beyond his palace walls. "David has returned!"

The words bludgeoned Saul and crushed all vestiges of the little happiness he had. *So, he has lived.*

"It seems your most prominent captain has returned," Rimmon said, his voice mirroring Saul's disappointment. He gestured toward the entrance to the courtyard. "Shall we greet him?"

Saul was barely able to keep his jealousy from his face. *David needs to learn his place.* He looked at the rest of the elders around him, all turning his way and awaiting his answer. "I am afraid I cannot." Saul nodded to Abner. "My commander and I have some reports to review. Movements of the Philistines in the wake of David's recent successes require my attention."

Rimmon only smiled. "I understand." He bowed, and the rest of the elders followed suit. Saul may have had an excuse, but he knew Rimmon could not lose face in front of the others. He *must* go watch as David returned. "We will see you soon, my king."

Another few moments and Saul stood the empty courtyard, save Jonathan, Benyamin, and Abner.

"Are you well?"

It was Abner who spoke. Saul looked at him. Abner was better at hiding it, but he had also begun to pity Saul. *Let them.*

"Well enough." He drew a breath to steady his beating heart. He had hoped to hear news of David's death, not be forced to celebrate his return. "Please bring Michal to my hall," he said. "And have David bring his lyre. Perhaps our mighty warrior should be reminded of how he came to be in my service."

THE MUSIC FILLED the air as David thumbed the strings. Despite Saul's feelings toward the boy—he would always be a boy, despite how he had grown into a warrior—he could not help but be soothed by the music. His jealousy, his envy, his fear, even his desire to see David dead—it all seemed to fade away as he sat and listened to David.

What is this? Why does this comfort me so?

David wore an alabaster white tunic that fell to his knees. His rough hair and beard were trimmed and oiled, and he had cleaned the filth of battle from his hands. Indeed, from where Saul sat, the boy looked the perfect picture of a musician. If one had only just met him, he would not have thought him a warrior at all. He began to sing, slowly and softly at first, and it only reinforced this image. As the song went on, his voice grew louder, filling the hall.

Let the godly sing for joy to the Lord; it is fitting for the pure to praise him. Praise the Lord with melodies on the lyre; make music for him on the ten-stringed harp. Sing a new song of praise to him; play skillfully on the harp, and sing with joy. For the word of the Lord holds true, and we can trust everything he does. He loves whatever is just and good; the unfailing love of the Lord fills the earth.

DAVID PLUCKED the strings without words for another long while. The sound echoed through the hall, and Saul found his eyes locked onto him. All the hate and anger within him—most of which was directed at David himself—was gone, replaced instead with both a peace and a longing he did not understand.

For the word of the Lord holds true, and we can trust everything he does...

Saul sat upright and shook his head clear. Samuel had been the word of the Lord, and he had made some unpleasant promises. *For the word of the Lord holds true...*

Let us hope not.

He cleared his throat once David finished and began to applaud. The others in the hall joined in, near a hundred of the town's elders tucked in between the acacia pillars. Their applause grew louder, faces beaming with pride at Israel's favorite warrior and musician. Michal stood beside him, her eyes locked on David with barely concealed infatuation. Both Benyamin and Jonathan had an admiration on their faces that Saul had never seen directed at him. Even Abner seemed pleased, and Saul had never counted him as a man who appreciated music. He felt more than a tinge of jealousy at their admiration.

I sat in utter fascination while he played. Why wouldn't they?

"Very well done, David," Saul said, his voice carrying over the applause and silencing the hall. He tried to conceal his mounting frustration, his renewing hate. He was shocked at how quickly he had gone from peace and comfort to envy and anger. It almost seemed he preferred the latter. "And it seems your coming bride enjoyed it most of all." He gestured to a now-blushing Michal and noticed with smug satisfaction that David's face had reddened, as well.

"I am happy she is pleased," David said as he set aside his lyre. He tried to meet Michal's eyes and failed. "She is more beautiful than a man like me deserves."

"Yes, she is," Saul said, drawing fake laughter from among the gathered crowd. "But it is her heart's desire."

David seemed to pause, unable to find words. Then he smiled, and it seemed as forced as Saul's own smile felt. "She will be taken care of, my king."

21

DAVID

"You fought Goliath."

David frowned as he looked at the fuzzy reflection of himself in the polished-bronze mirror. "I know, Abishai."

"You led fifty men against two hundred Philistines."

"I know, Abishai."

"You have seen more battle in five years than most men see in their lives."

"Do you have a point?"

He felt his friend's hand on his shoulder. "I have never seen you more nervous."

I am not nervous, David thought. *I am heartbroken, about to wed a woman I do not love.*

He buried the thought and turned to Abishai, who had cleaned up better than David had ever seen him. His long, unkempt hair was braided and combed and oiled. He wore a soft gray tunic of the highest quality. He even smelled of frank-incense. David nearly smiled. He had never seen his friend so dressed.

"Is it because she is so beautiful?" Abishai asked with a sly grin.

It is because she is not Abigail. And yet David knew he would have to eventually get her from his mind.

"Perhaps," he lied.

Abishai let out a long and dramatic yawn. "Three men come upon a river in the forest."

David did not immediately respond. He stepped away from the mirror and walked out onto his balcony. Dozens of his most loyal men stood in ranks below—men he had trained with, had battled with. They were to be his wedding procession as he retrieved his bride.

"And what did they do at this river?" David finally asked.

"Well, the river was wide and raging. They could not cross."

"Why did they need to cross?"

"It does not matter *why*." Abishai stepped outside and leaned against the railing. He followed David's gaze to the people below. "It's a joke, David."

He grinned, thankful for his carefree friend. "Ahhhh. I thought I knew these men."

Abishai rolled his eyes. He turned and leaned his back against the railing. "The first man prays to Yahweh: 'Please make me strong enough to cross this river.' Yahweh answers, and the man swims across before sundown."

"A generous gift."

"Indeed. The seconds asks, 'Yahweh, please make me strong and give me the tools to cross this river.' Yahweh again answers, and the man builds a boat and crosses before midday."

"A wiser prayer."

"We must always pray to Yahweh with wisdom. And so, the final man prays, 'Yahweh, please give me the strength, the tools, and the *wisdom* to cross.' Yahweh turns this man into a woman. She walks a few hundred cubits down the river and crosses at the bridge."

Despite his mood, David couldn't help but smile. "So, a woman is wiser than a man?"

Abishai patted him on the shoulder. "It is good for you to learn this before you are wed." He walked back inside. "Now, let us go and get your bride."

The walk through the streets of Gibeah was the most trying walk David had ever experienced. Abishai stood at his side, his cousin and confidant and closest friend. Nearby was Ira, insisting on his presence despite David's many arguments. And behind him, trailing in practiced unison, were his men. Their armor gleamed; their swords and speartips shone in the sunlight. They presented themselves as if for a king, and yet David felt nothing but shame.

These men, these warriors, had risked their lives to bring David to this moment. Some had fought and bled to pay Saul's bride price. Yet David did not want the bride. These men had bled for nothing. The woman he wanted—the woman he loved if he dared think the word—was instead given to a fool only to spite David.

He tried to put aside his shame as the men and women of Gibeah began to fall in beside him. They cheered and sang and danced, and soon there was a great crowd following David to Saul's palace. And now, standing up beside his shame rather than putting it aside, David felt a fraud. Men and women he did not know—indeed, that he likely never would—had dropped what they were doing to follow him, to show their support for his marriage. They wished nothing more than to share in his happiness. Yet it was not real happiness, but merely walls of counterfeit happiness he had built to hold together his broken heart.

I am a mess, he thought.

You are looking for purpose in the wrong place.

David nearly stumbled at the voice. He hadn't heard it in

some time and had certainly not expected it now, as he was about to wed.

Where do I look?

Yet the voice was silent. Yahweh, it seemed, expected David to know the answer.

And I should. Shouldn't I?

He dwelled on the words of Yahweh as he finished his walk, only putting them aside when he came into sight of the gate to Saul's courtyard. He had a bride to take, whether he wanted her or not, and it was time. All he could do now was try. Perhaps a happy marriage was indeed in his future. Who knew the plans of Yahweh?

Certainly not me.

He stopped when he reached the gate, his men falling into such a perfect formation behind him that he would have been proud under any other circumstances. Abishai patted him on the back, a broad smile on his face, and then he stood at the head of the men.

David took a deep breath, trying and failing to steady his beating heart, and then walked through the gate and into the courtyard. Saul himself stood on the palace steps, Michal at his side and Benyamin at their backs. Twin lines of fully armored troops stretched out from the steps, forming a small path between them that would lead David directly to his bride. One of the lines was headed by Jonathan and the other by Malki-Shua.

Michal beamed. She was indeed beautiful, and David felt for the first time that he could make this work. He tried his best to mimic the smile, though he was sure that he looked to be grimacing. Eventually, given time and care, the smile could be real.

"My king!"

The shout came from outside the courtyard, an urgency in it that made even David stop. All eyes turned toward the gate as a man—dressed in the armor of Israel—stumbled into the courtyard.

"My king," the man shouted, tripping over himself as he rushed toward Saul.

Saul pounded down his palace steps. "Have you lost your mind?!"

David moved aside as Saul rushed by him, Benyamin following quickly behind.

"This is a wedding!"

The man swayed as if drunk, and David looked at him—truly looked—for the first time. The man's tunic was bloody, his helmet cracked and ruined. Saul stopped short as he noticed the same thing. For a long moment, no one moved.

"Philistines," the man said, his voice strained. "At Beersheba..." He swayed once more, tried to steady himself with his spear, then collapsed in the middle of the courtyard.

22

SAUL

Saul was again in his council chambers. Abner was present, as well as Jonathan, Benyamin, and Malki-Shua. Saul had personally requested Rimmon to join him, as well as Doeg. Baanah and Recab were still in the south, fighting the Amalekites. And sitting still and observant directly across from Saul, was David. He shared the confidence of Doeg, though David's irked Saul in a way he could not define.

"He is stable," Jonathan said, interrupting Saul's thoughts. "And speaking."

"And?"

"He is confident in his numbers: at least one hundred chariots and near six thousand Philistines are on their way to Beersheba."

Abner leaned forward. "That cannot be right," he persisted. "They have always had chariots, but over a hundred? How can that be?"

"I cannot say if he is right, only that he believes he is."

Saul scoffed. "There are few facts that can fight belief."

"Does it matter," Malki-Shua said. "Can we not match that number?"

"We can match the foot soldiers, given time," Abner said. "But we have precious few chariots."

Now Malki-Shua scoffed, a near-perfect imitation of Saul. "I do not understand. I have faced chariots before, and I did not quiver in fear."

Abner pinched the bridge of his nose. "You have faced maybe ten chariots. One hundred will tear through our ranks. They are easily worth fifty soldiers each."

"But we must fight," Malki-Shua persisted.

"He is right," Rimmon said. "We cannot delay in our response. We must strike quickly if we are to save our people."

"But that is the problem," Jonathan said. He gestured to the map before them. "The majority of our captains are spread out, and with them our warriors and chariots, few as they are." He waved his hand at the western border. "We have men in Shechem, En-dor, and Kadesh. They are in constant skirmishes with the Philistine armies there." He pointed to the east. "En-Gedi is garrisoned against the Moabites." He sat back and waved a hand at the southern border. "And we still have Rimmon's sons facing the Amalekites to the south."

His son's mention of the Amalekites made Saul squirm. "There is a lot of talk of what we cannot do," he said. "What *can* we do? What do we have?"

"I have over a thousand men under my command," Malki-Shua said. "Israel's strongest and bravest. We can march the day after tomorrow."

"I can match that number," Jonathan said. "Though I also need a day to gather them."

Saul turned to Doeg and Rimmon. "And you, Doeg of Edom? You are here by personal request. I assume it is because you are useful."

Doeg shrugged. "I command a small force of one hundred men. Not as sizeable as the king's sons, but they are well trained and loyal to me. And we could march today. Within the hour, if needed."

"We will soon see how well trained they are." Saul finally turned to David. "And you?"

David was silent for a moment, his ears perked as if he heard a noise no one else did. "There are near three hundred still under my command," he said. "We can also leave within the hour. All are in Gibeah."

Abner turned to him. "That makes near three thousand. If we add in our standing army of three thousand here in Gibeah—"

"I will not leave Gibeah undefended," Saul said. His tone left no room for discussion. "One thousand of the army must stay behind."

Abner frowned yet said nothing. "Then that puts our total force at near five thousand within a day." He sighed. "If we send runners tonight and scour the nearby villages, we can more than double that, likely bring our forces above ten thousand men within another day. But we do not have that much time. If we delay, the Philistines will reach Beersheba ahead of us." He pointed to the map. "Beersheba is on a hill. Strong, defensible walls surround it. But it has little army to speak of. If we do not march *today*—indeed, right this moment—then we will lose it. And when we *do* arrive, we will be the ones fighting against those walls."

"Send me," David said. All eyes turned to him. Saul felt his hands form involuntary fists at the sound of his voice. "Send me and my men."

"I thought you had fewer than three hundred."

"I do. But we can leave immediately."

Rimmon made a noise somewhere between a scoff and a laugh. "Three hundred? David...I understand you to be a great warrior. But taking your small band of three hundred against six thousand? And over a hundred chariots?" He scoffed in full this time. "Not even you are so blessed."

But David did not give in. He leaned over the map, an intense look in his eyes that caused even Saul to listen. "I would not engage them, not directly." He looked at Abner. "But the biggest threat is the chariots, correct?"

Abner nodded. "Yes…"

"What if I could at least take those out? Perhaps even delay them enough for the city to still be defendable once the army is assembled?"

Rimmon snorted a laugh. "Forgive me," he said, covering his mouth with a hand. "I mean no disrespect, but no amount of tactics and subterfuge will help so few men even delay six thousand. They will simply ignore you."

"I can be insistent."

"I see that. But what you are saying is suicide."

Not a bad thing, Saul thought, his mind already at work on a plan.

David eyed Rimmon, and for the first time, Saul saw genuine anger behind his always perfect demeanor. "We go to battle with the Living God of Israel. If it is my time to die, then I will gladly give my life for him."

Abner frowned. "We all hope that is not the case, David. Israel will sorely miss you."

Perhaps too much. Saul eyed his sons, his plan beginning to come together. He turned to David. "It is not an unsound plan," he said abruptly. "David can be as a dog to the Philistines while my sons assemble their men. At the very least, he can delay their assault on Beersheba long enough to assemble the army. In two days, we can march at the head of ten thousand and crush them, chariots or no."

"My king," Doeg said. "What would you have me do?"

Saul looked at Rimmon first and then to Doeg. "What would you do?"

"I would join in the fighting, now if I could. Let me join with David's men, supplement his forces."

David looked immediately put off by the suggestion. "I would prefer my men remain as they are," he said. "We have fought together long and—"

"Doeg will travel with you," Saul said, the kernel of the plan in his mind finalizing. "There is much at stake, and I will not deny help. You have your duties," he said, his eyes on David. "See to them. You are dismissed, David. I would have a moment with the rest of you."

David rose, gave a curt nod, and then was gone.

Saul looked at those around him. He was about to give them an order he was unsure they would all follow. His eyes fell on Abner, his most trusted companion. Whether he agreed with the command or not, he would not deny him. Rimmon was of no concern. He has already shown that his loyalty was to Saul. The Edomite, as well. If he had been willing to slay Abigail simply to upset David, Saul's next words would mean nothing to him. Benyamin stood behind him, silent as a statue. He would disagree, but he would do nothing about it. Yet there were his sons. Malki-Shua would be easy to sway, but Jonathan and David were as brothers. He would likely not agree so quickly. They were all staring at Saul, waiting for his words. *I guess we will see.*

"The son of Jesse must not return from Beersheba."

Their reactions were much as he had suspected, a mixture of real and feigned surprise.

"What...what do you mean?" Jonathan said. "Not return?"

Saul eyed his son. "David is a great risk to our kingdom. He has just wed into my family." *At my request.* "He has become great friends with you, Jonathan, with the obvious goal of usurping your future throne. He has gained the favor of the people. He's amassed a small army of followers. He cannot be allowed to return from Beersheba. This is our only chance to be rid of this…this jackal."

Jonathan opened his mouth to speak, but Rimmon was quick to interrupt.

"A prudent decision, wise king," he said. "You have my assurance"—he gave a slight nod toward Doeg—"that it will be carried out."

There was a long silence in the room.

"It is not an unwise move," Malki-Shua said, though the words seemed forced. All eyes turned to him. "David is a born leader, a man with a great reputation. But he is also ambitious. When offered Michal's hand, he fought two hundred Philistines with only fifty men. A bold move, yes, but brash and foolish. A grab for the throne does not seem far off."

Saul nearly smiled. He had expected to have to convince Malki-Shua and Jonathan both, rather than have Malki-Shua convince Jonathan for him.

"Wise words, son." He turned to Abner. "What say you?"

The stoic commander said nothing at first. He made a show of thinking and then rested his elbows on the table. "David leads men like no other. I cannot say whether he will leverage that for a grasp at the throne, but I *can* say that if he did, he would likely succeed."

"I believe that settles it," Saul said. "The son of Jesse will not—"

"No."

Saul looked at Jonathan. "What?"

"You cannot do this." He stood. "He has not wronged you, and what he *has* done has benefited you greatly. We have all seen him in battle, how he takes his life in his hands every time he fights. He fights for Yahweh, and Yahweh fights with him. He has done no wrong. Let the king do no wrong by killing an innocent man."

"It is not a matter of what he *has* done, Jonathan, but what he has yet to do."

"And we do not know what he is yet to do. How can we murder him for it?"

Saul's jaw clenched in anger. "I am protecting the throne, *your* throne."

"Does Yahweh not choose the king of Israel? Does Yahweh not raise us high and bring us low? If David is to be the next anointed one of Israel, who are we to stop it?"

Saul stood with such a jerk that his seat clattered to the floor behind him. "You forget yourself!"

Jonathan was not deterred. "I forget nothing, father. Rather, I remember why we are here. Why *you* are here. It is the hand of Yahweh that placed you on your throne." He stepped around the table and fell to a knee before Saul. "And I pray that you do not forget that hand."

He looked down at his son as he bowed low. Anger boiled inside him; his hand almost drifted to his sword. Jonathan was the only problem, the only one unwilling. A quick thrust would end it, would silence this rebellious child. For a moment that perhaps lasted too long, he debated. Thoughts swirled in his head. The image of his son bleeding on the floor came unbidden to his eyes, though he did not immediately push it aside.

What am I doing?

The now-familiar red haze faded, and he looked at his kneeling son. He could not kill him, even if it led to David's death. But now he could not follow through with his order, either. He could not command David's murder when his son would speak so eloquently against it. Even a hint of disagreement could lead to rebellion. David, it seemed, would live.

For today, perhaps.

"Stand, Jonathan." His son stood, and they eyed one

another. The room was silent as Sheol for the length of several heartbeats. "You speak wisely," he finally said, the words tasting like vomit in his mouth. "As surely as Yahweh lives, David will not be put to death."

Yet.

23

DAVID

DAVID PRESSED the heavy oak doors open and stepped into Saul's empty hall. Pale moonlight—*was it already night*—streamed in through the high, square windows and lit a dozen tables, all set for what was supposed to have been a glorious feast. He had no idea where Michal was, did not really care. For the first time, David was thankful for the Philistines' interruption, though if he was honest with himself, he did not feel prepared to fight such numbers.

Yet Yahweh did not stutter.

Indeed, David did not think he had ever heard Yahweh more clearly. *Go to them*, he had said. *You will strike them with a mighty blow. Beersheba will not fall.*

How he would strike one hundred chariots and six thousand men with such a blow was still beyond him.

Abishai was sitting alone at the bottom of the palace steps twirling his knife on his fingertip. He sheathed the blade and stood as soon as he heard the doors open.

"Where are the men?" David asked, not slowing as he leaped down the steps.

Abishai fell into step beside him. "At the arena, awaiting

word. What happened?"

"The Philistines are moving on Beersheba. They will be there in a day."

"How many men?"

"Six thousand. And a hundred or more chariots."

Abishai did not falter for a moment. "What do you need me to do?"

David felt a swell of pride in his friend. Many would balk at those numbers. Indeed the king seemed to have.

"I need you to gather the rest of the men. We leave within the hour."

They parted for a moment as they rushed around a man pulling a cart. "That is fewer than three hundred men."

"Then we fight with fewer than three hundred men."

They had reached David's home, but Abishai grabbed him by the arm and stopped him from entering the courtyard. "Against six thousand soldiers? And over a hundred chariots?"

"We have no choice."

"We can assemble the army."

"Saul is already doing that. He will depart in two days, perhaps sooner, with the full force of the Israelite army."

Abishai looked confused. "Then...then why are we leaving now?"

"If we do not at least slow the Philistines, then they will take the city, and we will be fighting them with walls between us."

"But...but attacking that many...and so many chariots. David, it is suicide."

"I do not choose the battles. I fight them."

"Who chooses them?"

He tensed. Abishai, of all people, knew the answer to that question. "Are you going to gather the men, or do I need to?"

Abishai frowned, his mind clearly searching for a reply. Then he smirked. "You know what I will say. But one day, you will have to tell me what the voice in your head is saying. Perhaps let me talk back to it."

"One day." He offered his hand, and Abishai took it. "Thank you, friend." Then David stepped into his courtyard, prepared to ask his men to risk their lives yet again.

THE CITY WAS FULLY asleep by the time David's men had assembled under the city gate. Lights had guttered out, the markets had long since closed, even the revelers from the wedding had made it back to their own homes or, in some cases, the inns they had stayed at. The only light in the city was from the dim glow coming from a dozen torches scattered among his men.

Despite the confidence with which he had spoken to Abishai, David's mind was full of doubt. Less than three hundred men were standing ready before him. Yet they were all looking to him as he stood beneath the high gates of Gibeah.

What do I do, Yahweh? Give me some guidance; show me this mighty blow I am to strike. I want to walk in your steps, but I do not see them.

He received only silence as he looked again at his men, at their steely gaze and intense focus. Surely these were the best soldiers in all Israel.

Now I only wait for Doeg and his brood of warriors.

He did not like the Edomite, yet he could not decide exactly why. Perhaps it was because he reminded David of Eliab. Perhaps it was because he'd bested David in combat, even if with practice swords.

But I think it is something deeper than that.

"That was an interesting wedding. I am glad for the invitation."

David turned and saw Ahimelech walking through the

gate. "It could have been worse," he replied as his old friend stopped beside him.

The priest laughed. "I do not see how. There are not a great many things worse than marching to war on your wedding night."

Ahimelech's unexpected appearance gave him a sudden need to share his doubt. He turned to the old priest, this man he had confided in time and time again.

"What am I going to do? How can I face such numbers?"

"I do not know the numbers you go to face, yet it does not matter. Remember Gideon."

"I doubt the Philistines will fall for the same trick twice."

"If you believe the story was about Gideon's trick, then you miss the point of the story."

David frowned. "That Yahweh was with him?"

"As he is with you."

And yet, for the first time in his adult life, David felt a sliver of doubt at that.

"You are torn," the priest said. "You have doubts."

The old priest was the most perceptive person he had ever met. "Perhaps."

"You do not trust in your role? In Yahweh's?"

He sighed and turned to look Ahimelech in the eye, aware that every one of the three hundred men were watching them speak. "I love Yahweh," he said, his voice near a whisper. "You know this. I would go to battle a thousand times with him at my back."

"Then why do you doubt?"

"I…" he trailed off, the image of Abigail with Nabal coming unbidden to his mind. *If I am doing Yahweh's will, why did he take her from me? Why punish both of us?*

"I don't know," he lied.

Ahimelech frowned. "You are a terrible liar."

"Is that such a bad thing?"

"I suppose not." He took the briefest pause. "Did you know that after Gideon's success he strayed far from Yahweh?"

He had not expected a lesson tonight, but he supposed he needed one. "I did not."

"After his victory, he took some of the spoils of his battle—the gold and fine linens from the Midianite kings—and made an ephod from it. He put it in Ophrah, his hometown, and worshipped this instead of Yahweh."

David frowned. "I had not heard that. Why do we speak of him as such a great man? A great judge?"

"Many of the judges had great flaws," he said. "Samson had his lust for women; Gideon's own son had a murderous lust for power. Gideon put his riches, his rewards for doing Yahweh's work, above Yahweh himself. He idolized them, eventually turning them into an object of worship."

"You fear I may do this?"

The old priest laughed again. He was in good spirits this night, it would seem. "I fear we all may. There is something in all our lives that threatens to take Yahweh's place. It is what holds us back, what makes us question Yahweh's commands. And it is best set aside."

Is Abigail mine?

He looked back toward Ahimelech. "You are full of advice, old friend."

"I do what I can," he replied with a smirk.

"Do you happen to know how I can stop one hundred chariots?"

He thought for a moment. "I'm sure you'll dig something up."

David had a reply on his tongue that was cut short as Doeg rounded the corner of the gate. He walked by the two of them, almost not even looking their way, as he guided a small group of a hundred or so men out into the field beside David's own. David watched as they strolled, all following their leader's casual gait. There was no uniformity, none of the discipline that marked David's own men.

"I'm afraid it is going to be a long night."

DAVID PATTED the earth with his shovel and brushed the sweat from his brow. The sun had risen to a few finger widths above the horizon and was throwing long, stretching shadows out over the field. He hadn't realized he could get so sore from something that was not battle, but the hard march through the night and the work they'd just put in had proved him wrong.

"Ever feel like you're digging your own grave," Ira asked.

David chuckled. "Often."

"This is never going to work," Abishai said.

David turned and looked out at the field. He could barely tell that they had been out there, and then only because he knew where to look. The four hundred of them had made a significant mess during the night and had subsequently spent the early morning hours cleaning it up. "That's what you said about my torches too."

"I did."

"Well, that worked."

He shrugged. "I guess." Ira snorted a laugh. Abishai looked at the young scout. "Want me to put you back where I found you?" Abishai asked.

"It's a little late for that," David said.

The three stood in silence for a long while, feeling the warmth of the morning sun spread along their backs as they kept their eyes on the west. Beersheba stood less than a league to the north, built atop a rising hillock, its high walls offering comfort and shelter. Shelter he knew they could not take, not if they wanted to defeat the chariots.

David looked at Ira. "The men are hidden?"

"Over the hill behind us."

"And our tracks?"

"Gone."

"That is good."

He heard footsteps, and Doeg was soon standing among them. He looked a formidable warrior. His men seemed to respond to him with respect earned only through years of battle, even if they lacked any form of discipline. David saw a bit of himself in the man. Only a bit, of course, because everything else about the Edomite reeked of violence and hatred.

"Are you sure of this plan?" Doeg asked.

Abishai laughed. "It's not going to work," he repeated.

David ignored his friend. "It will work," he said to the Edomite. "Have faith."

"I am in short supply of your faith."

"I have noticed."

"Is that a problem?"

"I do not trust a man who has no God."

"I serve your king. Is he not your god's anointed one?"

"Serving a man and serving Yahweh are different."

"Yet, I am here by your side nonetheless."

"That was not my decision."

Doeg laughed. "You do not like me, do you?"

"I do not know you. And I prefer to fight with men I trust."

"You will know me eventually, son of Jesse."

"And the trust?"

There was a long, uncomfortable silence until Doeg simply shrugged. "Who can say?" Then he was walking back up the hill toward his men on the other side.

"*I* do not like him," Ira put in.

There came a low rumble in the distance. A silence fell over them as they stared expectantly at the horizon. The ground began to tremble, softly at first, then picking up until pebbles and small rocks started shifting on the dirt. Then the

Philistine army streamed into view. They appeared as silhouettes along the western horizon, ghosts rising up from Sheol and marching toward them. After a long while, he could make out their weapons, the glint of spears and shields and helmets. He could hear the rattling of armor and the crunching of boots on the hard ground. They seemed to never end, filling the landscape in either direction, row upon row of armed and armored Philistine soldiers.

But his eyes were not drawn to the soldiers, not to their weapons or armor. Instead, his eyes fell on the line of chariots riding at their head.

Ira sucked in a breath through his teeth. "That is a lot of chariots…"

"I told you this isn't going to work," Abishai said.

David drew a breath and handed Ira his shovel. "See to the men. Have them assemble and be sure the Philistines see us when the time comes."

Ira turned and ran up the hill, disappearing over its top. David began to walk toward the Philistines, choosing his footfalls very carefully as he made his way across the field. Abishai fell into step behind him. Two of the Philistine chariots peeled off from the main body and rode confidently toward them. David's eyes were on the field, watching as the chariots approached. The chariots stopped fifty cubits from them, and David breathed a sigh of relief.

Time to pick a fight.

"Welcome to Beersheba," he shouted. "Have you come to take in the sights? Perhaps see the well of the oath dug by my ancestors?"

One of the men stepped down from his chariot, handing his helmet to the man who held the reins. "We have certainly come to take *something*, son of Jesse," the man shouted back. "But I was hoping for the entire city, well and all."

They recognize me everywhere.

"Then you are going to be sadly disappointed."

"Are you not going to quote your Moses to me? Offer me a place among you?"

"Your kind has long turned a deaf ear to my offers of peace, and I have ceased giving them." He turned and looked behind him just in time to see his small band—along with Doeg's—creep up over the hill. "So, I brought some friends."

The Philistine commander looked on without expression. Once David's soldiers had filed into place, he gave a small smile. "Do you think me a fool?"

"I do," David said. "But why do you ask?"

"I have heard about you, giant slayer. Your love for traps. Your love for ambushes and subterfuge. I suppose you need it, with such a pitiful king and such pitiful men."

He made a show of looking back at his men. "My men are not pitiful," he said, choosing not to defend his king.

"Everyone knows of your tricks. They are not new. You want me to look at your men, perched atop a hill, and assume you have thousands more on the other side."

David shrugged. "I care not what you think. Only that you turn around and leave."

He stepped forward, a smile growing. "But I am no fool. My scouts watched your men approach. They watched you arrive last night." He opened his arms wide. "This is *all* you have. This is *all* your men."

How long did his scouts watch us?

"It is Yahweh who owns the battle, Philistine. Numbers do not matter."

"I was told you were clever. Is this the best you have? Hiding on a hill and hoping I cower? Have you run out of tricks to try? No night assaults as we siege your walls? No torches hidden among pots?"

"I only use tricks when I feel a need."

The man frowned. "I was also told you were overly confident, giant slayer, but I did not think you were insane."

"Perhaps I am confident because I always win, Philistine."

"We will see about that."

David lowered his voice. "Abishai."

His friend stepped forward suddenly and hurled his spear. The commander ducked on reflex, but the weapon soared by him and caught his driver in the chest, sending him flipping over the railing. The commander turned and sped back to his chariot, seizing the reins and driving it back to his army, his helmet clattering out of the back of the chariot.

"Do you think that will work?"

David shrugged. "I hope so. The Philistines are not known for their restraint."

"What if their scouts stayed after we made camp? What if they saw us through the night?"

David had opened his mouth to speak when a horn rang out from the Philistine army. The line of chariots rumbled across the field toward them in a cloud of dust.

"I guess that answers that question," Abishai said.

Together, the two sprinted back across the field, again carefully choosing their footfalls. Ira was waiting for them at the top of the hill. "I see they took the bait," he said.

"Their commander seems to have an anger problem," Abishai said.

David watched the chariots speed across the field, nearing the place where the dead driver still lay with Abishai's spear in his chest. The line began to stagger, breaking into a giant wedge shape. The dead man's body bounced as the lead chariot tore over it. They were coming closer now, close enough for David to almost see the drivers' faces and the foam in the horses' nostrils. The ground shook beneath his sandals from the thunder of the hoofs pounding on the hard desert ground. The dust from their charge nearly blotted out the army behind them.

Suddenly the lead chariot's horse disappeared in a cloud of dust and dirt. The chariot flipped end over end and landed with a horrendous cracking as if a mighty oak had splintered in two. Vicious screams came from both horse and man as the wreckage tumbled another dozen paces before skidding to a ruined halt.

As if the first chariot unleashed the floodgates of disaster, the entire line fell to similar fates as they crashed through the holes David and his men had dug and concealed the night before. The morning air was filled with cries of pain and snapping of timber and roars of crashing chariots.

"By Yahweh, that is terrible."

Abishai's words summed up David's own feelings. He could only nod his agreement. The cloud of dust rolled over the chariots, and soon David saw nothing, only listened as man and animal cried out in pain. Then seven chariots emerged from the dust and continued their mad charge up the hill, no doubt filled with rage as their fellow soldiers died around them.

David drew his sword and held it aloft. "Now!"

His three hundred Israelites hurled three hundred spears. They landed almost in unison, a concussive thud of wood and bronze and iron. Fewer than a tenth met their mark, but that was all that was needed. Rider and horse alike were struck, some pinned in place and others sent careening off into the dirt. All that was left of the vicious charge was the sounds of wailing and whimpering and the dust falling to the ground.

"Huh," Abishai said. "It worked."

There was a roar from across the field, and the ground beneath them shook as six thousand Philistines began their charge.

"Time to go?"

David nodded. "Absolutely."

Ira blew a horn, and three hundred Israelites ran in the opposite direction.

24

SAUL

THE MEN WERE ARRIVING in the hundreds now, entire towns emptying themselves of their fighting men with a tenacity that shocked even Saul. In the past, it had seemed close to torture to get these men of Israel to come to battle. Now they flooded in as if Saul was offering them gold and not blood.

It was Jonathan's fault that they were coming so quickly. He had led the charge, traveling firsthand into the settlements within a half day's ride with word that the army needed assembling. He also told the tale of David's heroism in riding ahead, risking his own life to slow the flood of the Philistine army.

They rush to David's aid but must be dragged to mine.

The entire spectacle made Saul cringe. He had agreed to send David ahead with the hopes the Philistines would handle his problem for him. And with Jonathan's rousing speech at the council, he could no longer count on his own men to take care of David, unless Doeg took matters into his own hands. All his hopes rested with the Philistines, as odd as that seemed.

And now he stood atop his high wall at the city's edge and watched as thousands of Israelites were organizing in the fields beyond. He'd raised his army as high as twenty thousand soldiers in the past, yet that had taken months of planning. While he was still nowhere near that number, the mass of soldiers he saw before him seemed impossible in a day. He watched as Abner turned away from the army and began to walk his way.

Saul absently twirled his spear as he waited for his commander to bring news of their total number. The spear never left his side now; from his throne to his dining table, he carried it. His feelings of insecurity had only grown since the counsel. He had risked much revealing his plan to his sons, and now he felt their eyes on him always. *They think me a would-be murderer, despite the fact I am protecting my throne.* Their *throne, in time.* But Jonathan could not see that. He was too full of bluster and zeal for Yahweh, and it was beginning to sicken Saul.

Abner stepped up and knelt before him. Saul still appreciated the respect he received from Abner, even if he no longer felt he deserved it.

"Rise, friend."

"We are nearing eleven thousand strong, my king. It may be time to prepare the march."

Eleven thousand? In a day…

David had left the night before last. Such a small band had likely reached Beersheba before sunrise. That meant David had been alone for less than a full day. *Not nearly long enough.*

"Perhaps we should make preparations to leave in the morning," Saul said. "With a good night's rest behind us, we will make better time."

Abner opened his mouth and then paused, clearly choosing his words carefully. "My king. It will be over two full days if we wait any longer, and it will take us that long just to reach Beersheba. I know what you wish to happen, my king, but…but we risk much in waiting."

"My son is not here, Abner. You do not need to speak in riddles."

He sighed. "Very well. David is resourceful. If you are hoping for the Philistines to kill him, then they will need more than a few days."

Saul almost smiled. "Are you suggesting we wait longer for our army?"

"No, my king. Only that we perhaps find another mission for David to fail at. One that does not endanger our own people."

"But he does not fail, Abner. This is what Jonathan does not see. David gets what he wants. He always has. And he wants my throne."

"I understand, my king. I share your mistrust. It's just…I do not wish for it to be so apparent."

Saul's grip tightened on his spear, and he felt a nagging urge to stick it inside Abner. "My wants and desires should not need to be hidden. *I* am the king. *I* am Yahweh's anointed. What *I* command should be obeyed, not questioned. Especially by my own blood!"

"I do not disagree, my king."

"Then, the army waits. We leave in the morning."

25

DAVID

THE CAMP, if it could be called that, was spread throughout the ravine in clusters, sleeping blankets bunched together around low fires that were nothing more than embers. David hadn't allowed any real fires for fear of being spotted. The men spoke in hushed, anxious voices as they ate and sharpened blades and counted arrows. Sunlight leaked in through the canopy of leaves in thin, ghostly beams of light that flickered in the floating dust.

"We cannot hide forever."

Doeg talking. His voice had come to grate at David with every word.

"We are not hiding," Eleazar said.

"They why do we sit in this crack in the earth? Why are there no fires?"

The ravine, with its thick canopy of trees and high, sheer walls, did indeed provide the perfect hiding place. Yet, so did much of the forest. The Philistines were six thousand strong. David doubted that they would venture into the woods in search of them, especially after the trap he'd set days before. And marching six thousand into the ravine would make their numbers near meaningless. They would barely be able to stand a dozen men across.

"Out of an abundance of caution," Eleazar answered. "The Philistines would be foolish to look for us."

Doeg grunted. "So, we look for them!"

David was looking down at the map laid out over the stump of a tree between them, barely giving any heed to Eleazar and Doeg's argument. With Abishai leading the scouts, Eleazar had been acting as his second-in-command for the last two days. And he and Doeg had not exactly gotten along. David renewed his focus on the map. Beersheba sat in its center, green swaths marking the surrounding farmland, a small rock on their current location.

"Are you suggesting we march at an army of six thousand with four hundred men?" Eleazar asked.

"If the choice is to face them like men or be found hiding like sheep, I choose the first."

"Dead is dead, whether you're a man or sheep."

David almost smiled at that as he finally spoke. "Without their chariots, they will likely proceed with more caution." He felt both Eleazar and Doeg look at him, his own eyes still on the map. He was speaking more to silence them than to say anything worthwhile. "And they have made no attempt to take Beersheba," he added. He was trying to work out his next move, but he was having trouble seeing it. He sighed and studied the map as if he could see the answer in its folds. "I wish Abishai would return…"

"We cannot sit and wait for your scouts," Doeg said. "We must make a decision!"

Eleazar scoffed. "An uninformed decision is a foolish one."

"The Philistines *must* know that the king is coming with an army," David said, more to himself than either of them. His eyes drifted again to the green that marked the farmland.

"Then we fight," Doeg said, slamming his fist on the stump

and shifting the map. David's face twitched with annoyance. "If the Philistines remain, then we can be sure they intend to meet Saul in open battle."

"By fight, you mean when Saul arrives," Eleazar said.

"I mean now!"

"If they stay," David said, "it does not mean they intend to meet Saul in battle."

"What else could it mean?"

He shifted his map back to where it was before Doeg punched it. "Look at all this farmland. Any farmer who values his life is gone or inside the city walls. Any that stayed are no match for six Philistines, let alone six thousand. Livestock and grain and goods just sitting, ready for the taking." He punched the green with a finger to emphasize his point. "That is where they will go. To pillage."

"And what can we do about it?" Eleazar asked.

Doeg almost smiled. "We fight?"

David wanted to tell him no just to tell him no but knew he was right. "We cannot sit in hiding while they pillage our land."

Eleazar frowned and looked at Doeg. "You will get your chance to show us you are a man."

"But we cannot fight them directly," David quickly added. "Eleazar is right; we cannot march against six thousand with a few hundred."

"So, what do you suggest?"

He studied the map, hoping something would become clear to him. "We need Abishai. We need to know where they are."

Doeg scoffed. "Your scout is dead, David."

His fist was moving before he could stop it, and Doeg was on his back. A dozen of Doeg's men standing nearby had swords drawn before he had even hit the ground. Eleazar stepped forward, sword in hand, and put himself between them and David.

Doeg just looked back up at him with a smile, a thin line of blood running from his nose. "He will not be the last of your men to die, son of Jesse." He stood and wiped the blood away, his eyes going to Eleazar and his own men. "Your man would stand between you and twelve swords?"

"Because he knows I would do the same."

The Edomite nodded to his men, and they sheathed their weapons. "My men are loyal, but I doubt many would take a blade for me. It is no wonder Saul wants you dead."

Before he had time to register Doeg's final words, time to consider what he had just heard, shouts came from the edges of the camp. They turned in unison to find Abishai stumbling through the ravine toward them, face and hair smeared with blood. David broke into a sprint, Eleazar and Doeg following close behind.

"What happened?"

Abishai fell to a knee. "Philistines," he shouted. "In the forest."

David helped him up. "How many? Where?"

"We are here, giant slayer!"

He looked to see the Philistine commander emerge through the brush at the far end of the camp. His men were on their feet in moments, swords and shields and bows ready. Then a line of Philistine soldiers stepped into view, then another, and another. Within moments, the ravine was filled with them, clogging it like a plugged drain. His men paused, ready to attack but awaiting David's command.

"Hold," he shouted, passing the wounded Abishai off to Eleazar and then rushing forward. "Hold!"

His men fell back into orderly lines, swords and spear tips bristling like thorns. David stepped to the front.

"David, son of Jesse," the commander said with a smile. "I was hoping I would find you."

"And you have," he said. His hand rested on the hilt of his sword. "What can I do for you?"

"You owe me a chariot driver."

Abishai shouted from the back. "You owe me a spear!"

The commander chuckled. "Call it even, then." He took a step forward and lowered his voice. "You know, after your little spectacle with my chariots, my men suggested that we retreat." He laughed. "Flee in the face of a few hundred Israelites. No, thank you."

"You can still leave," he said. "And your men will still live."

The commander laughed again. "You know you cannot win this fight."

David looked over the commander's shoulder and to the men lined up just beyond. His estimation before proved to be close: the Philistines could fit no more than ten men across. "My shield is God Most High."

"Let us hope he is a sturdy shield," he said, turning and walking back into the forest. "Kill them all."

The Philistine battle lines slowly marched forward, and David hoped his men remembered their escape plan. He did not need to defeat the Philistines, merely to stall them.

"Arrows!"

From the back of the battle lines came a flurry of arrows. Some lodged themselves into the low-hanging branches, and others flittered off into the forest, but perhaps a dozen met their marks and bit into the flesh of the oncoming Philistines. The living stepped over the dead and did not falter, only kept coming.

"Again!"

More arrows, more dead, more Philistines taking their place. Always more.

"Spears!"

The spearmen stepped forward and took the first two

ranks, David and the others with swords falling behind them. The spears rose together and created a wall of thorns.

"Forward!"

David cleared his mind as they marched forward, preparing himself for the upcoming battle. That steely focus came over him, that familiar strength filled his tired limbs. He tasted the air, heard the Philistines' footsteps, the breathing of his own men. His skin tingled as he waited for the battle, ready to cause chaos.

There was a mighty crash as the Philistines slammed into his spearmen. Blood laced up and painted the forest red, grunts of pain filled the ravine, and men died by the handful. David's men held their ground, causing more damage than they took, but there were thousands of Philistines, and it did not take long for the sheer weight of their numbers to punch a hole in the line of spearmen. Within moments, the entire ravine plunged into mayhem, and dozens of individual skirmishes erupted around him.

An ax came from overhead. David sidestepped as the axhead plunged into the earth below. He brought a knee up into its owner's face, crunching through bone and teeth. He drew a dagger and dragged it over the man's throat, kicked him off to the side, then felt his body turned by those otherworldly hands and saw another Philistine charging at him, armed with a spear. He hacked at the spear and narrowly knocked it aside. The spear missed him by a handbreadth, digging itself into the wall of the ravine. David grabbed the spearman by the back of the head and used his charging momentum to slam him into an exposed root. As he fell back, he plunged his sword into his chest.

"Archers!"

David looked up just in time to see the high walls of the ravine lined with Philistine archers.

"Shields," he shouted, realizing immediately that he did

not have one. He dropped low and pulled the body of a dead Philistine atop him as the archers fired. The ravine was filled with the cries of dying men—both Israelite and Philistine—as arrows rained down on them in the hundreds. The tip of one poked through the corpse covering David with enough force to dig into his bicep. He grunted and kicked the dead man off him, the arrowhead ripping from his arm.

"Archers!" he shouted. "Archers, ready!"

A dozen of his own bowman rose and fired up toward the Philistines, nearly every arrow finding a mark. Dead men fell into the ravine, but the gaps in the lines of archers were filled almost instantly.

There are too many.

The thought was fleeting as another Philistine charged him. David parried a strike and jabbed with his dagger, cutting a gash in his stomach. The man fell, clutching as his insides spilled into the dirt.

"David!" Eleazar grunted up beside him, bloodied spear in hand. "They are ready!"

David ducked a strike and caught another on the edge of his dagger. He looked deeper into the camp and saw that indeed his men had rope ladders slung up at the back of the ravine. Philistine archers were rushing across the edge, trying to get to the ladders and cut them down.

"Retreat," he shouted, stepping inside the Philistine's guard and stabbing him through a pair of ribs. Warm blood flowed out onto his hands, and he left the dagger inside his victim. "Protect the ladders!"

Eleazar ran back into the camp and scooped up Abishai, draping him over his shoulder and guiding him toward the ladders. His wounded cousin still held his spear, jabbing out at Philistines even as Eleazar carried him across the battlefield. Those of his men still breathing pulled away from the battle and followed. He lifted a spear from a dead Philistine and threw it toward the archers at the top of the ravine. It slammed into the lead archer and sent him tumbling backward. More spears and arrows flew overhead and peppered the archers atop the wall.

David scanned the living for Ira, but he found no sign. His men were rushing across the ravine, arrows raining down and Philistines in pursuit. Doeg was still locked in battle, three enemies surrounding him and poking at him with spears. He rushed one of them, swatting the spear aside and splitting his skull with a heavy ax, and then David lost sight of him behind the wall of men.

Eleazar returned to his side, no longer carrying Abishai.

"Where is he," David asked.

"Up the ladder," he said, shouting over the din of battle.

As the rest of his men rushed toward the ladders, they stepped into the pursuing Philistine army, using the confines of the ravine as their ally. He knew he and Eleazar could not hold them off forever, but he prayed they could hold them off long enough for his men to finish the retreat.

David reached out and caught the shaft of an incoming ax. He pulled hard, but the Philistine refused to let go and lurched forward with his weapon. David's sword hacked down and cut his arm off at the elbow, and the ax and arm fell together into the dirt. Another Philistine entered his peripheral view. David twisted aside, the head of another ax roaring by and digging into the first man's ribcage. He reached out and grabbed the ax just below the blade, wrenching it free. As he spun to turn it back on its owner, a warning screamed in his mind, this time not for his own safety.

Eleazar!

He pivoted and buried the ax head into the skull of a Philistine. The man twitched once, and his own weapon went wide, just missing an unaware Eleazar.

A fist crunched into David's cheek, and stars filled his eyes.

He turned back to the man he'd stolen the ax from only to receive a knee in the stomach. Another pair of punches came in quick succession, and David was weaponless on the ground and gasping for air. He reached for his sword, fumbling in the grass and leaves. He heard the twang of a bow and felt the sting of an arrow slice into his arm. The arrow went all the way through, pinning it to the ground. He ignored the pain, reached out with his good hand and snapped the shaft of the arrow in two before ripping his wounded arm free. A boot crunched into his ribs, flipping him onto his back. He stared up at the Philistine, breathless and bleeding and still clutching the broken shaft of the arrow. The Philistine lifted David's own sword and stabbed down. David twisted aside, and the blade dug a full arm's length into the dirt. He rose with a jerk and jabbed the Philistine in the throat with the broken arrow shaft. The Philistine gurgled once, thick, black blood running down David's arm, and then collapsed on top of him.

"David!"

He shoved the man off him and saw Eleazar standing at the rear of his retreating men.

"Let's go!"

They were nearly all up the ravine now, only Eleazar standing at the bottom and waving him frantically over. He stumbled across the grass, arrows whistling by, each one feeling closer than the last.

Something hard struck him across the back of the head. He collapsed into the dirt, then rose to his hands and knees and looked again at Eleazar. He was still screaming, but David heard nothing but a high whining in his ears. His vision was blurry, his hands shook. He tried to stand, tried to force himself to his feet, but he felt another crack against his skull, and everything went black.

26

SAUL

THE FIRE CRACKLED from the torches and filled the large tent with smoke and ashes. The smoke floated up to the opening at the top of the tent and escaped out into the forest. Saul picked at the cheese and bread before him with little interest, taking his time as he selected his meal. Around him, he felt the eyes of his counsel as they waited.

Let them wait. What have they done for me? Fought me at every turn? Sided with David whenever they could? His eyes drifted to Jonathan, and more than a little anger flowed in his veins. *And my son most of all.*

They were camped in the forest outside Beersheba and had received no word from David or his men. Saul picked up some cheese and laid it on a hunk of bread. He ate slowly, deliberately, before finally looking to Abner.

"And the scouts have not returned?"

"Not all of them, no."

"And the ones that have?"

"We still cannot find the army."

Saul shook his head. "We lost six thousand Philistines and one hundred chariots?"

Jonathan stepped forward. "Actually, father, we *have* found the chariots."

Saul's ears perked in interest. "And?"

His son gave a haughty smile. "They have been destroyed."

"Destroyed?"

"Yes. They are no more than wreckage scattered around the fields before Beersheba. It was wise to send David ahead of us." Jonathan was smiling in full now, clearly proud of his friend.

"We still have six thousand Philistines to find," he said, his eyes fixed on his son. "Do not celebrate just yet. What of the city?"

Malki-Shua spoke now. "The city is safe."

Saul rubbed his temples. "This doesn't make any sense. Why come all this way and leave the city?"

"Perhaps they have fled," Jonathan said. "Saw they could not contend with even a few hundred of Yahweh's warriors and decided against fighting an army they knew would come."

Rimmon shook his head. "Doubtful. The Philistines are prideful, arrogant. Not unlike your friend David. After losing so many chariots, they would not let a slight like that go. More than likely, they are pursuing him as we speak." He and Saul made brief eye contact.

Pursuing David?

"Rimmon is right," Abner said. "The Philistines would know the size of David's band and know they only need to find them to overtake them. And any Philistine commander would know the worth of David's head."

"We need word from the rest of our scouts," Saul said.

Jonathan eyed him with distrust. "So, we do nothing? Has this been your plan all along?"

Saul clenched his jaw as he held his anger in check. "Watch yourself, son."

"It is you I need to watch, father."

"Enough!" Saul jerked to his feet. "I do not care if you like me, Jonathan. I do not care if you trust me. I do not care how you feel. But you will respect me. I am the king, *Yahweh's* chosen, and so long as I sit this throne, you will speak to me as a king. Is that clear?"

Jonathan did not reply.

"Is that clear!"

"Yes, father."

"Yes, *my king.*"

He drew a breath, his nostrils flaring in anger. "Yes, my king."

Shouts came from outside. "Go see to that, Jonathan."

He gave a curt bow and disappeared outside. The tent filled with palpable tension and thick silence.

Abner cleared his throat. "What orders do you have for the army?"

Saul sat back down, his mind still focused on his disobedient son. "What say you, Abner?"

"We do not know where the Philistines are, but we cannot sit idle. I suggest we proceed with caution. Move slowly and keep our flanks protected as we approach Beersheba."

Wise words, but not in the vein of what Saul wanted to hear. He looked at Rimmon. "And you?"

Rimmon threw a glance at Abner. "I also suggest prudence. Though perhaps even a touch more than Abner. I suggest we await the scouts."

Much better, he thought, turning his gaze finally to Malki-Shua.

"And you?"

His son was silent for a moment as he seemed to be gathering his thoughts. Even his less intelligent son knew there was more at stake here than merely the Philistines. "I want to fight, father. I want to shed Philistine blood. But I do not want to see our army ambushed." He paused, obviously weighing his words. "A slow advance seems wise."

The Philistines were likely pursuing David. As soon as Saul's army—swollen to over thirteen thousand now—appeared before the city, no matter how slowly they marched, the Philistines would likely give up their pursuit and retreat.

And I cannot have that.

"We do not know where the Philistines are, but we know where they are *not*," he said. "And they are not endangering Beersheba. The risk of being caught on the move is too great. We stay here until we receive word from the scouts. *All* of them." He looked again at the tent flap. The shouting outside had long stopped. "Malki-Shua, see where Jonathan has gone."

His son stepped outside, leaving the tent silent. He returned a moment later, leading a pair of familiar faces inside. One he recognized as one of David's men. The other was Doeg. Both looked fresh from battle, scrapes and bruises and bloodied bandages covering their bodies.

David's man rushed forward. "We must go! We must leave now!"

Saul frowned, and Rimmon stepped forward. "Watch yourself. You address the king."

"But they have David," he shouted.

Have David? Saul had to put forth considerable effort to hold back a smile. "What of the rest of your men?"

Doeg answered this time. "Dead."

"All of them?"

He shrugged. "A dozen or so are getting patched up now. Some of them will be dead either way."

David's man looked angry, a rage that Saul was all too familiar with simmering just beneath the surface. "We must go now," he said between gritted teeth. "David has little time."

Doeg scoffed. "David is dead."

David's man lurched over and threw a punch at Doeg. The

bigger man sidestepped it and cuffed him on the back of the head, sending him sprawling into the dirt.

"Enough," Abner shouted. He stepped between them just as David's man charged in again. He stopped, gave an angry look around the tent, and then stormed out.

"He's a little emotional," Doeg said.

Abner sighed, throwing a sideways glance at Doeg. "Tell us what happened."

"David had the smart idea of hiding in a ravine for two days, just waiting. Fool. Philistines found us, slaughtered our men. I escaped with a dozen or so of David's men. They took David alive." He grinned. "Mostly."

"Did you see where they went," Abner asked. "Where the army took him?"

He nodded toward the tent flap. "He wanted to follow, so we did. We saw where they camped."

"Where are they?"

"They went north around Beersheba, through the forest, until nightfall. We followed them to a clearing about a half day's walk from here. They made camp for the night, and then we came looking for you." He chuckled. "For help. David's men still think there is a chance at saving him." He scratched absently at a cut along his cheek until it bled and then looked at the blood on his hand. "I can take you to them if you're looking to fight. I got a pretty good score to settle myself."

They have David. "We must march," Saul said. "But I will not rush into a trap. We move slow, deliberate." He looked at Malki-Shua. "Organize some more scouts. Follow Doeg and find this camp." He turned to Abner. "Form up the army. We march at midday."

Finally, he turned to Jona—

"Where is my son?"

They all looked around the tent. "I...I don't know," Abner said.

"He ran off," Doeg said. "When we told him about David."

"Ran off?"

Doeg just shrugged.

Saul and Rimmon shared a look, and then Saul stormed outside, the others following behind. The camp was spread out before him. He looked frantically for signs of his son.

"Which way?" He turned and looked at Doeg. "Which way?"

He looked casually around and then pointed off to the right.

Saul looked where he was pointing, tried to remember what was in that direction...

The horses!

They found the clearing where they'd kept the horses at the edge of the camp. Saul's chief herdsman was standing in the center of the field. There were still horses within the fence, yet he could see many of them were gone. The herdsman was digging at something with a shovel and only looked up when Saul was within striking distance. The herdsman immediately dropped to a knee.

"My king."

"Where is my son?"

The herdsman remained on his knee, though he looked up to Saul. "He...he left, my king. Only a few moments ago. He and twenty others."

"Did he tell you to where?"

He looked back down at the ground. "He did not, my king. I thought not to question."

Saul felt his anger boil inside him. "So, you allowed my son to take our horses, *my* horses, and did not inquire as to why?"

"I...he...I did not..."

Saul looked at Doeg. "Congratulations, Doeg. You are my new chief herdsman." He looked back to the kneeling man.

"Find something useful to do in this camp, or I will find a hole to hide you in."

The former herdsman nodded furiously and then crawled away, not rising from his knees until he was well away from the field.

"Was that necessary?" Abner asked. "You cannot have expected him to question Jonathan."

Saul glared at Abner. "Yet, I can expect you to question me?"

Abner frowned, though he said nothing.

Rimmon cleared his throat. "My king, what will you do about Jonathan?"

He was likely rushing off to meet the Philistines, to save David. He and twenty others attempting to face an army of thousands. They could mount up, pursue Jonathan. Yet even if he was able to gather enough men for the remaining horses, they would still be facing an army of thousands with only a handful of warriors. And by then, Jonathan would be beyond reach, anyway. "We cannot catch them," he said, almost to himself. "There is nothing we can do."

DAVID

DAVID'S BREATH blew back into his face, hot and dusty and thick. He tried to draw another breath but only sucked in a mouthful of coarse cloth and gagged. He coughed and spat and nearly vomited into the cloth before he could get it from his mouth. Everything was a black blur. He realized absently that his eyes were closed, opened them, and found everything a brown blur. The cloth ran up from his mouth over his eyes and ears and head. It ran down under his chin and was cinched tight around the neck.

A sack, then.

He heard nothing but his heart beating in his head and the muffled sound of voices not far off. The ground was hard beneath him. His wrists were chafed from fraying ropes that bound them together behind his back; he was tied like a sheep for the sacrifice. He tried to lift his head, slo—

Sharp pain shot up his spine and slammed into the back of his eyes. Sparkling red lights filled his vision. His world was no longer a brown blur but a crimson one. He squeezed his eyes shut and gritted his teeth against the pain, a low moan escaping his lips. The muffled voices around him cut short, and all was silent except for the throbbing of his head.

A foot hit him in the ribs. He tried to double over, but the ropes pulled tight, and he managed only a heavy wheeze that drew laughs from the men around him. Another foot stomped down on him, and he could no longer hold back the vomit at the edge of his throat. It came up like a fountain, a mixture of blood and bile hitting the sack over his face and then mashing into his nose and eyes. He gagged again and tried to blink the vomit from his vision, but the now-soaked sack clung to his face like a spider's web.

Suddenly the sack was yanked free, and his world changed yet again, this time from blurred crimson to blinding white light. He rolled to his side and blinked until his vision cleared, tears stinging his eyes alongside the vomit. The laughter around him grew louder and clearer.

"Good morning, giant slayer."

His entire body ached, his head throbbed, his vision was blurred from tears and bile, yet he somehow managed to turn his head up. The Philistine commander was standing over him, the dripping sack in one hand. He squatted down and wiped David's face somewhat clean with the backside of the sack.

"I said, good morning. Does your god smile on poor manners?"

David spat once more into the dirt, ignoring the pain that screamed at him. "My God...smiles..."

He was unable to form any thoughts, and his words trailed off.

"He smiles?"

He drew a deep breath, his lungs swelling with fresh air. His head began to clear, the pain fading just enough for coherent thoughts to form. David looked again at the Philistine commander. "He smiles...on the righteous."

"On the righteous? Is he smiling now?"

"Remove these ropes...and we can find out."

A few laughs and taunts came from around him. David glanced to his sides and saw he was surrounded by Philistines, a perfect circle formed around him. The commander smiled. He threw the sack aside and drew a sword—David's own sword, he realized.

"Very well."

He stepped forward and sliced the ropes free, then tossed the sword into the dirt beside him. David's hands tingled as the blood rushed back to them. He lunged for the sword, but his feet gave out, forcing him to crawl to it, dragging himself over the dry desert sand. When he finally reached it, the commander was standing back at the edge of the circle.

"I am Phicol, commander of the Philistine army. We all already know who you are."

David grunted as he pushed himself to sitting. "Sometimes, I wonder myself."

"Don't we all. Yet you have done many great things, son of Jesse."

Using the sword as a cane, David stood on trembling legs. "Have I?

"You have killed hundreds of my men, have you not?"

"I'm not done yet."

Phicol chuckled at that, a lighthearted sound that seemed drastically out of place. "If the stories are to be believed, you and fewer than twenty men assaulted a camp of two hundred. And won."

"It was closer to fifty."

"And Goliath! He was a big one, wasn't he? Yet you dropped him with only a sling and a stone. Impressive."

"His own sword did most of the work."

"I remember. And what is this story I hear of a young David killing a lion with his bare hands? This, at least, is untrue."

"I had some stones then too."

Phicol laughed, louder and more robust this time. "It would seem." He looked down the line of warriors. "Who would like to be the one who slew the giant slayer?"

A Philistine soldier stepped forward. He was as broad at the shoulders as Eliab, a long vicious-looking spear in one hand and a shield in the other. His face was scarred, and David could tell immediately that this man was a warrior. Not simply a soldier in the army, but a warrior. A man who had seen battle and come out stronger for it.

"I thought he'd be bigger," the Philistine said. His voice was like iron being sharpened, grating and rough and dangerous.

David closed his eyes. *Contend, Lord, with those who contend with me; fight against those who fight against me. Take up shield and armor; arise and come to my aid.*

When he opened his eyes, he saw the Philistine waiting patiently.

"Are you done," he asked.

David didn't immediately answer. Instead, he drew a long breath and held it. He felt Yahweh's calming presence fill him. The pain faded to the back of his mind. Beginning in this feet and working to his fingertips, strength crept through his body as the shaking slowed and stopped. His grip tightened on his sword as he lifted it from the dirt and held it purposefully before him. Finally, in a long exhale through barely parted lips, he let out the breath he was holding. The Philistine's eyes widened noticeably at the sudden change in David, who gave a small smirk.

"I suppose."

The Philistine charged in, jabbing with his spear. David pivoted and let the jab go wide, welcoming that deadly strength as it coursed through his veins and filled his weakened body. His feet shuffled, and he lashed out with his sword. His blade bit into the wooden shield, chips and splinters flying off. He wrenched it free, spun away as the Philistine tried to ram the rim of his shield at him, and swung low to hamstring the Philistine and drop him to his knees. He continued his spin, and his sword whipped around and cleanly sliced the warrior's head from his shoulders. Blood erupted like a fountain as his body fell to the sand, crashing down in a cloud of dust. One of the legs gave a light twitch, then all was still but for the flowing blood.

There was stunned silence from the men of the circle. A handful of heartbeatsthudded in David's head like a drum before Phicol gave a slow applause.

"Well done, giant slayer. Who is next?"

Another Philistine stepped forward, his eyes on his dead companion. "He was a fool," he grunted, tossing aside his own spear and pulling his sword free. "You cannot fight a duel with a spear."

O Lord, do not forsake me; be not far from me, O my God. Come quickly to help me, O Lord my Savior.

The Philistine came in slowly, sword and shield in constant motion. David watched his movements, how he carried himself, how he handled his weapon. When he was close enough, the Philistine struck, thrusting hard and fast. David sidestepped, felt his sword arm move on its own as Yahweh guided him. The blade swiped sideways and caught the tip of the Philistine's sword, twisted once, and drove it down into the ground. His other hand shot out with a strength he did not own, grabbed the rim of the shield, and twisted. He heard the man's arm crack as the shield spun upside down. He swept out a foot and kicked him in the back of the knee, pulling down at the same time. The Philistine crumpled to the ground, and David stabbed straight down, his sword slicing through his ribs and puncturing his heart. He coughed once and then went silent.

This time Phicol laughed. "Perhaps two?"

David felt some of the air go out of him. Two Philistines stepped from the circle, one with a spear and one with a sword. Both held shields out in front of them and began to march forward in unison.

O Lord, be not far off; O my Strength, come quickly to help me...

The spear darted in, and David parried. The sword came right after, and he felt his legs moving, stepping him just out of its reach. His free hand shot up and grabbed the shaft of the spear. He jerked it and used it to parry the second strike from the sword, his own sword jabbing at the spearman with a speed that surprised even him. Blood shot back at him, and he ignored it, ducking another strike from the oncoming sword. He jerked on the spear and rammed it into the shield of the swordsman. It broke through the wood and into the Philistine's hand. He opened his mouth to scream, but David's sword was already moving. It caught the Philistine across the side of the face, and blood and bone and brain spewed into the air. Both men collapsed together. Again, there was a long silence.

"By Dagon, that was impressive."

David's breath was ragged in his throat as he turned to Phicol. "May I leave now?"

He smiled, seeming to enjoy watching his own men die. "Archer!"

An arrow whistled from somewhere, and David's hand shot out snatched it from the air. He looked it at for a moment and then tossed it aside. Phicol's eyes widened with surprise.

"Very well," he eventually said. "Perhaps four will be enough."

They came out in unison as if they had planned to face David together beforehand. Two with spears and two with swords, all with shields. They spread out and circled him.

You are a shield around me...

The spearmen came in together, one on either side of him.

The swordsmen were a step behind. David picked a spearman and lunged, reaching out and catching hold of his spear by the shaft. He used it to block one swordsman while his sword shot out to parry the other. He pulled down on the spear and spun, his sword following and slicing the spearman down his spine. The man stumbled once and then fell into the dirt. Behind him, he heard the commander laugh and clap.

You armed me with strength for battle...I pursued my enemies...I overtook them...

Without pause, David leaped to the swordsman on his right. He hacked in a hard, vertical slash. The Philistine raised his shield to block, but that otherworldly strength was behind the blow, and his sword split the shield down to the boss at its center, cutting through wood and flesh. The Philistine lurched back with a scream, jerking the sword from David's hand as the weapon stayed lodged in the shield. David stepped forward and kicked the shield. It slammed back into its owner, the stuck sword piercing the Philistine's neck. He gurgled once, dropped his weapons, and then collapsed onto the hard-packed dirt. David pulled his sword from the shield, then grabbed the fallen Philistine's weapon, as well. He turned, a sword in each hand, and faced the remaining two.

The two living Philistines backed off in opposite directions. David chose the one with the sword and sprinted in. He ducked a jab and rolled inside his guard. His blades lashed out together and separated the swordsman's legs from his body. He fell with the rawest scream of pain David had ever heard.

They cried for help, but there was no one to save them...

The final Philistine was shaking so hard the tip of his spear was wobbling. David hurled his stolen sword. It clanged off the Philistine's shield, but David was right behind it, hacking the spear from his grasp. It fell to the ground, and the Philistine gripped his shield with two hands and raised it to block. David grabbed the rim of the shield and jerked it free as if stealing a toy from a toddler. He tossed it aside and kicked the Philistine hard in the chest, sending him rolling along the hard desert ground. David followed and plunged his sword into his chest, twisted once, and pulled it free. The Philistine went pale in an instant.

David turned to find Phicol still smiling widely.

"Are you satisfied," David shouted, dropping his sword beside him. "Does this please your foolish gods!?"

"Dagon does enjoy a good sacrifice, though we were hoping it would be Israelite blood and not Philistine." He looked over at the one David had cut the legs from and frowned. He was still screaming, clutching at his stumps and rolling in the dirt. Phicol drew a small dagger and jammed it into the dying man's chest, burying it down to the hilt. The dying man gurgled for a handful of heartbeats and then fell silent. "Though there is still a chance at that."

The circle of Philistines parted, and a hooded man filled in the gap. The man stumbled, but a Philistine grabbed him by his bound hands and pulled him upright. Phicol sliced the rope binding his hands. He wrenched the sack off his head and kicked him into the center of the circle.

Ira blinked in the sunlight. His eyes went wide as he saw the Philistines around him. He turned, eyes meeting David's.

"Don't do this," David said, looking beyond Ira and to Phicol. "If you wish us dead, then do it yourselves."

"That clearly hasn't worked." He threw the sword onto the ground beside Ira. "Now, you two will fight, and at least *one* Israelite will die today."

"Plenty have already died."

"I want only one more."

Ira was on all fours beside the sword. "They...they want us to fight?" he asked.

David didn't answer.

Ira looked at the sword. "I'll not fight you."

"Nor I, you."

Phicol stepped from the circle. "Then you will both die."

"We will both die either way."

"What if I promise to let the winner go?"

David spat into the dirt. "That is what I think of a Philistine promise."

"You wound me, giant slayer. I armed you, sent only a few men after you. If I wished you dead, I would have done it already."

"You wish me to suffer."

"Have you ever killed a friend, giant slayer?"

"Why would I?"

Phicol stepped forward. "I have! Our god is not pathetic like yours. He is not weak and merciful. We cannot sacrifice animals to appease him. He desires the blood of man!" He looked down at his hands and seemed to only now notice the blood on them from the legless man he had stabbed. He wiped them clean on his tunic. "I have killed many men I considered my friends to appease Dagon. Now you will do the same. One of you must die, so the other may live."

"Mercy is not weakness," David said. "And I'll not fight my friend to appease a god that does not exist."

"Then you will both die."

Ira's hand drifted to the hilt of the sword. He looked at David. "You must live," he whispered. He whipped the blade up and rammed it into his own stomach.

"No!" David ran forward, catching Ira as he fell to the ground. Warm blood filled his hands. Ira's bruised and beaten face was pale, blood running from the corners of his mouth. His lips moved yet made no sound, his gaze was fixed over David's shoulder, locked on nothing. "No. No, no no..." David lowered his head until it rested on Ira's. He felt the boy trembling, felt his skin already going cold.

"That does not count."

David looked up at Phicol.

He looked mildly upset. Annoyed. "You did not kill him," he said. "It does not count."

David ignored him and looked back at Ira. The trembling had become a violent shake, his pale face alabaster white. Yet his eyes were now in focus, locked onto David's with a fierceness that startled him.

"I'm…I…" the boy whimpered. Ira's hands were pawing at him, struggling to grip David's torn and bloody tunic, struggling to hold on to this life.

David had no words and only lowered his head until it rested again on Ira's. "I'm sorry…"

I'm…I'm so confused…I heard you. I know I did. You sent me here, sent me to battle. Ira's pawing slowly weakened until David no longer felt him move. He placed a hand over Ira's heart and felt its weak and dying beat. *First, you needed a shepherd, then a musician, and finally, a warrior. Do you now need dead men? Can our bones praise you? Can our corpses sing of your glory?* He felt Ira's heartbeat one final time. Then silence. He held his breath, waited for an answer from Yahweh. *I'm so lost…Why? Why am I here?*

This is where I need you, David.

But why? Where is this mighty blow that I am to strike?

Do you trust me?

What?

Do you trust me?

David felt something stir inside him that he'd never felt before. He thought of loving Abigail only to lose her. He thought of being forced to marry Michal in her stead. He thought of his men rotting in a ravine not far away. Now he held Ira, still a boy, having just breathed his last because he'd followed David to battle.

Because you *told him to follow me!* You *told me to take him in! And you ask if I trust you? I am surrounded by death and disappointment, brought on by my trust in you! And you test me still?!*

"It is a shame." Phicol bent down and plucked the dagger from the soldier he had killed. "I would have let you live had you been the one to strike him down."

David glared up at him. He was dominated now by hatred. It felt like a fire on his flesh, a burning from within. Yet this one was different. This fire was not fueled by Yahweh but by rage and hate and loss. He gently laid Ira aside and climbed to his feet. His hands balled into angry fists.

I am done. Find someone else for your calling, whatever it may be.

He received no response. Indeed, he expected none.

Phicol was grinning. "Is your god smiling now?"

David ground his teeth. "I wouldn't know," he said, his voice barely above a whisper. "It's just us now."

"Is that so?"

Phicol lunged forward suddenly, the dagger aimed at David's chest. David's arm snaked out and caught his wrist. "There are no gods here, Philistine." He bent his arm back, heard Phicol whimper. He leaned in close. "I have sent them away. We are alone."

"Archer!"

An arrow dug deep into David's lower back. He looked down, saw it poking through his side just under his ribs, more dumbfounded than in pain. He released Phicol, and the commander fell back.

"Sword!"

A sword clattered to the ground beside him, and Phicol lifted it. "Now you die, giant slayer."

He lunged back in, the blade coming down in an overhead strike. David almost didn't move; he'd become so accustomed to that strength filling him, Yahweh's hands guiding him. But it was gone now. As he'd just told Phicol, he'd sent it away.

At the last instant, he raised a hand in defense and caught

hold of Phicol's forearms, the blade shuddering to a halt midswing.

"Perhaps I will die, Philistine," David said. "But you will come to Sheol with me."

"Archer!"

This time David sidestepped, never releasing his grip. The arrow whistled by and plunged into Phicol's chest, high and near his collar bone. Both the sword and dagger fell from his hands. He looked down at the arrow in his chest, then raised his eyes to David.

"You can kill me," he said, his voice raspy and strained. "But you're going to die too."

David pulled him close. "I don't care." He headbutted Phicol at the temple, and the Philistine's head snapped back with enough force that David dropped him. He bent and lifted the fallen sword, turned it blade down, and rammed it through Phicol's heart.

Pain erupted in David's leg, and he dropped to a knee, one hand still on the sword. He looked down, saw yet another arrow sticking from his thigh. Before he registered what happened, another arrow struck him in the shoulder and spun him. He felt his knee pop, the world spin around him, the hard dirt slam into his back.

I am done. All done. It is time to rest now. He felt a weight lift from him, a weight he had not realized was there. *It is my life leaving me,* he dimly thought. *This is death.*

A figure stood above him, sword gleaming in the sunlight. It was a Philistine, a soldier, but beyond that, his comprehension was failing him. The sword rose, glimmering and shining like a jewel. He closed his eyes. *I am done...*

Then the voice spoke.

I am not done with you.

There was a thud nearby, and David opened his eyes to see the blue sky again, the Philistine soldier gone.

I still need you, David.

There were shouts, the shuffling of feet, and then the sounds of battle. David looked up and saw Israelites on horseback crashing into the circle of Philistines. The last thing he saw before slipping into unconsciousness was Jonathan at their head with a bow slung across his back and a sword in his hand.

28

SAUL

SAUL STOOD on the small hill at the edge of the camp, the ever-present Benyamin right behind him, and scowled at the horizon. He could see the outline of Beersheba far to the west, but more important for him was the forest north of it. The forest faded into a broad desert, and his eyes never left that expanse, straining to see his son's return. The sky was beginning to purple in the east as dusk approached.

It had been hours since Jonathan had snuck away with twenty men, rushing off to face six thousand Philistines with the hopes of rescuing David. Jonathan's return was unlikely, and he was not sure if he wished his son success or not. Saul felt torn between his hatred of David and his love of his son.

A love he has been testing lately.

"Have you seen any sign?"

Saul looked back to see Rimmon stepping up the small hill to join him. "I have not."

"What will you do if he returns?"

Rimmon had become adept at reading Saul's thoughts. "I am torn, old friend."

"I would imagine so. The death of an enemy is hardly worth the death of a son."

"It would not have come to that if he had not rushed off like a fool."

"Jonathan is passionate, that much is true. We need only direct that passion."

Saul scoffed. "It is directed at David as if that jackal were already king."

"The shepherd will never be king."

Will he? Can I stop what Yahweh has started? But he already knew the answer, and he did not like it. "Not while I live."

The horizon began to shimmer, and Saul took a step forward. The shimmering cleared, and soon he could see the distinctive shapes of horses approaching.

He turned to Benyamin. "Have Abner ready some men. Be prepared."

Benyamin nodded and ran off.

"Jonathan, perhaps," Rimmon asked.

"We shall see."

"What will you do if it is him? And if he brings David with him?"

"I will celebrate my son's life," he said. "As for David, there seems to be little I can do."

"But you are the king," he said. "Yahweh's anointed. Regardless of how righteous David appears, he was not chosen. *You* were. You can do whatever you wish."

Saul regarded him for a moment. Samuel's words echoed in his mind: *"The Lord has torn the kingdom of Israel from you. He has given it to another—one who is better than you."*

He has given it to David.

"I wish it were that simple, friend."

The two watched in silence as the horses continued their approach and the sun set. When Benyamin returned, they had only the light of the moon and stars to see by.

"My king," Benyamin said, only a hint of hesitation in his voice. "Abner has suggested we venture back into the camp in case it is the Philistines."

Saul's face remained hard. "I'm not going anywhere."

A pair of horses split off from the rest and rode hard toward them, one of them pulling far ahead of the other. As the first rider neared, Saul recognized him as Jonathan's armor-bearer. The horse stopped in front of Saul, and the rider dismounted, dropping immediately to a knee before the king.

"Jonathan requests the physician be ready," he said, breathing heavily. "David is badly wounded."

Saul looked beyond the rider and toward the second one still approaching. He could clearly see Jonathan sitting tall on the horse, though now he could also make out a body draped across it.

"My king?"

Saul looked down at the first rider and then turned to Benyamin. "Get the physician."

SAUL STARED down at the battered and bruised body. Countless bloodied bandages were wrapped around countless wounds. A heavy, padded cloth had been wrapped dozens of times around his chest and gut, the right side stained red and thick with blood. The face was bruised and battered and broken, barely recognizable.

But it is recognizable. I see the face of my enemy, still breathing.

Jonathan had already recounted what had happened. How they had found David, moments before a Philistine was about to kill him. How they had struck into the unsuspecting army, Abishai and Eleazar standing over him long enough for

Jonathan to secure David onto his horse. How they had fled, leaving a broken and shocked Philistine army behind.

"Tell me about his wounds."

Everyone in the tent turned to look at Saul. Jonathan was there, as well as Abner and Malki-Shua. A pair of physicians in bloodied tunics were standing over David's unconscious body.

Saul looked at the physicians. "His wounds?"

They exchanged a glance, and then the older of the two stepped forward. "He is badly wounded, my king." He pointed to several of the bloodied bandages. "A blow to the head. A pair of bruised ribs. However, these are not as bad as they look. The more serious ones are here," he pointed to the bloodied cloth that wrapped around his chest and gut. "Puncture wounds. One coming from the back and another from the front. Both piercing cleanly through. His lungs and heart were spared somehow, as was his stomach. It is a miracle he lived through the initial wound and a miracle he has not died from loss of blood."

"So, he will live?"

"I cannot say for sure, my king. Wounds like this can be difficult to heal. Even with the best care, it is in Yahweh's hands now."

So, he will live. Saul tried to hide his anger, but his teeth began to grind together. "Thank you. You may leave. I would have some words with my counsel now." He locked eyes with Jonathan.

The physicians nodded and perhaps said something that Saul ignored. Then they were gone, leaving the four of them standing over an unconscious David. The tent was silent but for his ragged breathing and the crackling of a nearby sconce. Outside Saul could hear the reveling of the men, all cheers after the heroics of their prince. Saul's eyes remained on his son.

"You snuck away."

Jonathan opened his mouth, but Saul cut him off before he could speak.

"You did not take counsel, did not inform anyone where you were taking your men."

"Father..."

"You left us without horses and attacked an army of thousands with twenty men."

"I had to go, father..."

"You had to do nothing."

"If I had done nothing, then David would be dead."

Saul took a big step forward. "Good!" The word echoed throughout the tent, bouncing off the fabric walls and ringing in his ears. "Then I would be rid of him and of your strange subservience to him. My kingdom would be free of jackals, and your mind would return. You are foolish, Jonathan. A boy. A child. An idiot!"

Jonathan stood his ground, his face reddening in anger. "I saved Israel's greatest captain. We lost not one man. Their army retreats as we speak, broken. I do not think me an idiot."

"You took your men without speaking with any of us. You rushed off to meet a stronger force. A much stronger force. It is a miracle you are alive at all."

"Perhaps, father. But I expect miracles. We fight with the Living God of Israel at our back. Something you have forgotten."

Saul's hand was moving before he could stop it. He backhanded Jonathan with enough force to send his son stumbling to the ground. "*I* am the king! Me! Not you, not David! *I* am the anointed one! Yahweh chose *me* to lead! Do you understand!? ME!" A red haze had begun to cover his vision as he felt his anger rise. For the first time, Saul embraced it.

Jonathan leaned on an elbow and touched his now-bloodied lip. "Then why can you not act like it?"

Saul began to step forward, but Abner moved between

them. "He is fresh from battle, my king," he said. "He doesn't know what he is saying. Let me see him fed and rested, then he will answer for his decisions."

Saul eyed Abner, his anger changing directions in a heartbeat. "You would stand against me, as well? Stand in the way of Yahweh's anointed!" His hand went to his sword, and then Malki-Shua was beside him.

"Father...don't."

Rage screamed through his bones. "And you? You would tell me what to do? My most foolish son!" He tried to draw his sword, but Malki-Shua's hand fell on his and pinned the tip of the blade in the scabbard. Saul's eyes darted around him, at his closest counselor, his sons. "You are *all* fools!" He shrugged Malki-Shua's hand from his and drew his weapon. Abner and Malki-Shua took a step back. "All of you, seduced by this jackal. This fake!" He pointed with his sword as he spoke, jabbing it wildly about the tent. "I am the king—Yahweh's chosen—and yet I am still being told what to do. When to fight. Where to fight." He placed the flat of the blade on David's chest hard enough for him to cough in his sleep. "Who I can kill." He looked at David's sleeping face, his hand shaking as he gripped his sword.

Jonathan stood. "Father...you cannot..."

"But I *can*. I. Am. The king."

Do it. A little jab, and he is gone forever. Kill him now.

He watched the blade rise and fall with David's fractured breathing, felt his hand continue to shake as he fought with himself about what to do. He drew in a deep breath, the anger fading enough for him to think straight. *The men will revolt if I slay David here.*

He pulled the sword back and sheathed it. "I *can*." He eyed everyone in the tent. "When we get back to Gibeah, things are going to be different. I will give a command, and it will be followed. Is that clear?"

All three men nodded.

"Good. The times of Saul the soft are over. This is *my* kingdom, given to me by the God you all serve, and I will run it as I please. And anyone who stands in my way will suffer." He pointed down to David. "Even Israel's favorite son."

29

DAVID

Davidʼs eyes fluttered open, and he felt the beginnings of consciousness as he stared up at a clear blue sky. He didn't know where he was and—for a fleeting moment—who he was. *I am a shepherd.* He was hot; he knew that much. He could feel a fire burning within him, sweat soaking a heavy blanket laid across him. He bent to move the blank—

Searing hot pain shot up his gut and into his chest, the urge to vomit nearly taking him. He squeezed his eyes closed, saw blinding white light, and bit a lip through the pain. The rest of his body parts began to one by one announce their pain, as well. His ribs throbbed, dozens of cuts groaned, even his feet hurt. He could not move his left leg.

And with the pain came his memory. He was not a shepherd—at least not anymore. He was David, Israel's greatest captain, fearless warrior, slayer of Goliath.

Yet I am no longer those, either. What am I?

After what felt like an eternity, the pain faded enough for him to think. He inched his eyes open and saw the blue sky, this time noticing that he was moving beneath it. His bed jostled, and he realized he was on a cart. He could hear the creaking of the wooden wheels as they rattled down some dirt path. He tried to lift his head to get a better view of his surroundings.

"Easy," a voice said, pulling the blanket down to his waist. His chest—heavily bandaged from navel to nipple—seemed to sigh in relief as the cool air touched what little skin was exposed. "Easy, David."

A familiar face leaned over, bobbing with the cart as he walked alongside it.

"Abishai," David said, his voice hoarse and scratchy in his dry throat. "You're alive."

"So are you."

More memories came back to him. "Barely. Anyone else?"

Abishai frowned. "Eleazar. A few others. Doeg is among them."

David drew a shuddering breath. The voices of his men echoed through his mind, their sounds of joy and pain, victory and defeat. So many lives blown out like candles, wasted like chaff, cast aside like trash.

Abishai glanced down at David's wounded body. "Do you feel as bad as you look?"

"I don't know how I look, but I feel like Sheol," he said, a fit of coughing taking him. His ribs throbbed with each cough, his gut burning. "They...they made me fight, Abishai."

His friend looked confused. "We all fought. Did you—"

"No. After they took me. They made me fight." He closed his eyes, could see Ira's pale face.

"Fight who?"

"They surrounded me and sent their soldiers at me one at a time," he said without opening his eyes. "They wanted Israelite blood for their god."

"They didn't get it," he said, setting a hand gently on David's.

How I wish that were true...

"They did," he said, his voice just over a whisper.

"I guess you bled a little..."

He felt a hot tear leak through his closed eyes. "They had Ira too." He opened his eyes and looked at Abishai, his face a blur now through the tears. "They wanted us to fight each other. I...I wouldn't do it. Ira...he..." He fell silent, the image of Ira bleeding out in his arms coming to him. He felt the boy's body go cold all over again, felt his heart stop pumping, felt his dead weight in his arms. "He took his own life."

Abishai's face dropped. "He...why?"

"They said if we fought, the winner would live." David looked away, fixed his eyes on nothing. "Ira thought me important enough to take his own life."

They fell quiet. David could hear the footsteps of others walking behind them. Laughter sounded in the distance. "He was a brave kid," Abishai finally said. His voice was as solemn as David had ever heard it.

Anger swelled up in him. "No." He looked again at Abishai. "He was a fool. Who am I? Who am I to deserve that kind of sacrifice?" His throat felt raw, but he didn't care. "I'm a shepherd, brought high because of a lucky shot with a sling. And they're dead because of me. All of them." He felt more hot tears coming, his breath catching in his throat. "I can't...I don't...I'm not even..." He pulled in a shuddering breath to steady his beating heart, held it for a long time, then gave a deep sigh. "I am lost, Abishai." He dropped his head back and stared straight up. "And I'm done."

There was a long silence, followed by, "You may be injured, but I'll not hesitate to smack you."

He looked at Abishai, saw an anger there he had never seen before.

"Ira took his life so you can live, and you lie here and belittle that sacrifice? And a lucky shot with a sling? The entire army of Israel stood shaking before Goliath, and *you* stepped up to meet him. As a boy!"

"A foolish boy."

"The world is full of foolish boys, David, and they do not often slay Goliaths."

"No, they do not. They take their own lives defending a shepherd."

"Ira was no fool. He knew exactly what he was doing. And the men around you? They are there because of you. You are their leader, and they would follow you to the gates of Sheol."

"They have!" His voice echoed around them. He could feel the eyes of others drawn their way. He didn't care. "They followed me—no, followed *Yahweh*! And now they are dead while I still draw breath. They gave their life. And for what? For a shepherd?"

Abishai leaned in close, his voice harder and more commanding than David had ever heard it. "Don't forget, David. Don't forget that you told me. You told me what happened when you were a child, how Samuel anointed you. How Yahweh chose you for something."

"I was chosen to lead men to their deaths?"

"You still draw breath," he said. "Your time is not yet over."

David sighed. "Yes. It is. I'm done."

Abishai scowled down at David. "You're an idiot, you know that?" David laid his head back down, ignoring the pain shooting through his aching body.

"They're dead, Abishai. Because I listened to Yahweh, because he chose me to lead them, hundreds of wives have lost their husbands. Hundreds of children have lost their fathers. I'm done asking people to die for me."

"Do you hear yourself," Abishai said, his voice rising. It seemed he no longer cared about those around him, either. "Do you not realize what would have happened had we not fought? Beersheba would have fallen. Everyone inside the city would be dead or enslaved. Saul's army would have had to face a hundred chariots. One hundred, David. And the Philistines would have had the city walls to defend themselves. Because of you, *thousands* of wives have *kept* their husbands, and *thousands* of children have *kept* their fathers. And you say they died for nothing?"

David sighed, even that burning his throat. "Perhaps you're right. Perhaps it was a noble sacrifice. Perhaps we did save lives. But I'll not ask that sacrifice again. Yahweh can do with me as he pleases, but I'll not lead men to die for me again. They can die for someone else." He closed his eyes. "I'm done having others suffer for my calling, whatever that may be."

Abishai opened his mouth to reply when a noise in the distance got both of their attention. David lifted his head and saw the walls of Gibeah approaching, their tops filled to the edges with women and children. Hundreds more lined the path leading to the gates. Their voices carried on the air and came rushing toward them.

"David! David! David!"

Abishai only frowned. He looked back at David and sighed. "They chant your name, David. They will follow you whether you would lead or not. And you think you're nothing?" He shook his head as he walked away. "You're a fool, at the least."

He watched his friend leave before looking again at the crowds around the city gate. His cart crawled its way through them. He looked at their faces, saw their joy at his return. He knew he should feel a swell of pride, of meaning, of purpose. But all he felt was pity, pity for these people who wanted so desperately for him to be something he couldn't be.

"David!"

His ears perked at the voice. This one he recognized, despite having heard it only sparingly.

"David!"

"Michal," he croaked.

She burst through the crowd, tears streaking her face, and

nearly threw herself on him. His cart rattled to an abrupt stop. His body screamed in protest at her weight, but he didn't care. This would be his purpose now, this woman. Yahweh had forced her into his arms. He would take this parting gift from Yahweh and make his own life, a life without battle, without the unseen forcing decisions upon him. He wrapped his arms around her and pulled her closer, her hair falling into his face, her scent filling his nose, her warmth strangely comforting him.

"I thought you were dead."

He squeezed her tighter, tears running down his own face now. "I was," he whispered. "But I'm back. I'm back, and I'm done."

She leaned back just enough to look into his eyes. "Done? Done with what?"

"I'm done," he said, pulling her back close. "I'm done fighting."

30

SAUL

SAUL SAT atop his horse and watched the procession enter the city. He could still hear the chants as David's cart was pulled through the gates, still see the women and children crowding around him. His own daughter walked alongside, her hand resting on David.

"The people are foolish, my king."

Saul looked at Rimmon, the only person within earshot of him. "I know."

"They know not what they say."

"Yes, they do."

"Yet they will forget this victory soon."

"Perhaps, but there will be another," he replied. "And another and another until the son of Jesse is in the ground." He drew a breath and let it out slowly, a calmness filling his mind that he had not expected. "I will let him heal. Then I'm going to kill him."

PART III

SIX MONTHS LATER

Saul tried to pin him to the wall with his spear, but David eluded him as Saul drove the spear into the wall. That night David made good his escape.

31

DAVID

Davɪᴅ's sɪᴅᴇ ached a little less today, just as it had ached a little less yesterday and the day before. He stood on his balcony, the cool morning air of spring kissing his bare chest. The bandage was no longer needed, though he often wished for it to hide the pair of gnarled scars, one just beside his navel and the other under his collarbone. He touched one of their puckered surfaces with a finger and remembered the searing pain he felt as the arrows had cut through him. He also remembered how he'd sent Yahweh away that day. He'd yet to hear the voice since.

He looked down into the training grounds. What remained of his men—and a few dozen newer recruits—were down below, training hard and filling the early morning with the sounds of mock battle. Practice swords banged together, arrows thudded into bales of hay, feet shuffled in the sand. He could smell the familiar scents of sweat and dirt and not a little blood. Practice swords they may be, but wood can pierce flesh all the same.

His eyes drifted to Abishai, leading the training. He walked among the men with confidence, correcting a stance here, straightening a bow there. David almost smiled at his cousin and longtime friend. He had taken over David's role without pause or delay, and the men had responded. He doubted Abishai had told them that David was quitting, that he was not merely filling in until David healed. Abishai would lead them now, and they were better for it.

How will they take it? As bad as Abishai?

He took one last look at his men and turned back into his room. Michal lay in their bed, her chest rising and falling with the gentle rhythm of sleep. He was trying to make her his everything, his new purpose, despite his mixed feelings toward her. She was beautiful and kind, nothing like her father. The more he learned of her, the more he developed a liking. She had only a passing knowledge of Yahweh, something he now viewed as a good thing.

Yet there was something still there, something keeping him from giving Michal his all. And despite his thoughts to the contrary, he knew what it was: He was still in love with Abigail.

He sighed and pushed her from his mind. He would never see her again; Yahweh and Saul had made sure of that.

"David?"

Michal sat up in bed and stretched, arching her back as the covers slipped from her body. David felt his face flush.

"Yes, my love."

She smiled at him. "Today?"

He nodded. He had promised her he was done, promised to lay down his sword and pick up a shepherd's crook. He was done being Yahweh's tool, and today was the day he would solidify that promise. Saul had summoned him to play the lyre as soon as the sun set, and he planned to speak with him after, to request a permanent leave from battle.

"I will go to your father tonight." He slipped into bed and pulled her close. "But I have business at home first."

THE LATE AFTERNOON sky was overcast when David stepped into the training grounds, the familiar feel of the dirt beneath his sandals making him more than a little nostalgic. The thought that this may be his final time stepping onto these grounds tugged at his heart. The men all stopped their training, turned his way, and broke into spontaneous applause. Abishai stood at their head. He clapped along with them, but his face was firm and knowing. He eventually stepped forward.

"All right, all right," Abishai said, looking back to the men. "Back to work. The sun is still up."

There was a mixture of laughing and groaning, and soon the sounds of training returned. David and Abishai turned away from the training grounds.

"Have you come to say goodbye?" Abishai asked, his voice cold.

"Something like that," David said. He felt a long sigh escape his lips. He had not been looking forward to this. Abishai had been faithful for years, loyal beyond reason, and now David was quitting. This was a conversation David had been avoiding since his return to Gibeah. *Since the last time we spoke…*

"I'm sorry, Abishai."

"Hmph. I bet." Abishai looked back up toward David's balcony. David followed his gaze and saw Michal, wrapped in a blanket and watching the two of them. "Not as much as you should be. Explain to me again why you're abandoning your men?"

"Abandoning them? How many have died because of me and my calling? And I do not even know what I am called to do. It seems I am called to lead people to the grave. They are the ones abandoned, Abishai. Not the living."

He nearly laughed. "Is that your justification? That's your

reasoning? That men will die? They have died since Cain slew Abel. Yet without your leadership, *more* will die."

"No more men will die because of what Yahweh asks me to do."

"Plenty *will* die because you do not do what he asks of you."

"That's not fair."

"Not fair?" He pointed back into the crowd of training soldiers. "How about leading these men, training and fighting with them for years, giving them a purpose, something to fight *for*, and then just leaving because you got hurt." He reached out and swatted David in his wound. "And it isn't even that bad."

"It's not my wound that finally beat me. It was the look on Ira's face as he died. He thought—"

"I know. You've mentioned it. He thought you were something you're not. Yet what if he was right?"

David was silent.

"And what about all the others? I've seen dozens of friends dead, hundreds maimed. Do they not matter to you?"

This isn't going well.

"What can I say? What can I do, Abishai?"

He scoffed. "What *can* you do? If you came down here for my blessing, you'll not get it."

"Abishai…"

"I've thought a lot about you these last six months. And I've finally figured it out. You're quitting not because of your wound or Ira or any of the other men who have died by following you. You're quitting because it finally got hard. You've lived a blessed life these last five years, fulfilling Yahweh's calling. You've won battle after battle, received blessing after blessing. Now, Abigail is off with Nabal, and you are forced into Saul's family. You were wounded, lost your first battle. Some of your men died, one of them in your own hands and by his own sword. Life is finally hard. Is it bad? Yes. Tragic? Yes. But shall we accept the good from Yahweh and not trouble? You are abandoning your calling for the sake of an easy life. And that is not something I ever thought to see. For that, you'll not get my blessing. You will always have my love, as hard as it hurts to give, but not my blessing. Go. Talk to the king. Live a good life, an *easy* life." He turned away from David and stepped back toward the men—*his* men, now. "I'll take care of them."

David watched him leave, his heart aching as if he'd been pierced anew. It took all he had not to stop him, not to join back in with the training. Perhaps Abishai was right, but had he not earned an easy life? Had he not given enough in service of Yahweh?

He let out another long sigh and then turned and left the courtyard, his lyre at his hip where a sword should be.

THUNDER ROLLED in the distance as David climbed the palace steps. Inside, the hall had changed little in the time he'd been absent. The acacia pillars still stood tall, the high windows still let in the golden evening light. It all felt smaller to David somehow, less impressive than it had before.

The only noticeable difference was its emptiness. Saul sat on the throne, twirling his spear as he always did, and Benyamin stood a step behind. The only other body was Rimmon, standing beside the throne with his hands clasped behind his back. The three of them watched as David walked the carpet and stopped a dozen paces before the throne. He bowed low.

"My king."

There was a long silence as David stared at the ground,

waiting for Saul to bid him rise. It felt an eternity before he spoke.

"Rise, David."

When he did, he noticed a fire in Saul's eyes that he had not seen before, a determined look that had long been absent from the king.

He gripped his lyre tighter, wishing for some reason he had his sword. "Is there something you wish to hear, my king?"

Saul's eyes narrowed, and his jaw worked behind tight lips. "You have yet to disappoint, my son. Play what you will." His voice was strained as if his mouth had difficulty making the words.

David drew a breath and began to pluck at the lyre. He found a gentle and familiar melody and let his hands work from memory over the strings. As he listened to the music, he closed his eyes and let the words come to him as they always had.

Yet he had no words. Nothing came. He had always found singing Yahweh's praises to be easy. Words just flowed from his mouth as if put there by another.

They were *put there by another*, he thought. *But I sent him away...*

He opened his eyes and realized he had stopped playing. The three men were staring at him with expectant looks, yet he only stared back.

I quit...why would he give me words to sing?

David cleared his throat and began to pluck at the strings again, yet this time he even had trouble finding a rhythm. He squeezed his eyes shut and concentrated, found himself barely able to strum a coherent flow of notes. And finally, he felt Yahweh put words into his mouth.

I am like the deaf, who cannot hear, like the mute, who cannot speak; I have become like one who does not hear, whose mouth can offer no reply. LORD, I wait for you; you will answer, Lord my God. For I am about to fall, and my pain is ever with me. I confess my iniquity; I am troubled by my sin. LORD, do not forsake me; do not be far from me, my God. Come quickly to help me, my Lord and my Savior!

THE LYRE STRUCK off key as he abruptly stopped playing on the final word. He opened his eyes and found Saul's gaze had changed from expectant to barely concealed anger.

"Why did you choose those words?"

He looked again to the king. "I...I do not know, my king."

Saul's lips twitched. "Play something else."

David nodded and gripped his lyre more firmly. His fingers struggled to find the strings. He drew a breath and closed his eyes. His hands ached, twitching awkwardly as they worked at the lyre, struggling again to find something. To be able—

Hands pushed him down, and David landed face first on the woolen carpet. He opened his eyes and looked back, tried to find his assailant, but there was no one behind him. He looked at the king and saw him standing, Rimmon and Benyamin both tense at his side. Yet something else was different, something missing.

His spear.

Saul's spear was gone. David turned and looked behind him again, this time noticing the spear sticking up from the floor only a few paces behind him.

He tried to kill me!

He rose and looked again toward the king. Saul turned to Benyamin. "Spear!"

His armor-bearer moved slowly but did not deny the king a

weapon. David shuffled back, still only dimly aware of the danger. "M-my king…"

"Silence!" Saul leaped from the throne and threw his new weapon. David ducked, and the spear lodged itself in the wall behind him. He looked one final time at Saul, who was now jerking awkwardly at the sword on his hip, struggling for some reason to draw it from its scabbard. Then he turned and fled the hall as Saul shouted madly behind him.

SAUL

"SPEAR!"

Benyamin hesitated for a fraction of a second before handing over his weapon. Saul snatched it up, silently swearing to kill his armor-bearer if David escaped because of that small delay.

"M-my king," David stuttered, the confused look on his face only serving to heighten Saul's burning rage.

"Silence!" He leaped from the throne—Benyamin's spear feeling foreign in his hands—and hurled the weapon. David ducked, and the spear lodged into the wall. He growled, reached for his sword, and felt a hand clamp down on his wrist. "Release me," he shouted, looking down to see no one holding him. His gaze darted around, trying and failing to find whatever was holding his wrist firmly in place. He jerked on his sword again, the unseen hand on his wrist, refusing to let go. "Wh-what is this!? Who is that?"

The grip on his wrist released, and his sword came scraping free, but when he turned back toward David, he found his hall empty and his door hanging open. He let out a long, growling shout and threw his sword across the hall. It spiraled end over end, eventually landing on his new carpet and tearing a long gash in the fabric.

He spun on Rimmon. "Which one of you did it?" He glared from Rimmon to Benyamin and back to Rimmon again. "Which one!?"

"My king?"

"He knew! He knew I was going to strike!"

Rimmon exchanged a glance with Benyamin.

"We are your most loyal, chosen by you to be here. Why would we warn him?"

"I don't know!" Saul was furious. He stormed across the hall and ripped his sword from the carpet. "But he knew! You saw him. His eyes were closed, yet he dropped just as I threw." He let out another low, rumbling growl as if he were a fearsome lion and not a scared fox. The noise only served to anger him more, and he felt his arm swinging, slicing and tearing further into the already ruined carpet.

Rimmon shuffled forward. "He…he looked as if he fell. As if he was pushed."

Saul knew what he was insinuating, and he didn't like it. He spun, his sword flailing out dangerously close to Rimmon, yet he didn't care. He no longer cared who died, what damage he did. All he felt was pulsing anger, throbbing hate. David was still alive and likely fleeing at this very moment.

Fleeing home…

The red faded from Saul's vision—not entirely, but enough —and he felt his senses return. "Doeg!"

The door behind his throne creaked open, and the massive Edomite entered. He sauntered around the throne and stopped before Saul. "You called?"

"Gather men," Saul said. "Take a dozen. No, two dozen. Go to David's house. He will not leave without seeing Michal."

"What of your daughter?"

Saul looked around the room, saw genuine concern on the faces of Rimmon and Benyamin.

Cowards. Afraid to do what must be done. These are my closest allies? These jackals? He looked at Doeg, not an ounce of care on his face. *This is a man I can trust.*

"She will choose her side. If she chooses right, then she will live."

Doeg gave a grunt of approval. "And if she chooses wrong?"

Saul felt no remorse. He was done letting his family slow him down. "Then do what you must. David must die."

33

DAVID

THE TRAINING GROUNDS were empty as David rushed through them, his sandals kicking up dirt and sand that caught on the rising wind and flew off into the night. He sprinted across the grounds and up the stairwell, kicked the door open, and stormed across the room to the chest in the corner. He dug through it, tossing aside ceremonial clothing and blankets, clay pots, and worn sandals.

"What are you doing?"

He glanced over his shoulder and noticed Michal for the first time. Her face was a mixture of mild irritation and barely concealed worry. He dropped a sandal and stood. "Your father," he said, still out of breath. "He tried to kill me."

The irritation became annoyance as the worry melted away. "Kill you? Really?" She sighed and walked over to the chest, closing the lid and frowning. "What happened, David? Where is your lyre?"

She doesn't believe me.

"I left it," he said. "When he tried to *kill me*."

She sat down on top of the chest and frowned. "What happened?"

He nudged her off the chest. "What do you mean, 'what happened?' He. Tried. To kill me!"

She watched him in silence as he dug back into the chest, finally coming out with his leather vest and battle sandals.

She looked at his gear and almost smirked. "You're going to go fight him?"

The thought had not even entered his mind. But he could, couldn't he? He could kill Saul and be rid of his jealousy forever. But quick as the thought came, he pushed it aside. "No. I'm going to run."

She snorted a laugh. "You're going to run? Where?"

"I don't know!"

She frowned as a moment of silence hung in the air. "Have you gone mad, David?"

He slammed the lid of the chest down. "He tried to *kill me!* Why will you not listen?"

A flash of anger passed over her face, and she opened her mouth to respond when the sound of voices came from outside the window. Together they stepped to the balcony, David staying low as he looked down into the training grounds. Doeg entered first. He held an unsheathed sword in his hand, the bronze glinting off the full moon. Behind him came a group of men, at least ten in total, several carrying torches.

He grabbed Michal's arm and pulled her back inside. "Do you see?"

The disbelief of a moment before was replaced with genuine worry for the first time since he had come home. "But…why…I don't…"

David took her hands in his. "He is a jealous man. He has hated me for a long time."

She just stared back at him, her face a blank mask. "I don't…" She shook her head clear and met his gaze. "Why are you running?"

"What?"

262 | BRYAN R. SAYE

"Why run," she repeated. "Why not fight?"

"There are at least ten of them, Michal. Probably more."

"I don't mean them. Run now, of course. But why not return to the palace under cover of night."

David felt his heart clutch in his throat. "And do what," he asked, hoping she would not say what he knew was coming.

"Kill him," she said without the slightest hesitation. "The people no longer support him. He is aging, failing as a king. Kill him."

The words shocked him, despite the fact that he'd had the very same thought, even if only briefly. Yet Saul was Michal's father. For David to think it was one thing, but her... Perhaps Michal had not been Yahweh's parting gift as he had thought.

"You want me to kill your father?"

"I want you to not run."

He shook his head in dismay. "I...I can't believe you would ask me to harm your father."

Her face went hard for the briefest of moments, a stunning reflection of the anger and heartlessness he had seen only an hour before on the king's face. Then she melted into fear and collapsed onto the floor, David only just catching her. They both knelt on the carpet as her head fell into his chest. "I don't want you to leave," she said, her voice cracking, tears wetting his tunic.

Her pleas softened his heart, if only just, but he knew he could not slay Saul. Michal's father or not, he was the chosen king of Israel. Turning his back on Yahweh's calling was one thing; killing Yahweh's anointed was another entirely.

"I can't do it. I can't kill Yahweh's chosen."

"I don't care about that. I don't care who is king and who is not, who Yahweh anoints and who he does not. I want *you*, David."

He had a sudden thought, and the words were coming before he could stop them. "Come with me."

She looked up, wet eyes wide. "Come with you?"

He nodded. "Run away with me."

"Where?"

He shrugged and almost smiled. He was excited now, excited at the thought of leaving all this behind and starting over with Michal. "I don't care. I can hunt, fish, shepherd. I can defend us. We can go anywhere you want. Judah, Gilead… Damascus, even."

"Damascus? Leave Israel?"

"Why not? Yahweh has abandoned me." *Not entirely true.* "His anointed hunts me. Let's leave. Start over. Just us." He smiled wider and took her hands in his. "We can make a life away from all this, Michal."

The corner of her mouth moved in the hint of a smile, and his heart raced. He could already see their home, built on the edge of a hill far away, a few sheep grazing in the field below. They would be poor, but he had grown up that way. All she had to do was say yes, and he would fight through a hundred men to secure their safety. All she had—

"I can't."

His smile vanished as if she'd slapped it away. She slowly pulled her hands from his.

"I'm sorry," she said. "I can't. I can't leave Israel. I can't live in hiding."

He felt hot tears and blinked them away. *Very well.* "I can't stay here, and I can't harm him. I have to run."

"I won't stop you."

There was a loud knock on the door, and David was on his feet. He looked at the door, watched it shudder as another loud knock sounded. His eyes fell to Michal. She was still kneeling on the ground.

Doeg's voice came from the other side of the door. "Michal! Open the door!"

She wiped a tear. "Go, David. Run. I will buy you time."

He knelt and pulled her tight.

"I'm sorry," she whispered.

There was another series of hard knocks. "Michal!"

David scooped up his vest and dashed onto the balcony, slipping it on as he moved. The colonnade ran along the edges of the training grounds, its roof level with the balcony floor. He stayed low and stepped to the railing, then leaned out to look down into the grounds. There were a pair of men below, torches in hand, eyes scanning the roof of the colonnade. He gripped the railing, preparing to jump over and make a run for it.

My sword!

He looked back into the home just as the door shuddered open and Doeg forced his way inside. Michal was lying on the floor where he had left her, new tears streaming down her face. David slipped to the edge of the balcony, pressed himself up against the wall and listened.

"Where is he, Michal?"

"He left," she said, sobbing louder now. "He is gone…"

"Where? When?"

There was near silence, Michal's fresh sobs the only noise.

"Where, Michal?"

"How should I know?"

David leaned forward and looked down into the training grounds again. The two men now had their backs to the balcony and were searching the opposite side. A loud smack came from inside, followed by the sound of Michal crying. David's hands clenched into fists. He edged back to the doorway, ready to leap back inside.

Then the voice, which had been silent for six months, spoke.

Run, David.

He froze.

You would command me? Here? Now?

"Where is he?!"

"I don't know!" More crying.

Run!

The voice was more forceful than it had ever been. He felt everything in him pulling him back inside his home, back to his wife. He knew he needed to run, but his feet would not take him.

"I tried to stop him, tried to make him stay," she shouted from inside. "But he said, 'Let me get away. Why should I kill you?'"

Doeg laughed at that. "He is more like me than he will admit."

GO!

His feet finally unstuck, and he stepped away from the open doorway. He leaped the railing, landing softly on the mud-brick roof of the colonnade. Shouts came from the courtyard, and he knew he was spotted. Forgetting silence, he broke into a sprint and jumped from the corner of the colonnade. Two more men were waiting for him, torches and swords in their hands.

David was on them before they could make a noise, jabbing one of them in the throat with the edge of his hand. He started to crumble, and David snatched the torch from his hand, deflecting a blow from the second man before stabbing him in the face with the torch. The man dropped his weapon and clutched at his face, his blood-curdling scream echoing into the night. David felt a moment of remorse for harming him, then remember that these were Doeg's men and not soldiers of Israel.

The two men from the training grounds stormed through the archway and charged him. David reached for one of the fallen men's swords when the twang of a bow sounded. An arrow skittered near his hand. He looked back to the colonnade he had just leaped from and saw a pair of archers standing on his balcony. Doeg was with them, his grip firm on Michal's bicep as she was dragged along. It was a sight that would be etched into his mind for the rest of his days: Doeg gripping her arm, her tear-streaked face clear in the torchlight, the lopsided, casual smile on his face.

I'm going to kill him, he thought.

Another arrowed flittered overhead, passing close enough for him to feel the breeze, and then the two men from the training grounds were on him. They tried to surround him, attempting to corral him back toward the training grounds and closer to the archers. David chose one and rushed, ducking a strike to come up inside his guard. His head smashed into the man's face with a sickening crunch. He grabbed the man's sword arm and twisted it back around, slicing downward and opening his midsection. Using the man's own arm, he lifted and parried the blow from the other man. The impact knocked the sword from the dying man's grip. He snatched it out of the air and brought it in a quick upward jab that sliced through the second man's ribs. Thick blood oozed out over the blade and soaked his hand up to the wrist. He released the hilt, leaving the sword sticking from the man's chest.

He looked back again at his balcony and saw the archers fire another pair of arrows that went far wide. Doeg frowned and disappeared inside with Michal. Every urge within David pulled him back toward his home, back to save his wife from Doeg's grip. There were shouts, and several more men ran from the training grounds. David glanced one last time at his now-empty balcony and then turned and ran into the night.

34

SAUL

THE MAN LAY STILL in the dirt, his bloodied face covered in cloth, chest rising and falling with the steadiness of sleep. Beside him were two more, one with his insides spread out around him and the other lying motionless in a pool of blood. Sitting in the dirt, not a dozen paces away, was the only conscious one of them, his own hands around a darkening bruise at his throat. Two guttered torches and a trio of short swords were scattered around them. Saul knelt and picked up one of the blades.

"Tell me again," Saul said, his voice calm and even and emotionless despite the rage roiling underneath. He turned to the man clutching his throat. "Tell me again what happened."

The man massaged his wounded throat. "He leaped from the roof," he said, his voice just above a whisper. "Chopped me here." He lifted his head and showed the bruise more clearly. It had spread in the few moments Saul had been here. "Snatched my torch and burned Abarron." He pointed to his sleeping friend. "Saw a bit of the fight afterward, but I was barely conscious."

Saul looked down at the blade in his own hand. The blade

was from Edom, just like the men around him. He was beginning to trust less in their skill, though he doubted his own soldiers would have fared much better against David.

"You let my enemy escape," he said. There were footsteps behind him and then the heavy shadow of Doeg. "You let the one who seeks the throne of Israel flee." He jerked forward and put the sword through the wounded man's throat, slicing off a pair of fingers from the hand that had been clutching it. He gurgled once, eyes wide in shock, and then fell backward into the dirt.

"You killed one of my men."

Saul looked and saw Doeg standing beside him, his hand firm on Michal's arm. His daughter's bloodshot eyes were wide, tearstains running down her cheeks.

"David killed two." Saul turned and looked at the man lying with the cloth over his burned face, watched his chest rise and fall. Before he knew what he was doing, his sword was moving, slicing at the sleeping man's face and chest; blood sprayed into the air in crimson arcs. The man jerked a handful of times and then went still, yet Saul hacked at the corpse until his arm grew weary. He finally stopped, his chest heaving, sucking in deep, ragged breaths, blood running down his face and chest like water. He stabbed down, piercing the sword through the man's ruined chest, and left it shuddering like a planted flag.

Doeg just shrugged. "I have others." He jerked Michal forward, and she would have fallen to the ground in front of Saul if Doeg had not been holding her so firmly. "Your daughter."

She looked around her, at the death that he had just brought, the death her husband had caused not long before. Her face was white as a lamb's wool. She finally looked up and into his eyes. Through the despair and horror, through the shock and dismay, Saul could see it. She had been his daughter long enough for him to see through whatever emotions were on the surface. She had let David flee, had probably encouraged it.

He looked at Doeg. "Leave us."

He released her arm. Michal fell the rest of the way to the dirt. She landed in the pooling blood of the men he had just murdered, whimpering and scooting away until she was nearly on top of Saul's feet.

"You let him go."

She looked up at him, fresh tears coming. "He…I… You…" She looked again at the death. "You murdered them…"

"Michal. Look at me."

She continued to sob, her head dropping into her hands. "You…you killed them…"

"Now!"

Her head jerked up, her red eyes leaking tears, and her face distorted by a cluster of emotions: pain and sadness and guilt and anger. "You murdered them! And you would have murdered David."

Saul knelt, eyes now level with his daughter's. "He is an enemy."

"Then why would you wed me to him," she asked, sobbing between words. "Why would you let me love him?"

He scoffed but said nothing.

"And now he's gone," she went on. "You gave me to him, and now you've taken him from me." She wiped her eyes. "Why do you hate me?"

His hand jerked out and cracked across her face before he could stop it. He did not even know if he would have stopped it if he could. Michal fell sideways back into the pooling blood, her white sleeping gown now completely covered in the gore. She didn't seem to care, only cradled her face in her hands and wept.

"You took him——"

"You're weak, daughter. Pathetic." He stood. "I'll find you a stronger husband."

Doeg was waiting not far off. He fell into step beside Saul, and the two took to the stairs leading up to David's home.

"I've already got scouts following him," Doeg said. "If you'll give me more men, we can pounce as soon as he stops."

"You can have them. Whatever you need, however many. The son of Jesse must die."

35

DAVID

DAVID KNELT at the foot of the acacia, his rapid breaths ragged in his throat. Sweat poured down his face and chest, soaking his tunic against his skin. His head was swimming as he tried to digest all that had happened. The scenes of the night replayed over and over in his mind. He could still see Doeg holding Michal's arm, gripping her and smiling down at him.

He looked to the east and saw the walls of Gibeah in the distance, saw his life as it had been. The dark thunderclouds that hung over the city had not yet reached the countryside where David was. His life in Gibeah was over, snatched away in a single night. He could not return to Gibeah, to Saul or his wife. Only death would meet him within those walls.

For nearly six years, he had followed Yahweh, had obeyed every command, every instruction. And he had been blessed for it. Yet he had refused Yahweh once, refused to keep fighting, refused to keep letting people die for him. And for that, Yahweh had taken everything. First Abigail, then Ira and his men. Last night he'd taken the remnants that David had tried to salvage.

Why are you doing this? What do you want of me?

The voice was silent.

Tell me why? Please!

Silence.

David stood and looked up at the sky. "What do you want from me!? Have I not given enough?!"

His only answer was a flash of lightning from within the storm clouds and the rolling thunder that reached him moments later.

"Why are you silent now when you have been with me so long?" He sat back against the trunk of the acacia, already knowing the answer to that question.

Because I told you I was done.

"I don't know what to do..."

Yet he did. There was still one place he could go, one person who was beyond Saul's reach. It was not Ahimelech; Saul could find him there. It was not Abishai or Jonathan; both men lived in Gibeah. Not even his father. Saul would check there, would kill his entire family if he found David had hidden among them. There was only one man in all Israel who did not fear Saul.

Samuel.

He stared one final time at Gibeah and sighed.

"To Ramah, then."

THE WIDE, low valley of Ramah stretched out before him, a complex of houses and buildings clustered in its center. The fields around the complex were barren of crops and instead filled with flocks of sheep. It was midday—two days since he had fled Gibeah—and the southern wind brought with it the familiar scent of a shepherd's work.

David inhaled the clear air and began to walk into the valley. A shallow creek followed him down, bubbling its way toward what looked like the heart of the complex. He passed a handful of sheep and a pair of shepherds, their watchful eyes never leaving David.

An old man was waiting for him at the complex's outer edge, and David stopped before him. The man was ragged, his cloak stained and worn and faded, his hair thin and patchy, the skin underneath spotted and leathery. His thin lips were pressed together in a frown, and the skin on his face seemed to struggle to remain attached to his skull. Yet there was a fire in his eyes, an awareness that seemed unnatural for the man's age.

He leaned on his cane and smiled, and David found a familiarity he could not recognize.

"I have been waiting a long time for this," the old man said. "Since I last saw you."

A flash of realization came. "Samuel?"

He nodded. Turning, he gestured into the complex. "Would you join me? I would prefer you were sitting when you heard the news."

News?

Without waiting for an answer, Samuel began to walk into the complex of houses, navigating narrow paths and alleyways until he came to a simple home with a courtyard. A pair of old wooden stools and a small table sat under a cloth tarp, and David was instantly reminded of Ahimelech's home. Two clay cups and a wineskin were already set on the table as if he was expected.

"Shall we sit?"

David nodded and wordlessly helped Samuel onto a stool before taking his own seat. For a long moment, neither spoke. Samuel stared expectantly at David.

Finally Samuel spoke. "Would you pour the wine?"

David looked at the wine and back to the prophet. "Of course."

He lifted the skin and filled both cups, then handed one to

Samuel. The old man sipped at his cup and smiled anew. "I love a good cup of wine." He took another sip. "It soothes the bones, calms an old man's nerves. Do you like wine, David?"

He took a cautious sip. "At times."

Samuel took another long drink and then held the cup in both hands at his lap. "That's good wine." He stared down the pathways they had come through, eyes distant as if he were remembering something.

David glanced back, followed his gaze, found nothing worth staring at, and then looked again at Samuel. He opened his mouth to speak, found he had nothing to say, and took another sip of his wine. They sat for another long while in silence.

"When I was younger, a boy," Samuel said suddenly, eyes coming into focus and looking at David with that striking awareness he'd noticed before. "I heard a voice in the night. 'Samuel, Samuel,' it said. I thought it was my guardian, Eli, and so I went to him. 'Here I am,' I said. He sent me back to bed, telling me he had not called me. Yet I heard the voice again and so returned to Eli. Again, he sent me back to bed. Three times I heard the voice, and three times I ran to Eli, only to be sent away each time."

David sipped his wine and continued staring at the old prophet. He had become accustomed to Ahimelech's teachings, and this sort of meandering story no longer bothered him. He felt confident Samuel would come to a point eventually.

"When I finally learned it was Yahweh and not Eli, I stopped and listened." He drew a breath, his smile breaking. "And he told me terrible things, things I had long known yet ignored fiercely. How Eli and his sons had soiled the tabernacle, how they had used the Ark of the Covenant as a totem, a charm. Something to be bargained with, to be used. Carried into battle as if the Ark itself were Yahweh and not just his dwelling. He told me how they would die." He swallowed hard. "And he continues to speak to me to this day. And I have not let a single word fall to the ground."

David had spent a great deal of time in the presence of Ahimelech and other priests and Levites, and so he knew the story of Samuel well. Yet he also knew it was often best to let an elder speak, to let him tell the story he is looking to tell.

"What happened," David asked. "To Eli and his sons?"

Samuel frowned. "Come now, David. You are not that young, and it was not so long ago."

David gave a weak smile. "Eli's sons were killed by the Philistines at Shiloh. When Eli heard the news, he fell and died as well, for he was an old man."

"See? There is no need to play games with me, David. Speak your mind."

"Very well. Then I am wondering what the point of this story is."

"The point, David, is that I took Eli's place. I was chosen to lead Israel due to the sins of Eli, whom Yahweh *himself* put in place. I did not want it, was not ready. But Israel needs a leader, David, one who is righteous."

"And I am still wondering about the point of this story. You led Israel well, for many years, until Yahweh appointed Saul as king."

"But now Yahweh is choosing a new king. Just as the sins of Eli forced me to lead, the sins of Saul will force another to lead in his stead."

The prophet fell silent, waiting for the words to take on meaning. David just stared back, confused, until suddenly, like a flash of lightning, he understood.

"Me?"

"You."

"*Me?*"

Samuel laughed. "Yes, David. You. You will be the next king of Israel."

The courtyard began to spin. The cup of wine fell from his hands and spilled onto the sand. He paid no mind to the wine, Samuel's words still ringing in his head. "But…but why?"

"Must you really ask?" Samuel's voice seemed distant as if coming through water. "Have you not already seen it in the dedication of your men, the baseless jealousy of Saul, your victory in battle? Everything you touch succeeds. Everything you do, you do well. And for Yahweh."

David could not believe the words. He put his hands on the small table as if it would help steady the spinning world around him. "I have done well?" Even his own words sounded distant. He physically shook his head clear, though it helped little. "There are many dead men of Israel who would speak differently if they still drew breath."

"Men will die, David. Have died since Cain slew Abel, as Abishai so eloquently put it."

David drew a deep breath and held it, and the world spun a bit less. "But I can't do it." His voice was barely above a whisper. The spinning world around him came to an abrupt halt that nearly knocked him from his chair. He looked at the prophet, feeling nauseous now that the world had stopped. "I'm not…I'm not strong enough."

"I know."

David scoffed, tears at the edge of his eyes. This conversation was getting more ludicrous with every word spoken.

"Do you think you have come so far because of your strength? Do you think yourself so great a warrior?"

He looked down at his scarred and calloused hands and said nothing. He didn't need to; both he and Samuel knew the answer to the question.

Yahweh has long guided my hands in battle.

"Your strength lies in your acknowledgment of weakness,

THE SHEPHERD AND THE KING | 277

that you *know* you are not strong enough. Neither am I. *He* is, though. *He* will be strong enough for both of you. Lean on Yahweh, David. Lean on him in life as you do in battle."

"But...but I have sent him away."

This time Samuel laughed in earnest, loud and long. "One does not send Yahweh away."

David looked again at his shaking hands.

Why? Why me?

I need a shepherd, David.

I was one.

But now it is my *sheep you must tend.*

"I don't...I can't..."

"Calm, David. Calm. Yahweh does not make mistakes. You must trust him."

"I did. I trusted him for a long time, and it did not end well. And now...king? Me?"

"You are fearfully and wonderfully made, David. Who else?"

David let out a long breath, and his shaking hands seemed to steady. He didn't know what to think, how to feel. The last few days had been a whirlwind, to say nothing of the months leading up to them. He felt exhausted, stretched beyond measure.

Samuel seemed to sense his thoughts. "I know you are weary, tired, but you cannot rest yet. You have much still to do, whether you believe Yahweh's word or not. Saul is coming, and will reach us within the hour. And he will not stop coming until one of you is dead."

He tensed, realizing for perhaps the first time that Saul would continue to hunt him. "I need a sword."

"No, you do not." Samuel's voice left no room for doubt. "Not yet, at least."

"When?"

"When you have given thought to whom you would use it

on. I knew of Eli's coming fate for years. Vengeance and justice are not ours to give. Eli did not sin against me, for man does not sin against man. Eli sinned against Yahweh, and the punishment is his to give. You shall not lay a hand on his anointed. He will take care of Saul in his own time."

"Then what would you suggest?"

"I can give you food and supplies. You should make ready to leave immediately, though you need not fear. Saul may be here, but he will be…delayed in reaching the city."

"Delayed?"

He smiled. "Delayed."

"How did he find me?"

"His Edomite slave had someone follow you from your home." He paused. "Saul knows, David. He knows you are to replace him as king."

"Then he must believe it more than I."

"He has believed it for quite some time." Samuel almost smiled. "Probably since the time I told him as much."

"What do I do? Where do I go from here?"

"That I can only guess at, I am afraid. I would run, were I you. Flee to the desert strongholds in the hills of Ziph. Seek the wilderness of En-Gedi, the caves of Adullam. You have distant relatives in Moab. There are many places Saul cannot take an army."

"Your advice is to run?"

"What is to be gained by facing him?"

"I can't just run. What of Michal? Of Abishai?"

"What of them?"

"I…I don't know. I wish to see them again, to explain this to them."

Samuel sighed. "Do what you think is best. But you *must* live. For the sake of Israel, you must live."

A man in a worn robe sprinted into Samuel's courtyard,

then doubled over, sucking in heavy breaths. "Saul's men... there are...hundreds...on the road."

David rose, his hand going reflexively to his sword and finding nothing.

"Calm, David." Samuel grunted as he stood. "As I said, I will delay them. Gather what you need and go."

"You will face Saul's men? Alone?"

He smiled. "You are not the only one who fights for the Living God of Israel. We merely have different weapons."

36

SAUL

SAUL SAT atop his horse and stared down at the small village, watched two hundred of Doeg's men marching through the shepherds' fields leading up to it. Doeg himself was standing beside him, his eyes on his men as they moved to surround the city. Another two hundred men were gathered behind them. The shepherds had long cleared the fields, guiding what sheep they could away from what they perceived would be an upcoming slaughter.

How did I not know he would flee here? That he would come to Ramah, back to Samuel?

"David knows we are here," Saul said, his eyes on the city. From a distance, he could see men fleeing the city in every direction, all of them running into the waiting arms of Doeg's men.

Men I have given him. Men from my personal guard. Men I trust with my life.

"He will get nowhere."

"I hope not." He looked at Doeg. "For your sake."

The Edomite only laughed. "I should tell you, now that we are alone, I cannot be threatened." He returned Saul's gaze.

His eyes were like ice, cold and empty. "I have been told by the gods how my life ends. Anat and Baal, El and Dagon. They speak to me. My life does not end today." He snorted another laugh and looked back at Ramah. "And it does not happen by your hand."

Saul felt his anger subside and fear take its place. "I thought you served no god?"

"I do not. They serve me."

"And my god speaks to you?"

Doeg smiled at that. "He is the only one who is silent. Often I wonder if he has any real power."

"And do you know by whose hand you will die?"

Doeg's eyes went distant for a moment. "I know not his name. I was told the man who will end me will be a great man, his name echoing among the greatest the world has ever seen. His house and kingdom shall endure forever." He grinned that haughty grin that Saul hated so much. "Only such a man can defeat me. Until I meet this man, I fear nothing."

"How do you know I am not that man," Saul asked.

Doeg looked at him and laughed. "I think not."

Despite the insult, Saul had no more words and only turned back to Ramah. All two hundred of his men were now on their knees, faces and arms lifted to the heavens.

"What is this," Doeg muttered, taking a handful of paces forward. "Why have they stopped?"

"Samuel." Saul dismounted and stepped forward. Standing at the entrance to Ramah, staff in hand, was an old man. He could see his face, could see his eyes locked on Saul's. "Samuel is stopping them."

"They stop for an old man?"

"You wonder about Yahweh's power, Edomite. Here it is." Saul felt his hands tremble, a new fear taking him. "Your foreign gods may serve you, but Yahweh serves no man. We will not see David today."

Doeg grunted. "We shall see."

He turned and signaled to the men still behind him. They quickly joined Doeg and began moving as the previous men had to surround the city. On the far said, Saul could see groups of shepherds escaping to the north, passing through the kneeling warriors.

David is gone...

Doeg's new group slowed as they neared Ramah and soon halted entirely. Doeg himself stopped a few paces from Samuel. They stood in silence, eyeing one another. Saul could see the glint of Doeg's drawn sword, could see the steadiness of Samuel's stance. Neither backed down, and time seemed to stop as Saul wished with all his might that Doeg would strike down the old man.

Then Doeg's sword fell, and he was kneeling, face and arms raised to the heavens. As one, the rest of his men followed suit, and now four hundred men stood around Ramah. He could hear the steady hum of their chanting from a distance, though the words escaped him.

There is no point in delaying this.

Saul stepped out into the shepherds' fields, walked along the creek's edge, and followed it to Ramah. As he neared the kneeling men, he could make out their words, four hundred of them chanting the same thing.

"Blessed are those whose ways are blameless, who walk according to the law of the Lord," they said together, their voices in perfect harmony, rising in steady praise.

Saul ignored them, weaving his way around them until he could see Samuel clearly. He stepped around a small pond, more puddle than anything, and onto the path that led into Ramah.

"Blessed are those who keep his statutes and seek him with all their heart," the chanting continued.

Samuel was smiling at him, a sad smile that spoke to Saul's

heart. He felt the fear return at the sight of his old adviser, felt a deep sorrow as he thought of the times when he was given the word of Yahweh, when he had been on the righteous path. Samuel's gaze was far too knowing for Saul's liking.

He stopped in front of Samuel, Doeg kneeling beside them.

"Shalom, Saul," Samuel said.

"Where is he?"

"Where is who?"

"You know."

Around them, the chanting grew louder, Doeg's voice resounding above the rest. "Blessed are those that walk in your ways."

"Why do you chase him?" Samuel asked.

"You know the answer to that."

The prophet gestured to those around them. "Can a man stop the Living God of Israel?"

"He can try."

Doeg's voice grew louder still. "You have given us your laws that are to be fully obeyed."

Despite every effort not to, Saul felt himself drop to his knees.

Samuel frowned. "A man can only fall on his knees in worship before God Most High."

Saul's arms rose to the heavens, and his gaze followed. He felt himself speaking. "Oh, that I had been committed to your ways, Yahweh! Then I would not be put to shame!"

He felt a presence on him like he had never felt before. Blinding light descended, though to Saul, it felt more like a shroud, like a shadow. It obscured his vision, burned his eyes. And yet they remained open. He knew it was Yahweh, knew it was the Living God of Israel descending to be with him.

And he rejected it with all his will.

Despite his inward rejection, he continued outwardly praising. "I will praise you with an upright heart!"

I will not.

"I will honor your righteous laws."

I will not!

"I will obey your decrees."

I WILL NOT!

"Do not utterly forsake me!"

He felt Yahweh's grip on his body release, and his arms sagged. His face turned to the ground.

He already has...I am utterly alone...

"You are not, Saul."

Samuel's voice. Saul lifted his head and saw the old prophet looking down on him.

"It is not too late."

Beside him, he heard Doeg continue to chant.

Samuel spoke softly, yet his voice carried over the noise. "Yahweh has chosen your replacement. Give him the crown; surrender to Yahweh's will."

Anger surged through Saul. "I do not care," he shouted, leaping back to his feet. "*I* am the king. *I* am the anointed one. If David wants the throne, he will have to take it with my blood."

Turning, Saul stormed away, the sound of continuous praise following him.

DAVID

Dᴀᴠɪᴅ sᴀᴛ in the shade of an oak, his back resting on the trunk and a handful of broken arrows scattered around him. He looked at the walls of Gibeah. He couldn't see the men on the wall, though he did see the random glint as the sun reflected off armor and spear tips. David felt fear at the sight of those walls.

Should I be here? What will Jonathan say?

David's gaze went from the city walls to the bale of hay just beyond the treeline. He could see Jonathan already firing his arrows, aiming for the hay and unaware that David was even in the woods. David watched and waited, counted the sixteen arrows. Once they had all been spent, he saw Jonathan sling his bow to his back and begin the long march to collect his ammunition.

David stepped from the shadows as Jonathan knelt to pluck his arrows from the hay. His friend paused. "David?" He dropped the arrows and walked around the hay. "David? Where have you been?"

Does he not know?

"At Ramah."

Jonathan's brow furrowed. "With Samuel? But…but why?"

"Have you spoken with Michal?"

He looked even more puzzled at the question. "Michal? Is she not with you?" He set the bow down against the hay. "What are you talking about?"

"Why would you think she is with me?"

Jonathan shook his head in confusion. "No one has seen her. Not since you disappeared near a week ago. What is going on?"

David drew a breath to steady himself, unsure how his longtime friend would take the news. "Your father is trying to kill me."

"I…no. No, he isn't."

"He is. He hurled a spear at me as I played the lyre, then sent Doeg to my home with a dozen men. He surrounded Ramah, tried to take it by force."

Jonathan shook his head, trying and failing to grasp what was being said. "No…he…he doesn't do anything without speaking to me, without taking counsel."

"Listen to me: there is but a step between me and death." He stepped forward, put a hand on his friend's shoulder. "Jonathan, tell me the truth. He gave this order before, didn't he? When I was sent to Beersheba?"

Pain appeared behind Jonathan's eyes, and David didn't need an answer. "I talked him out of it. I explained his mistake, explained that we cannot stop Yahweh. I…"

"Cannot stop Yahweh?"

Jonathan sighed. "He believes you are going to replace him as king."

David tensed. "And what do you believe?"

"I don't pretend to know Yahweh's mind. I am not Samuel. I am not Ahimelech." He paused. "I am not you."

"Me?"

He almost laughed. "You cannot pretend with me. I have

known you a long while." He stepped back and sat upon the bale of hay. "You hear his voice. Do you deny it?"

"I...I don't deny it."

"How long?"

"Since I was a child. Fifteen."

"And what does he say?"

David scoffed. "What he says is often confusing."

"Are you to replace my father?"

Here it is. The moment of truth. "I have been told as much."

Jonathan drew a long breath. "What do you need?"

David's heart clutched in his throat. What he had done to earn such friends was beyond him.

"You must speak to your father, hear it for yourself that he plans to kill me. Go and find him, tell him you saw me and let me return home to Bethlehem. Your father's reaction will be telling enough."

"And what of you?"

David looked around the field and back into the forest. "I will wait here for you, and we will see what Yahweh has in store for us."

SAUL

THE HORSE SWAYED beneath him as Saul rocked his way through the gates of Gibeah. There was no hero's welcome, no women or children heralding the king's return. Not a single person did more than step aside as he rode through the streets of his hometown. He felt as if he were nothing.

The streets would be filled if it were David returning.

The anger in him was reaching new intensity, had become so constant that he no longer remembered being at peace.

Not since David last played for me.

The thought only heightened the anger. *I do not need him.*

But he did, and he knew it. Israel needed him. Without David as king, Yahweh would not bless this land, would not guarantee them victory in battle.

I do not need him *either.*

And again, he knew he was lying to himself. But what else could he do?

Saul's palace rose before him, and he dismounted, barely noticing as his stablemaster took the reins and guided the horse away. He mounted the steps and entered his hall, found it packed as usual. Minor prophets—frauds, mostly—and village and tribal elders filled every cubit of space. Their conversations stopped momentarily as he entered, all eyes turning his way. Saul felt exposed, raw, in need of washing and a fresh change of clothes. Then their attention drifted away and returned to their conversations.

Jackals...

He passed through the hall and the back door leading to the palace corridors. He walked them in silence, the only noise that of his footsteps and those of Benyamin walking behind him. He found himself standing before a heavy cedar door, a recently added lock securing it from the outside.

"Key," he said, holding an open hand to Benyamin.

His armor-bearer produced a long copper key. He felt the heavy tumblers rattle as he slid it into the lock. A hard twist and he had the door open, revealing Ahinoam and Michal sitting on a bed across the room. His wife shot him a glare that would have cut to his heart if he could still feel it. Michal's eyes were red, her face pale and sunken.

"Leave us," he said, eyeing his wife.

"You will not—"

"Leave us!"

She stood and marched across the room. Her face was firm, challenging, and Saul nearly flinched.

"You will not order me. I am your wife, not a prisoner."

Saul drew a breath and looked back to Benyamin. "Take my *wife* to our quarters."

He stepped around Saul and started to take hold of Ahinoam's forearm. She jerked back and slapped him, and Benyamin froze in place. The red outline of her palm was already forming on his cheek.

"You will not touch me."

Benyamin looked at Saul, confused and unsure. He clearly did not want to hurt her. Saul spoke again, each word its own sentence. "Take her to my room."

Benyamin hesitated, and then his arm snaked out and latched onto her wrist, gentle but firm. She tried to wiggle away, but his grip was unrelenting.

"This will be easier on both of us if you cooperate," Benyamin said, his voice on the edge of pleading. "Please…"

"This will be easier if you let me go!"

Benyamin sighed and pulled her close, wrapping his arms around her and lifting her off her feet. "Come, my lady. I do not like this any more than you."

And then he was carrying her down the corridor, kicking and screaming the whole way. Saul shut the door, and the room fell into silence. He looked at Michal and felt a twist of sorrow in the parts of his heart that still worked. He pushed the feelings aside and stepped resolutely across the room.

"He is gone," he said, his voice hard. "Gone forever, now."

Michal choked down a sob. "You killed him?"

Saul barked a laugh though there was nothing funny. "Not yet. But we will. This is my land. I will find him, and he will die."

"He's done nothing wrong…"

"Has he not? How does no one see through him but me?"

She only sobbed more. "I love him…"

"Love?" Saul scoffed. "You're a child. You do not even know what love is," he said, his voice rising despite himself. "He *used* you, Michal. Used you to get to the throne."

"No…he loved me…"

Saul's fists clenched at his side. "He loves himself," he said. "He is a selfish, scheming jackal."

"How do you know? How do you know he seeks the throne?"

"Look at him, Michal. Do you not see his cunning? Do you not see his guile?" Saul was shouting now, his voice nearly breaking as his stress rose. *But she must see,* he thought. *She must understand that I've done this to protect her, to protect our rule.* "He has wed you to take my throne." The statement was far from the truth, but even Saul was beginning to believe it.

"You brought me to him…"

"He seeks my throne. This I know for sure."

"But how?"

"Samuel told me!" His voice echoed off the stone walls, bouncing back at him so that he could hear the words for himself. *Why did I say that…*

"Samuel? He…he told you David would seek the throne?"

He paused and drew a breath, steadying himself before he continued. "It matters not," he finally said. "I did not come here to speak of David but rather of you. I have found you a new husband."

Her eyes went wide. "Father, no…"

"Palti, son of Laish of Gallim," he said, turning toward the door.

"No…"

"He is a good man, Michal." Saul opened the door and stepped through. His daughter's face was buried in her bed, the sound of sobbing filling the room. "Better than you deserve."

The door shut with a heavy thud, and Saul secured the lock. He drew another breath and stood there by the door. His head sank, falling onto the heavy cedar with a crack. He felt weak, used, tired. *I cannot keep doing this…*

If you want to be king, you will.

He stood straight and stared at the door, stared at nothing. *Do I?*

He turned and started the short walk back to his quarters, thinking on that question the entire time. Ahinoam was sitting on his bed—what had once been their bed—with Benyamin standing by her. Saul tossed him the key.

"Take her to her daughter," he said. "And then fetch Doeg. I have need of him again."

She stood, her glare hard enough to cut glass. He only frowned, too exhausted now to deal with his wife.

"I hope you are happy," she said, stomping by him with Benyamin in tow. He watched them leave, watched his own door shut.

"I can't remember the last time I was happy," he said to himself. He sighed and looked at his bed, wanting nothing more than to crawl under the cover and let the day pass him by. It was not yet evening, and he'd already had enough disappointment to last him the year.

I had him...had him in my grasp.

Samuel. The fake, the fraud.

Yet he had seen them, all of them, bowing down to worship Yahweh rather than seize David. Indeed, he had done the same thing. Samuel was no fake. And he was clearly opposed to Saul.

I am ready for this day to end...

He drew a breath, drew in what strength he could, and stepped up to the wide window that overlooked Gibeah. His hand reflexively grabbed the spear that was propped in the corner, his fingers closing around the shaft and holding it as if it were a comfort object. This window was the highest point in Gibeah, and he could see far across the city. His eyes drifted over his city, over each house and each farm and each shop. The sun had nearly set when his eyes fell on a small open area with stone walls and a dirt center.

David's training grounds.

His fingers ached, and he looked to find them white from the force with which he was squeezing the spear. He eased his grip but did not drop the weapon.

There was a knock on his door, and his mind finally pulled away from his own thoughts.

"Enter."

The door creaked open, and Doeg stepped in. He sauntered up to the window with Saul, not bothering to kneel, not bothering to acknowledge he was in the presence of a king.

If he wasn't so useful, I would have him killed too.

"You needed me?" he asked.

Saul looked back out at Gibeah. "I need you to go to Nob."

"Nob?"

Saul nodded.

"Why?"

"I made you my chief herdsman because you are useful. And now I wish to use you further. I want to give you men, supplies. I wish to make you a captain."

"And these things are at Nob?"

Saul sighed. *For someone so useful, he knows so little about this land.* "Nob is where the tabernacle is, where my high priest is."

"I don't serve your god."

"But you serve his king. And to serve beyond that of chief herdsman, you will need to at least appear to serve Yahweh."

"Why?"

"My people care little who my chief herdsman is. But if an Edomite leads my men to battle without the appearance of fighting for Yahweh, they will lose their minds." He paused, almost smiled. "Will your gods have a problem with that?"

He scoffed. "As I've said, I do not serve them; they serve me."

"Good. Go to Nob. Seek Ahimelech or his son Abiathar. They will show you what needs doing."

Doeg left without another word. Saul turned back to the window when he heard more footsteps approaching.

Will this night never end?

He turned to see Jonathan standing in the doorway. Saul tried to keep his displeasure from his face. His son had become something of a bother as of late. So far, he had been able to plan David's death while Jonathan was away, either training his men or practicing his archery outside the city walls. He knew the time was coming, however, when he would have to let him in on his plans.

He will not like it.

Who cares if he likes it?

Saul looked more closely at his son. He was not sweating, but there was a sheen to his face and arms.

"Training again?"

His son forced a smile and nodded. "Yes. One can never be skilled enough."

Saul laughed before he could stop himself. "I thought Yahweh went ever before you? I thought your abilities did not matter?"

Jonathan frowned at that. "Yahweh has blessed us with our abilities. He has given us the strength to go to battle."

He turned again to the window. "Then why do we need him to go before us?"

"We must make use of our gifts. Yet we must always remember that they were given by Yahweh."

"What good are our gifts?" He looked at his son. "What good is your skill with a bow? Either Yahweh will bless you, or he will not, right?"

"We must walk in his steps to be blessed, father. And I do not imagine he desires lazy servants who do not train."

"We train for battle so that Yahweh may bless us in battle. But we are not to rely on our training in the battle, only on Yahweh?" He scoffed. "Do you not see the folly in this?"

"What would you suggest?"

He stepped away from the window, the spear dragging on the hard stone. "That we train and fight for ourselves."

Jonathan tensed. "And walk not with Yahweh? He chooses the victor, knows the outcome before the battle begins."

"Precisely. What can man do?"

His son looked confused, doubtful. Indeed, Saul himself wasn't even sure what he was saying.

"Man can walk humbly with Yahweh," Jonathan said. "He can do nothing else."

"What will you do, I wonder, when he decides he no longer wishes to bless you?"

Jonathan did not hesitate. "I will find my sin and repent, offer burnt sacrifices to him, and renew my obedience."

Saul snorted a laugh and found himself repeating Samuel's words. "Does Yahweh delight in burnt offerings and sacrifices as much as in obeying his commands?"

His son was silent for a moment. "Are you well, father?"

"No." He turned back to the window and found himself leaning on the spear like an old man on a staff. "No. I am not."

There was a long silence as Jonathan joined him at the window. Together they stared out at Gibeah, not a word said between them for several minutes. It almost felt comforting to have his son silently keep him company. The sun was entirely gone now, only the light of the moon and a handful of burning fires lighting the city. Saul's eyes were drawn again to David's training grounds, shrouded in darkness now that they were empty.

"Where are you," he found himself saying out loud. "Where have you gone?"

"Father?"

He sighed. "I have not seen David for some time," he lied. Then a thought came to him. "Do you know where he has gone?"

Jonathan did not answer for a moment. "He is in Bethlehem," he finally said.

"Bethlehem?"

"He asked to see his family, to offer sacrifices alongside his father and brothers. I bid him leave a few days ago."

Saul turned to his son, felt a rage running through him. He knew it was a lie, knew David had been in Ramah.

"A few days ago? You…you saw him? And sent him home to Bethlehem?"

He hesitated again, perhaps realizing his lie was caught. "Yes."

Saul spun, the tip of his spear lashing out and tearing Jonathan's tunic. His son leaped back and patted his chest, though there was no wound.

"What are you doing?"

"Disciplining a lying son!"

He stepped forward and jabbed with the spear, but Jonathan ducked out of the way, leaping back and putting space between them.

"What are you talking about?"

"You son of a whore!" He jabbed again, met only air as Jonathan dodged toward the still-open door. "I know you've sided with him. You know where he is!"

"I…I don't!"

"You lie!" Saul felt the strength go out of him. "Don't you understand? Don't you see? You will never be king so long as he lives. Your kingdom, *my* kingdom, will die with me."

"If it is Yahweh's will."

"No!" He slammed the butt of the spear into the stone floor. "Why can no one see it? Why does no one fear him?!"

Jonathan did not flinch. "I have seen him in battle, father. And I fear him. Or rather, I would if he were my enemy."

"He is!"

"He is not. I've never seen a man more after Yahweh's heart."

"No. He is a jackal. A fake! Send for him! Bring him to me!"

"So you can kill him?"

"Of course, you idiot. He must die!"

Jonathan inched forward, though the door was still only a few steps away. "Why? What has he done?"

"He has taken everything from me. Even my own children."

Saul hurled the spear across the room. It skimmed over Jonathan by a handbreadth and lodged itself into the table behind him. His son took one look at the spear and one more at his father and then he was gone.

He has taken everything. Saul dropped to his knees. *Michal. Jonathan. Ahinoam.* He felt hot tears in his eyes, the first real sign of emotion he had shown in years. *Everything...*

But he will not take my throne.

DAVID

Night had fallen by the time David saw the figure approach. There was an urgency to his step, though he wasn't quite running. Even in the darkness, even from a distance, he could tell it was Jonathan. And he could tell his conversation with his father had not gone well.

He has learned the truth.

David stepped from the woods and stood beside the bale of hay as Jonathan approached. Once he was close enough, David could see that his face was red, that his tunic was ripped open. There was no blood, but that did not stop David from rushing forward.

"What happened?"

Jonathan fell to his knees in front of David.

"I am sorry," he said, his voice choked. "I am sorry for what my father has done. He is…he is gone."

David stood beside his kneeling friend. "What are you saying?"

"My father…he wants you dead. He knows you are to take his throne."

Take his throne. The words still sounded foreign to David. *Not foreign. Impossible.* "I only want to live, Jonathan. I cannot say what will come tomorrow."

Jonathan looked up and met David's eyes. "How can you not? Yahweh has promised you the throne. My father is clearly no longer meant for it. Who but you?"

"You, Jonathan. Why do you not wish it?"

He looked confused. "Has not Yahweh promised it to you?"

David was silent.

"You must be king, David. Do you not see? I...I cannot take what is not mine."

And there it is, David thought. Though he had not verbalized it, Jonathan had been his last excuse, his final reason to deny the throne. Yet David could only look at him, the prince of Israel kneeling before a shepherd. He found his heart in his throat.

"I have been blessed with such friends as I cannot understand."

Jonathan finally stood. He held out his hand. David took it in his.

"May Yahweh be with you as he was with my father, so many years ago."

"I'll not forget you, friend. I'll not forget what you've done for me."

They embraced, holding each other close. David felt hot tears in his eyes as they pulled apart.

"Remember me, when you are king," Jonathan said. "Remember my family. Do not look on them as enemies, as my father looks at you. As Yahweh cuts off your enemies, do not count me among them."

I will not be king, he thought. Yet he could not say that, not after Jonathan's words. "Never," he said. "But I would ask more of you."

"Anything."

"Find Abishai. Explain what has happened, how I have fled. Tell him I am fleeing to Adullam, to the caves there. If he still wishes to fight with me, even as the outlaw that I am now, that is where I have gone."

"Of course."

He thought of leaving a final message for Michal, a final goodbye. But what would he say? She had denied him, chosen to remain behind and let him flee. There was nothing left to say between them. He looked one last time at Jonathan. Then he turned and left his home for the final time.

THE TABERNACLE WAS SPREAD out in the valley below, where the rising sun cast long, stretching shadows. The low fabric walls stretched into the distance, a small opening facing him. There was no cover, and David could see the altars and burning fires and even the tent for the Holy of Holies. He knew the Ark of the Covenant lay in the Holy of Holies, that place untouchable by the feet of most men. It was the dwelling place of Yahweh, the home of the Living God of Israel.

The town of Nob stretched beyond the tabernacle. He heard the bleating of sheep, the banging of a blacksmith's hammer, the rattle of carts, and even the laughter of children. From his vantage point, he saw Ahimelech's home near the center of the small town. He walked down the hill toward Nob.

Priests and Levites scurried about the courtyard within the fabric walls, seeing to the sacrifices and praying with the people, some from Nob, yet most having traveled from afar. Smoke rose from an altar, the scent of burning lamb coming to David's nose. He paused at the entrance to the tabernacle. Something was drawing him, forcing him to look. He had no sacrifice, no purpose within its fabric walls, yet he stood in silence, eyes on the tabernacle courtyard.

Then he saw him, grinning and kneeling before Abiathar. Doeg winked at David before Abiathar poured a horn of oil over him. David watched in stunned silence as the anointing was finished and Doeg rose slowly, letting the oil run over him.

What is he doing here?

David walked around the tabernacle and almost ran into Nob. Children called to him from the streets, laughing and clapping once they saw him. He slowed enough to greet them, everything inside him urging him forward.

Ahimelech cannot know I am running; cannot know he is helping me escape. Saul will kill him if he does. Yet I have no food, no weapon.

When he finally reached his friend's home, he found him sitting in his courtyard. Ahimelech looked up, and their eyes met. David expected a smile, the same warm greeting he always received when visiting Nob. Yet Ahimelech looked fearful, apprehensive. He looked worried.

Does he already know?

"Greetings, David," he said, warmly enough. "What brings you here?"

David stepped into the courtyard, hesitating before taking a seat. "I…" *I what? What do I say? I'm running from the king, can you help me?* "Saul has sent me on a mission."

Ahimelech looked beyond David to the fields in the distance. "I see no army. He has sent you on a mission alone?"

"I have told my men to go ahead of me." He swallowed, sweat running down his face.

He looked at David's belt. "And you left your weapon with them?"

David frowned; he knew his friend was aware of his lies. "I left in such a hurry." He looked down. *I want to tell you. I want your help. Need it. But I cannot risk your life.* "I…"

"David. Look at me."

He lifted his head, met his friend's eyes. Ahimelech studied him, ears perked as if listening to an unseen voice.

Does he hear the voice too?

Then a smile broke on Ahimelech's face. "What do you need of me?"

David exhaled and was once again thankful for the friends put in his path. "I need a weapon. And if you have some bread to spare."

"For your men."

He nodded. "For my men."

Ahimelech smiled. "I have but one sword, the sword of Goliath," he said.

The name brought a flood of memories. He saw himself a young boy, standing fearless in front of a giant. He remembered the strength, the conviction, the presence of Yahweh as he faced Goliath. He felt the heavy sword in his hand as it swooped down and separated the giant's head from his shoulders, felt his blood boiling and his skin burning from the unseen power, felt the rush of the Israelite army storming by him and tearing into the ranks of the frozen Philistines.

Ahimelech stood, shattering his memories, and David followed the old priest inside and saw him open a chest. "I cannot lift it, but it is in there."

David stepped around him and pulled the sword free. It was wrapped in cloth and sheathed in a heavy scabbard. He slid the material aside and slowly pulled the sword free of its scabbard, the blade hissing its way out like a snake warning him to step away. It tapered to a point, not forward curving like Israel's own weapons. He swung it once, twice. Though lighter than he recalled from his youth, the blade was still massive, nearly the length of one of David's legs.

It was a blade for a giant.

"I think you will need to wield it with both hands," Ahimelech said.

David nodded his agreement. "I am thinking that, as well."

"It is yours if you want."

"There is none like it." He sheathed it again and slung it over a shoulder. "Thank you."

"Let us get you some bread. For your men, of course. Then I will walk you out of the city."

It was nearly midday when the two of them were finished, standing at the opposite side of the city from where the tabernacle lay. Ahimelech looked at him.

"A mission from Saul?"

David nodded.

"And you are going to meet your men?"

"I…" David trailed off. "I am hoping so."

Ahimelech drew a deep breath. "I think this will be the last time we see one another. At least in this life."

"I hope that is not so."

The two embraced. *Again, I am saying goodbye to a friend, another who seems willing to face Saul for my sake.*

With those final thoughts, David bid farewell. He turned away from Ahimelech, from Nob, and began the long walk toward Adullam.

40

SAUL

SAUL SAT in the shade of the tamarisk tree. The bark was rough against his back, though he was thankful for the shade as the sun continued its descent from the midday sky. It was hot now and would only get hotter as summer began in earnest.

The walls of Gibeah stood tall and proud behind him. Five hundred of his personal guard stood in formation not far from the walls, weapons and armor glinting in the sun like the army of Yahweh that they were. But Saul paid them no mind. He did not care about the soldiers or the high walls. He looked instead at the dozens of elders and tribal leaders milling about him, all standing at the edge of the shade. Rimmon was here, as well, along with Benyamin, Abner, and Malki-Shua, the four of them the only ones in the shadow of the tree alongside him.

Let them simmer, he thought, looking with disdain on the men around him. *Let them burn. Let the heat work their minds and hearts as they stare at the strength of Gibeah. Maybe then someone will finally have the guts to speak out against David.*

"Listen," he shouted, not bothering to stand. "Men of Israel. Men of Reuben, of Simeon, of Dan. Men of Benjamin," he said, looking to Rimmon. "David, son of Jesse of Bethlehem, has sinned against the king, and as such, has sinned against Yahweh. He seeks the throne! He seeks to rule Israel in my stead. To remove the chosen king, the one anointed by Samuel so many years ago."

There was hushed chatter among the elders. Saul let them whisper to one another for a moment before continuing.

"He has fled!" They all fell silent. "He has left his fellow troops, left the men of Israel. He has abandoned his wife, my own daughter. David is an outlaw, a jackal, a traitor to the kingdom of Yahweh!" He paused and let the words sink in. "And I believe most of you knew this was coming."

This time the hushed chatter became outcries. Angry voices rolled over each other, each claiming innocence, each pledging loyalty. He let them yell for several moments, his eyes scanning them for any sign of deceit. "Silence! Will the son of Jesse give you fields? Will he give you vineyards? Will he make you commanders of men, leaders in the armies of Israel? Is this why you have conspired against me? My eldest son is absent today because of the covenant he has made with the son of Jesse. Not one of you is concerned, not one of you could see his treachery, and now he lies in wait for me, looking to end the life of the chosen king of Israel!"

Their shouts rose again. More cries of innocence and loyalty. Some went so far as to relay their newfound hatred of David. All lies, Saul knew. Whether they were guilty of conspiring with David or not, he didn't care. That wasn't why he had called them.

"Enough! Who among you knows where he is? Who knows where he has gone?"

Silence.

"A reward has been offered for the head of David. Fields and land and men. The one who finds this jackal will be a mighty man in Israel for years to come. His family will be counted among the most blessed!"

A voice cried out from behind him. "I think I can help you with that!"

Saul turned to see Doeg near-running across the field in their direction. He stopped beside Rimmon.

"You know where David is?"

Doeg smiled. "I know where he *was*, just yesterday."

"Where?"

"He was at Nob, in the home of Ahimelech."

"Nob? The tabernacle?"

He nodded. "He supplied him with bread and gave him a sword."

"And you did not kill him?"

"I did not think you would want the blood of your god's priest on my hands."

Saul jerked to his feet. "I care not about the blood of men!" He glanced at the elders around him. "If he has conspired with the son of Jesse, then he is no longer fit to care for the tabernacle!" He looked at Abner. "Get these men ready," he said, pointing at his guard standing in front of the walls. "We march now! To Nob!"

———

SAUL SAW the tabernacle at the foot of the hill, the smoke rising from the altars and the Levites and priests rushing about. Beyond the courtyard was the inner tent, and he could almost feel the presence of the Ark of the Covenant within. He looked at the town of Nob, at the men, women, and children slowly wandering to the town's edge, all staring out at Saul's small army.

But mostly, Saul's eyes fell on Ahimelech. The old priest stood before him, flanked by Doeg and Benyamin. His face was firm, his eyes meeting Saul's. The man looked to be nearing a century in age, yet he stood with a purpose and a determination that nearly made Saul falter.

"Listen now, Ahimelech, for I will not ask a second time."

"Of course, my king."

"Where is he?"

"Who, my king?"

Saul glared at him. "Do not play foolish with me, priest."

"I am not intending to, my king."

"Why have you conspired against me? Why have you given David food, given him weapons? Why have you helped the one who wishes to kill the king of Israel?"

"Kill you?" Ahimelech nearly scoffed. "Who is more loyal than David? He's your own son-in-law. A highly respected, valiant warrior of Yahweh. He has fought countless battles for you, my king."

"And yet he wishes to take my throne. And you have helped him."

Ahimelech looked around him, to Rimmon, to Abner, to Malki-Shua. He looked confused, puzzled as if one of them would speak for him. "This is not the first time I have helped David. He is in your service, one of your chosen captains. I have given him assistance many times as he marched to and from battle." His eyes drifted to the army behind Saul, to Doeg standing firm at his side. "I assure you, my king, I know nothing else of this whole affair."

Saul stood in silence for a long while, eyes locked on Ahimelech's. *Does he lie? Does he know David is to take my place?* His memory flashed to Samuel, to that day in the tent when Yahweh had cast him aside, when another had been chosen to replace him. *They are all the same. Priest, prophet. It makes no difference.* Ahimelech shuffled uncomfortably, his gaze finally falling to the dirt.

Then a new thought came to him, one that was not his own. *It is not too late, Saul.*

He looked around him, yet no one met his eyes. *What?*

It is not too late.

Too late?

Spare him. Renounce your throne, my throne. Allow my servant David to sit on it.

Saul's heart stopped. *Yahweh?*

Spare him, Saul. It is not too late.

He opened eyes he hadn't realized were closed, found Ahimelech staring back at him.

"How did you do that?"

"It was not me. Yahweh still loves you, still wishes you to hear him."

Anger sprang from within him like a fountain. "No! *I* am the king! And I will always be the king!" He drew a breath, tried to steady his now-shaking hands. "You will die today, priest. You and your family."

Ahimelech only looked disappointed. "It is not too late, my king."

"But it is. For both of us." He looked at Malki-Shua. "Kill him."

Ahimelech closed his eyes, prepared for death. His lips moved in what was likely his final prayer, his head turned up toward the heavens as he waited for the sword that was coming.

Yet nothing happened.

Saul looked back to his son. He was still standing where he had been, though his hand had moved to his sword. "Son? Kill him!"

"I…I can't kill a priest, father. I…I can't…"

"Can you not?" He marched to his son, put his hands on his shoulders. "Can you not?"

He drew the sword a quarter of the way. "I…"

"I have hopes for you, son. Hopes you will lead in Jonathan's place." He met Malki-Shua's eyes. "He is weak, afraid. You must be strong for the throne, must take what is yours." He pointed back to Ahimelech. "He helped an enemy. He *is* the enemy!"

The blade snapped back into the sheath. "I can't, father. I'm sorry."

Saul shoved him to the ground and turned to Abner. "Kill him!"

Abner frowned in disappointment. "You know I won't."

He spun back, eyes falling on Ahimelech. The priest's head was still upturned, still looking to the heavens. His eyes were open now, and his silent prayer was beginning to form a whisper.

"May all the kings of the earth praise you, Yahweh. May they sing of the ways of the Lord."

Why does no one obey me? Why has my own family disowned me? It is not too late...

Saul looked at Doeg. *It is.*

"Kill him."

The Edomite shrugged, and then his sword hissed from its scabbard, looping cleanly through the air and taking the head from Ahimelech in a single motion. Blood sprayed up, covering Saul from neck to navel, splattering into his face and eyes. He didn't bother wiping it away, his eyes drifting to the tabernacle and the town of Nob.

"Kill them all."

Doeg shrugged again and then turned and began a slow walk down the hill. Behind him, the army went into motion and followed the Edomite into Nob.

41

DAVID

DAVID'S FEET shuffled in the sand, the sun beating down on him. He'd long removed his tunic and wrapped it around his head, his bare chest and arms bearing the brunt of the heat. It was the middle of the third day since he had left Nob. Some of his travel had been through forests and plains and mountain passes, but this final day was through harsh desert as he traveled south along the foothills of Adullam, eyes peeled for the network of caves he knew existed.

I seek caves to hide in, like a rat.

It was late afternoon when he came across a line of cliffs, their faces pointed east. Through the shimmering heat, he could see the cave entrances dotting the cliffs, nothing more than dark shadows on an otherwise bright and rocky landscape.

He chose the largest of these entrances and continued walking. His mind wandered as he trudged on, meandering among his past, lingering on his mistakes. He wondered if Abishai would come, if his friend had forgiven him.

Faces passed before him. First Abigail, his dove, his perfect one, his first love. He saw her smiling wide, eyes meeting his.

He could feel her warmth on his skin, smell the scent of her hair, feel her breath on his face. David had thought her a reward for doing Yahweh's work, but she had been taken by Yahweh's anointed. Saul had sent her away with Nabal simply to spite him.

He knew Michal should be on his mind, not Abigail. She was his wife, his *true* reward for fighting Yahweh's enemies. At least, according to Saul. Yet as he trudged through the desert, he realized that he'd never really loved her, not like he had Abigail. And that only made his heart ache all the more.

Next, he saw Ira. David saw him as he was, a smiling youth, eager to please and eager to learn. Then the smiling face shifted, twisted in pain, and he looked as David had seen him last—bloodied, pale, dying. *So many have been killed because of me.*

David stopped and swore that if he was indeed to be king, if he was truly chosen to shepherd Yahweh's sheep, he would forever remember the men who got him there, the men who gave their lives so David could fulfill Yahweh's will. These men would be honored as mighty men, men worthy of having their names etched into the history of Israel, forever remembered alongside the words of Moses.

He stopped walking at the entrance to a cave. It sloped down into the mountain, disappearing almost immediately into darkness and shadow. He dropped his pack and the sword of Goliath—*the sword of David now*, he told himself—on the ground beside him. After a few moments, he pulled out one of the many thick sticks he had collected, along with a skin of oil, a length of cloth, and his fire-starting stone. He wrapped the fabric around the stick and poured a bit of oil over it. After another few moments of working at the stone, he had a burning torch. Putting the pack and sword back over his shoulder, he stepped cautiously into the cave.

It wasn't nearly as deep as he'd expected; it ran perhaps a

hundred or so cubits into the cliff before leveling out. Yet once inside, he could see another pair of entrances as the cave branched off. Down one, he saw a pillar of dusty sunlight shining through a surface crack. He chose this one and ventured on until he stepped into the light. From there, he saw another handful of similar branches. Some shone with daylight, and some slanted up. He followed one of the latter until he emerged again into the desert sun. A quick look down the cliff face revealed another dozen entrances.

It didn't take him long to retrace his steps, and soon he was back where he'd started. He chose a hill and climbed to the top to survey his surroundings. The sun was near setting with perhaps another two hours of daylight left, and he could just barely make out a thick forest to the southeast. He was running dangerously low on supplies—he was out of bread and had very little water and salted meat left. Though he could not stay in the forest—there were too many hunters who might see him —a quick trip could provide him with enough food and water for a week, at least.

He was about to begin walking down the hill toward the forest when a pair of dots appeared on the northern horizon. He squinted, shielded the little bit of sunlight from his eyes.

Horses?

He scurried down the hill, almost sliding at the steeper points, until he was back at the entrance to his cave. He tossed his pack inside, ducked into the shadow, and gripped the hilt of his blade as he watched the two riders approach. They weren't riding directly toward him but heading in the general direction of the caves. As they neared, he was soon able to make out their faces.

Abishai? He leaned forward slightly. *Is that…Abiathar? Ahim-elech's son?*

David stepped from the cave and into the fading light. "Abishai!"

The riders stopped and spun, searching for his voice.

"Abishai!"

Abishai finally saw him, and the horse broke into a sprint, kicking high plumes of dust and dirt into the air behind him. Within moments he'd skidded to a halt, dismounted and was standing before David gasping for breath.

"I didn't think…I'd find you…so fast."

David smiled, and they embraced. Abiathar walked up beside them, leading the reins of both horses. His face was drawn, eyes red.

"I'm happy you did," David said. He turned to Abiathar. "Tell your father I am grateful when you see him next."

Abiathar held his gaze, his lip trembling. "He's dead," he said.

David's heart dropped to his stomach. "Dead…"

"Saul and his Edomite slave killed him."

He fell to his knees, his mind reeling. "I…saw him there. When your father helped me, I saw Doeg. I didn't think…" He swallowed hard, the desert around him spinning. "I didn't think Saul would kill a priest."

"He did."

David looked up, saw a mixture of anger and sadness on Abiathar's face. "This is my fault," he said. "Saul is seeking my life. I should have known." He stood, met Abiathar's gaze. "I'm sorry."

Abiathar worked his tongue in his mouth, eyed David. His eyes moistened, and he blinked away tears. "Saul did this," he said. "I'll not hold you accountable for a wicked king's actions."

"I thank you for that, but the fault still lies with me. I was reckless seeking help from your father. I did not tell him much, sought to deceive him so he would not have to lie before Saul." He shook his head. "That did not work." He offered his hand. "I ask you to stay with me if you would. I will keep you safe."

314 | BRYAN R. SAYE

Abiathar forced a smile and took David's hand. "I will. After all, a king needs a priest."

EXCERPT FROM THE RISE OF DAVID

All those who were in distress or in debt or discontented gathered around him, and he became their leader.

DAVID

"Benaiah?"

The man nodded.

"And you are from the south?"

"Kabzeel."

"The far south, then."

"Near Edom."

David frowned at that. "I have unpleasant memories of people from Edom."

"As do I. I fought in many skirmishes along the southern border. A border that has steadily been pushed back."

"You fought in the king's army?"

"When he deemed it time to fight. He has been obsessed with you for some time now."

"Regrettable for both Israel and myself, I would say."

"Indeed."

"And why do you seek to join me?"

"I was told to."

"By who?"

"Yahweh spoke to me through a dream."

David raised an eyebrow. He immediately thought of Ira,

saw his pale face fading before him. "Is that so? Did he say why?"

"You are to be king. He said that you needed a bodyguard."

Abishai snorted a laugh behind him.

"As I've heard, on both accounts. But we shall see." David nodded toward Abishai. "Go with Abishai. He will find you a place to call your own."

Benaiah nodded and lifted his pack.

"Come," Abishai said. "We'll find you some rock to lie under."

David watched the two of them disappear down one of the many tunnels. He stood in the main cave he had discovered on his first day here, though now he was far from alone. It felt significantly smaller.

"That makes near four hundred."

David turned to find Eleazar standing beside him with a strip of leather and a scribe's pen. He sketched a few marks on the leather and then looked up at David. Eleazar had come shortly after Abishai, along with nearly a hundred of David's soldiers. In the two years they'd spent hiding in the caves, Eleazar had become indispensable.

"That is a lot of men," David said.

He looked about the opening. The dozen or so men within it were only a fraction of the band that had gathered around David. Most had come out of desperation, suffering from crushing debt or some other kind of distress. Some were thieves who had come begging for forgiveness. Abiathar had seen to their atonement, and the men had been trained in the way of war. Others still had come simply out of discontent with the king. From what his scouts and spies were reporting, Saul was so absorbed with finding David that Israel's borders had shrunk over the last two years, land falling to the Philistines or Amalekites or—like Benaiah's home—to the Edomites.

"They will keep coming," Eleazar said. "So long as Israel continues to disintegrate, the men will search for a new leader."

He still did not like the idea that he was to be king, yet the men would not let go of it. "In time, Eleazar."

"And how much longer do we hide in caves?"

A fair question. One that I do not have an answer to. "I—"

"David!"

They turned in unison as Abishai came charging back in.

"Abishai?" David stepped toward him. "You were gone for two minutes. Why are—"

"Jonathan has come again," he said, gasping for breath. "He is…he is on the surface."

Outside, the familiar desert stretched beyond sight, the sand fading into the horizon. Now, however, there were men camped in front of several of the cave openings. There were perhaps a dozen small camps, all neatly hidden among the rocks and hills. Most of the men were camped inside the cliff in caves like the one David was just in.

They found Jonathan sitting on a small boulder. He was holding a hand out, palm up, and his horse was gladly eating whatever he held. He turned when he heard them step out into the desert.

"Greetings, David," he said, lowering his head in a short bow.

"You need not bow, old friend," David said, joining him on the boulder. "I'm no king."

Jonathan smiled. "Yet."

"Yet," he repeated with a sigh. *Or ever.* "What news do you bring?"

Jonathan looked into the cave behind him. "There are two things. Which would you hear first?"

"Is there any good news?"

His friend thought for a moment and then shook his head.

"Then, does it matter?"

"I suppose not." He cleared his throat. "I have found Michal."

That gave David pause. "And?"

"She is married."

To his surprise, he felt only mild disappointment at that. Mixed with that was a surprising feeling of relief. He had tried to love her, had spent the better part of six months as her husband, albeit most of it in his bed healing. For the most part, he had succeeded, though he always knew she could only ever have half his heart.

David put her from his mind. "I suppose we both knew that was coming. What other news do you bring?"

"It appears my father has found you."

"Found us?"

"Well, Doeg has. One of his scouts, at least. He is on his way now to report your position."

"How much time do we have?"

"That depends on how many men my father wants to bring. He'll know you've gathered a small force about you. He may simply take the main army from Gibeah and march as soon as he can."

"Then we must leave with haste."

Jonathan only nodded.

"There is your answer." He turned to Eleazar. "It appears we are done hiding in caves."

ACKNOWLEDGMENTS

There are far too many names to mention in order to acknowledge the many people who have helped me get to this point. First thanks should always go to God, whose word and presence have gotten me through more than I care to admit. He also brought me my wife, Jessica, who has a way of encouraging me and challenging me in the same moment. I would not be the man I am without her. Additionally, I owe a great deal of thanks to Andrew Cowen, the first person to read this book all the way through. This minor feat meant more to me than he knows (and I'm sure he appreciated that the manuscript came assembled and without the need for dowels).

A special thank you to my editor, Alison Imbriaco, who did an amazing job with the first draft (I apparently have an unnatural obsession with ellipses and the word 'eye'). She saved the reader from much distress.

There were also many books that aided with the writing of this one. Two that were especially helpful: *David, Saul, and God: Rediscovering an Ancient Story* by Paul Borgman, and *Warfare in the Old Testament: The Organization, Weapons, and Tactics of Ancient Near East Armies* by Boyd Seevers. Borgman's insight into the minds of David and Saul was priceless, as was Seevers' detailed account of ancient Israelite warfare.

Being a self-published work, I feel a need to express gratitude to the many services made available that helped bring you the product you currently hold. While I will not list them by name, I hope fellow authors looking to self-publish their work will find encouragement to pursue their dream.

ALSO BY BRYAN R. SAYE

THE KINGS OF ISRAEL

———————

The Shepherd and the King
The Rise of David

THE CRUSADERS CHRONICLES

———————

Storm of War

Dorylaeum

Shadows of Antioch (coming soon)

DID YOU ENJOY THIS BOOK?

Your feedback helps me provide the best quality books and helps other readers like you discover great books.

It would mean the world to me if you took 2 minutes to share your thoughts about this book. You can leave a review with amazon at the link below. Also, if you like, you can send me an email with your honest feedback.

https://www.amazon.com/review/create-review?&asin=B096FYKS2B

ABOUT THE AUTHOR

Who is this guy?

Bryan currently lives in Idaho with his wonderful wife and two amazing children. He's a happy follower of Jesus, a proud member of the United States Air Force, and an often disappointed but always dedicated fan of the Jacksonville Jaguars (This is our year!).

He started his writing career late in life (if you consider almost 40 late), mostly because his little buggers wanted to eat everyday and have health insurance. His daughter says he can't talk without teaching (and no, he's not a teacher). According to his son, if you want to know anything else then you'll just have to meet him (come to Idaho, it's not that cold).

What does he write?

By drawing on real events and stories from history, Bryan writes quality fiction with powerful character arcs that display and encourage real change. Though always reflecting a Catholic worldview, he strives to write fiction that is accessible and relatable to people from all faiths and cultures that excludes no one.

For further information and updates, visit www.bryanr saye.com, or follow the social media links below.

f facebook.com/BryanRSaye

a amazon.com/~/e/B08Z3QHJWG

Printed in Great Britain
by Amazon

50040123R00189